SPECTR
SERIES 2

VOLUME 2

Also by Jordan L. Hawk:

Hainted

<u>Whyborne & Griffin series:</u>
Widdershins
Threshold
Stormhaven
Necropolis
Bloodline
Hoarfrost
Maelstrom
Fallow
Balefire

"Eidolon" (A Whyborne & Griffin short story)
"Carousel" (A Whyborne & Griffin short story)
"Remnant" written with KJ Charles (A Whyborne & Griffin / The Secret Casebooks of Simon Feximal crossover)

<u>Spirits:</u>
Restless Spirits
Dangerous Spirits

<u>Hexworld</u>
The 13th Hex
Hexbreaker
Hexmaker
A Christmas Hex
Hexslayer

"Heart of the Dragon" (short story)

JORDAN L. HAWK

SPECTR
SERIES 2

VOLUME 2

INCLUDING:
BREAKER OF CHAINS
SHAKER OF EARTH

SPECTR

SPECTR: Series 2, Volume 2 © 2018 Jordan L. Hawk
ISBN: 9781719958240

Cover art © 2018 Lou Harper

Edited by Annetta Ribken

BREAKER
OF
CHAINS

CHAPTER 1

CALEB SAT IN the passenger seat of the government-issued sedan, his hands folded in his lap and his gaze directed out the window. Silence pressed down on him with palpable weight, like a freezing wet blanket draped over his shoulders. He glanced at John for the fifth time in as many minutes, but his boyfriend's eyes remained fixed determinedly on the road.

Normally, the drive into SPECTR-HQ was filled with the sort of idle talk couples shared when they lived together: when to do the grocery run, whose turn it was to cook, were the clothes still in the dryer. Or else they shared chatter about whatever case they were working, or even companionable silence.

They wouldn't be working any more cases together. And this silence was anything but companionable.

Gray roused, a tendril of distress uncoiling through Caleb. *"John is angry with us."*

The drakul had five thousand years' worth of memories gleaned from the corpses he'd inhabited. None if it had prepared him for the reality of having the person he loved most in the world pissed at him.

John's got a right to be angry, Caleb replied silently. *We lied to him.*

For good reasons—or so they'd seemed at the time. To protect Yuri and Drugoy, the only other living drakul they'd ever met. The only other one in the world.

If SPECTR found out about Yuri and Dru, they'd have to run, or else find themselves dropped into some sort of black ops prison. John was already in trouble with the district chief; it hadn't seemed fair to force him to keep a secret as big as a living drakul on the loose in Charleston. So Caleb and Gray told him what felt like small, innocent lies, and it worked. At least until the point when John found himself face-to-face with Drugoy.

"He agreed to keep our secret," Gray said uncertainly. *"Why is he still angry with us?"*

Just because we talked him into keeping Yuri and Dru secret doesn't mean he's not upset we lied in the first place.

Unhappy restlessness exuded from Gray, like a tiger twitching its tail. *"I do not like it. I do not wish him to be angry with us anymore."*

Like I do. Caleb sighed mentally. *Keeping something so big from him was your idea in the first place. But I agreed, and now we're both paying the price.*

"What did he mean?" John asked. Caleb jumped at the abrupt breaking of the silence, but John didn't seem to notice. "The other vampire. When he said I was 'one of yours.'"

A white bandage covered John's nose, and black circles showed beneath his eyes. Exhaustion tugged down the corners of his mouth. He kept his gaze fixed on the road, still not looking in Caleb's direction.

Maybe if Caleb could answer John, it would put them back on John's good side. But unfortunately Caleb didn't know.

"Ours," Gray had said, when Drugoy approached John. A strange flare of jealousy had accompanied the word, Gray abandoning their kill to put himself bodily between Dru and John. Dru had instantly backed off, to the point of surrendering control to Yuri.

Gray? What was that all about? Do you know what he meant?

"John is ours," Gray said, as if it were the most obvious thing in the world.

You were jealous, weren't you? You didn't want Dru near John.

"I wished him to understand John is ours. And I did not wish John to go with Drugoy instead."

Caleb rolled his eyes. *Are you serious? I don't think Dru wants to steal our boyfriend.*

"It is not…like that." Caleb could almost feel Gray struggling for the right words. *"John is ours. But Zahira is ours as well."*

The fine hairs tried to stand up on Caleb's neck. *I don't understand. You're not…interested…in her.* Gray wasn't one for hiding his feelings, even if he'd had the option in the shared space of their brain.

Gray wasn't gay—didn't seem to be much interested in the idea of sex at all if it didn't involve John. Caleb might feel a flare of attraction toward a nice ass in tight jeans strolling down the sidewalk, but Gray was indifferent to mortals in general. As for gender, drakul apparently didn't have any inherent understanding of the concept, and regarded the whole idea as mortal nonsense.

"Of course I do not wish to sleep with Zahira. But she is our mortal."

No way was Caleb going to share that with anyone else until he had some clearer idea of what it meant. "Gray is being confusing," he said aloud. "Not on purpose—it makes complete sense to him. But I don't understand. Yuri might, though. I'll ask him."

John's knuckles tightened on the wheel at the mention of Yuri's name. "Yuri Azarov. Drugoy. The Lake Baikal vampire."

"They weren't actually encased in tons of concrete and dropped to the bottom of the world's deepest lake," Caleb corrected. "Yes, the Soviets summoned Dru from the etheric plane and put him in Yuri. But they didn't go insane the way Forsyth did. They realized their commanders had grown afraid of them, so they ran. The Lake Baikal story was just that—a story, made up to keep the men in charge from being executed."

"Etheric beings can't survive on this side of the veil without going mad," John said. He still hadn't looked at Caleb. "Not without some sort of cushion, like Gray had, to ease them into it."

Caleb frowned. "What the hell, Starkweather? Are you saying Yuri lied? It doesn't make any sense. Why would he lie about Dru coming straight from the etheric? When I told him about Gray's corpse-hopping days, he seemed more revolted than anything. I'd bet my bottom dollar he wasn't faking."

"You're betting a lot more." The sedan slowed as they approached the gate leading to the SPECTR parking lot. "If something goes wrong…"

"Like what?" Caleb threw up his hands in despair. "They've been together for sixty years, John. *Sixty!*" And their body still looked twenty-something, but Caleb wasn't going to even think about that right now. "If Yuri and Dru were so damned dangerous, we would have heard about them by now. If they were going to run mad and start eating everyone in sight, they would have done it decades before you and I were born."

They pulled up to the security hut, and John rolled down the window. Normally he exchanged pleasantries with the empath gate guard, but today he only held up his badge and grunted. The guard peered at them with a furrowed brow, but didn't say anything. He'd probably heard Barillo was punishing them for the publicity surrounding the grendel case.

John remained silent as he guided the car down the spiral ramp into the underground parking garage. When he parked the car beside a line of identical sedans, Caleb let out a frustrated sigh. "I'm sorry Dru scared you. He didn't mean to. He's no more inherently dangerous than Gray is. And before you can say anything about drakul and danger, let me remind you that you regularly let Gray fuck you into the bed."

Thank God, it got a small laugh from John. "Sean thought I got off from the danger."

"Sean was an asshole." Who'd taken an indefinite leave after nearly getting killed on Fort Sumter. "Not to mention wrong about pretty much everything ever."

"I know." John rubbed at his eyes. "All right. Let me meet this Yuri and Dru, when we aren't fighting a raging NHE."

Relief sluiced through Caleb's veins. "Of course. I'll text Yuri, set something up for tonight." He hesitated, before putting a hand to John's shoulder. "Listen…I'm sorry we lied to you. You were already in trouble with Barillo, and Gray just didn't think it was a good idea. We didn't want to make things worse. We love you."

"I know." John leaned over and brushed his lips against Caleb's. "I love you guys, too."

Gray perked up. *"John has forgiven us?"*

Looks like.

"We should get moving," John said reluctantly. "You don't want to keep your new partners waiting."

Caleb's mood instantly soured. "Oh joy," he said, opening the car door. "I can't wait to see what delightful surprise Barillo has in store."

For the fourth time in an hour, John found himself staring blankly at the empty desk across from him. The one where Caleb ought to be sitting.

His thoughts raced around and around in circles. The grendel, forcing Gray to reveal himself at Caleb's PASS meeting. The chaos and terror when the grendel came for the coach. The moment when John found himself face-to-face with another drakul and realized it wasn't Gray. The pain in his broken nose.

The look the other drakul had given the blood streaming down his face from said broken nose. As though he'd been thinking about taking a taste.

"Gray just didn't think it was a good idea," Caleb had said.

Up until then, John assumed Caleb was the one who decided to lie to John about the other drakul's existence. Gray wasn't a creature of deceit. Or at least, John hadn't thought so.

Maybe he'd been wrong. After all, Gray hadn't exactly blurted out his feelings for John, back when he still thought John meant to exorcise him into a bottle. Perhaps keeping silent on certain things came naturally to him, after so many years as a lone hunter.

A lone hunter in the mortal world, anyway. Not so much in the etheric one, apparently. *"I knew him once, John,"* Gray had said. *"Beyond the veil."* Gray and Drugoy had hunted together, in the strange dimension etheric entities inhabited. The storm and the earthquake.

Shit. Was that part of the problem? This Drugoy was Gray's…what? Ex? What would that even mean? No one knew how Non-Human Entities reproduced, and even if they did, Gray had only said they'd hunted together.

John took a deep breath. This was stupid. He wasn't jealous. Scared, though…hell yes.

So what was he going to do about it?

There came a knock on the open door, and Karl Rand stuck his head inside. "Got our list of exorcists?"

Hell. John had been sitting there woolgathering instead of working. "Just about," he said, as he pulled up a list of exorcists in the greater Charleston area.

Barillo had assigned John and Karl the task of finding the exorcist who summoned the grendel on behalf of one Michael Langen. Mike had wanted revenge on the two students who beat him for being an empath, as well as the college administrators who covered it up to save his attackers' athletic careers. On his own, Mike might have summoned a less powerful NHE like a therianthrope, or even a wendigo. But a grendel would be too strong for anyone but an exorcist to bring through the veil.

Barillo hoped finding the exorcist would take the attention off the college, whose powerful alumni had been embarrassed by the exposure of the cover up in the press. Which meant John and Karl didn't have any time to waste.

If they failed…John didn't know, exactly. His career was probably over as it was. Barillo would never let him back into the field. But he'd find some way to punish John. He might even try to use Caleb and Gray as a way to do it.

"Got the list," John said. He glanced up and found Karl frowning at him slightly.

Damn it. Karl was an empath, and a good one. He had to be sensing how much turmoil John was in at the moment. There was no sense lying about it, since Karl would suss out the lie easily enough, but telling the truth was out of the question. No one could find out.

If Barillo found out there was a second drakul, the chief would do everything in his power to capture or destroy it. And if he knew Caleb had concealed Drugoy's existence, Caleb might never see the light of day again.

At the same time, John was uneasy about letting so much raw power loose in Charleston without SPECTR's knowledge. Getting to know Yuri might help. But considering his job, John wasn't used to simply taking people at their word.

Even if the official story was wrong, there might be something to find in the files on the Lake Baikal vampire. Something about who Yuri Azarov had been before the experiment. If John went poking into classified information unrelated to his case, though, Barillo would find out and want to know why.

An idea began to take form in the back of his mind. For the moment, however, he pushed his chair back. "I say we start with exorcists nearest the college and work our way out from there."

Karl's features smoothed over. It went against protocol for an empath to ask about any troubled emotions he sensed, unless there was a legal need to do so. "Sounds good. I'm ready to start when you are."

Caleb sat in one of SPECTR's bland conference rooms. Two men stood across from him, both with the standard-issue buzz cut and dark suits, their arms crossed and their gazes hostile. Because of course Barillo had made sure to fuck Caleb over as badly as possible when assigning him to a new team.

Caleb's path had crossed those of Special Agents Ericsson and Steele before, most recently at the site of one of the grendel's kills. Thanks to Gray, Caleb's senses were far more acute than an ordinary person's, and had allowed him to overhear what they really thought about him. Namely, that he was a freak. A thing.

Gray roused. *"I do not like them."*

We don't have to be friends. We just have to get along, so Barillo doesn't make things worse for John.

"I don't know what things were like with Starkweather," Ericsson said, glaring down at Caleb as he spoke. "But we do things different. By the book. Got it?"

Caleb bit back a sarcastic reply. "Got it."

Ericsson didn't look convinced, and Steele's scowl deepened until his frown lines had frown lines. "The chief chose us to keep an eye on you. And that's what we're going to do. So we've got some rules for you to follow."

Wonderful. "I'm the best at following rules," Caleb deadpanned.

Steele's gray eyes matched his name, and were just as warm. "You'd better take this seriously, Jansen. You don't want us to tell the chief you aren't cooperating."

Anger coiled through Caleb. This wasn't fair. He ought to be meeting with John and Zahira, working together to stem the sudden outbreak of possession that had the Charleston office stretched to the limits. Instead, he was stuck in a conference room listening to these two clowns.

But he didn't have a choice. For now.

Until he had a chance to talk to Yuri and Dru again, anyway. Learn from them.

"And then we will leave these mortals?" Gray asked hopefully.

Eventually. We have to be smart about this, though. No one in SPECTR could suspect they were thinking about doing a runner. *For John's sake, we have to go along with this nonsense a little longer.*

Gray huffed and sighed, but settled down. *Very well.*

"Tell me what these rules are," Caleb said aloud, trying to keep his voice level. Meek.

Ericsson studied him with a narrowed gaze. "Rule number one: we don't so much as glimpse the *thing* living in your head. Steele here has an itchy trigger finger. At the first sight of fang, he's under orders to fill you full of lead, no questions asked."

The hell? Caleb sat forward, leather coat creaking. "The whole *point* of having Gray in the field is so we can use his powers to catch NHEs. If you won't let him manifest, it's going to make everything harder."

"Don't care," Ericsson said. "So I suggest you figure out how to make the best of it. Rule number two, you keep quiet unless one of us asks you a question. Rule three, you address us as Special Agent or Sir."

Caleb bit his lip against a dozen smart-ass replies which came to mind. Ericsson seemed to take his silence as agreement, because he went on, "The rules will be added to as needed. Oh, and starting tomorrow, I don't want to see that freak getup. You'll wear a suit like everyone else."

Now this was a bridge too far. No damn way was Caleb wearing a suit every day. "The coat is to keep me from being torn to shreds when we're fighting a demon."

"I didn't ask you a question, Jansen," Ericsson snapped. "Suit and tie, and do something about your hair. Now, we have our first assignment. So get off your ass and follow us."

CHAPTER 2

JOHN PULLED THE sedan to a halt in front of a stately old home converted to a law office. Karl leaned forward from the passenger seat, eying the discreet sign outside.

"It seems a bit…high end…for a college student on a scholarship," he suggested.

John's fingers ached. After a moment, he realized he was gripping the steering wheel too tightly. "Agreed," he said, taking his hands from the wheel and unsnapping his seat belt. "But we need to be thorough. We already went through the list of student exorcists when we were hunting down the grendel. I've tried to find out if Mike knew any exorcists outside of class, but it hasn't panned out yet."

In point of fact, he'd tried calling Nigel Legare, who headed up the PASS group Caleb belonged to. Mike had been a member before Caleb joined, dropped out for a few months, then returned possessed by the grendel.

No one in PASS was an exorcist, though, which meant they hadn't known Mike was possessed when Gray manifested in front of them. They panicked, tried to defend Mike from the monster they believed had come to kill him. Or kill them all.

John understood, or tried to. In the ordinary course of things, NHEs equaled madness and death. It made sense they hadn't listened when Gray tried to explain.

Caleb acted like it didn't matter, but John knew they'd broken his heart.

Needless to say, neither Nigel nor Caleb's friend Deacon, nor any of the other PASS members, were returning John's calls.

"Geographic proximity is all we have right now." John climbed out of the sedan, and Karl followed suit. The late August sun blazed down, the air so thick with humidity it felt like stepping into a sauna. "Starting with Amelia Wagner, Esquire."

The foyer of the grand old house had been transformed to a waiting room decorated in keeping with the era the home was built in. Dark, somber tones dominated, no doubt meant to impress on clients this was an office where serious business took place. An ornate 19th-century desk sat across from the door, a slender woman seated behind it.

"How can I help you, gentlemen?" she asked with a dazzling smile.

John took out his badge and held it up. "We're here to speak with Ms. Wagner. Official business."

To her credit, the secretary remained unfazed. "One moment, and I'll see if she's available."

The receptionist picked up the phone and murmured into it, too low for them to hear. After a brief wait, she put it down and said, "Follow me, if you please."

She led them back through sumptuous hallways. The occasional open door revealed offices lined with books and what looked like a law library. The carpet muffled their footsteps, and the atmosphere was one of intent work.

They reached the end of the hall, and she knocked on a door. "The SPECTR agents, ma'am," she announced.

"Show them inside," said a voice from within. "You may go back to your desk—we won't be needing any refreshments."

John stepped inside, followed by Karl. An antique desk carved from teak dominated the room. Behind it sat a woman whose proportions matched the impressive desk. Her expensive yellow suit contrasted beautifully with her dark brown skin.

"May I see your badges?" she asked in a pleasant voice.

"Special Agent John Starkweather, Strategic Paranormal Entity ConTRol." John passed his badge over. "And this is Agent Karl Rand."

"An empath," Wagner said, her eyes going to Karl's green armband. "I take it this isn't a social call."

"We need to ask you some questions. Not about a client," John added hastily. Unless she failed to tell the truth, and they needed to dig deeper, anyway. "You're an exorcist, correct?"

"Correct." She opened a drawer and took out a purse that probably cost more than John's monthly salary. After a moment of fishing around in it, she handed over her registration card.

He compared the number to the one he'd recorded before coming here. "Ms. Wagner, have you summoned any sort of Non-Human Entity in the last two months?"

Her face stilled. "Ah. So I was right."

John exchanged a glance with Karl, who looked equally confused. "Right about what?"

"There is someone behind this outbreak of demons. And you're looking for them."

It was as though a cold finger trailed down John's spine. "What do you mean?"

"I can read the papers, special agent." She sank back in her leather chair. "Charleston is reeling under a wave of possessions. Do you expect me to believe that many people suddenly took it into their heads to summon demons on their own? No, someone is behind it." She shivered. "An exorcist. Making deals, offering 'help.' Maybe just stuffing them into people, I don't know."

John swallowed against a suddenly dry throat. "And do you have any guesses as to who this might be?"

"Someone with a much stronger talent than I'll ever have." Her dark eyes glanced at him, then at Karl. "For the record, I have never summoned an NHE."

"And you don't know anyone who has?"

"No."

Karl nodded. "She's telling us what she believes to be the truth."

"Thank you," John said. "We're sorry to have taken your time, Ms. Wagner."

Her expression remained distant. "I'm only glad exorcists can't be involuntarily possessed. It helps me sleep at night."

Neither Karl nor John spoke until they were back in the sedan. Karl broke the silence first. "Do you think she's right? That there's an... epicenter...to this outbreak?"

John tapped his fingers on the steering wheel. "I'd like to say no. It couldn't happen. But then I remember Howard Brimm and his army of ghouls."

Karl shuddered. "Just interviewing one of his victims was bad enough. Sheffield, I think her name was? The idea a SPECTR agent, even an ex-agent, would stoop so low as to force NHEs into people..."

"Brimm had succumbed to paranoia. This...if true, it's a lot bigger than anything he did." John let out a sigh. "I don't know. People look for patterns where there aren't any. It might not be anything. No mastermind, just a bunch of desperate people acting independently."

Karl smiled wanly. "Nice try, John, but I'm an empath. It's not easy to lie to me."

"I didn't convince myself, either." John reached for the list of names and addresses lying on the dashboard. "I'm keeping it in mind as something to dig into. If there is some kind of mastermind behind the outbreak, this is as good a way as any of uncovering them."

"So on to the next address?"

John put the car into gear. "On to the next address."

Caleb sat relegated to silence in the back seat of Ericsson's sedan. Steele and Ericsson rode in the front, joking, chatting, and generally pretending Caleb didn't exist. Which wasn't the worst option, to be honest.

"You ever manage to score with that chick?" Steele asked his partner. "The one in the band with the dumb ass name? Twisted Rapid or some shit?"

"Oh, yeah," Ericsson said with a laugh that made Caleb want to take a shower.

"You seeing her again?"

"Nah. Turned out to be a whiny bitch."

"Better off without her," Steele said sympathetically.

Caleb ground his teeth together. If he had to listen to these chucklefucks much longer, he was going to reach over the seat and knock their heads together. Maybe some sliver of decency would rattle loose if he did it hard enough.

Gray stirred restlessly. *"I do not like these mortals. I want John and Zahira back."*

You and me both. But we have to play along, at least for a little while.

Ericsson took the Cooper River Bridge to Mount Pleasant, and thence to Patriots Point. Caleb had come here once with John and Sean, doing the tourist thing shortly after relocating to Charleston. The huge aircraft carrier anchored there had been vaguely interesting, but Caleb had spent most of the afternoon nodding dumbly while John spewed statistics about the fighter jets displayed on her flight deck.

Ericsson parked in the lot, but rather than make for the aircraft carrier or museum, he led the way to a grassy area where civil war cannons stood in a line, pointed out toward the harbor as though ready to hold off an assault. A number of cops milled about, the familiar yellow police tape fluttering in the breeze.

"You have a body?" Ericsson asked the cop who appeared in charge.

The cop nodded and pointed. "One of the tour guides spotted something odd from the causeway leading to the battleship."

"It's an aircraft carrier," Caleb said.

Steele and Ericsson both shot him a nasty look. "Go on," Steele said to the cop.

"They thought it was a dead animal, down in the marsh grass. A dolphin maybe, given the size. They didn't want any tourists to pitch a fit, so they called security and asked them to do something. A guard went down to shove the remains into the river, or bury them, whatever. That's when he realized it wasn't a dolphin."

"So what do we have?" Steele asked.

"Human remains. One arm, some organs, part of the back, with the front of the torso hollowed out. Fresh kill, and something chewed on it but good." The cop shrugged. "I figured it was one of yours."

"Might be. Might not be." Ericsson shrugged. "A human killer might have chopped up a body and dumped parts here, only to have gulls or fish feed on it."

"But you'll be able to tell, right?" the cop asked, a trace of worry in his voice.

"Maybe." Ericsson took a stick of gum out of his pocket and popped it in his mouth. "It'll have to go to forensics to be one-hundred percent certain."

Apparently Ericsson didn't realize why Caleb was in the field to start with. He waited until they started away from the cops, then said, "No need to wait on forensics. I guess Barillo didn't share, but Gray can smell demons, and—"

Ericsson came to an abrupt halt, forcing Caleb to sidestep to keep from walking into him. "Keep it to yourself. I already told you, we do things by the book."

Steele snorted, as though he'd made a joke. Ericsson cut him a sharp look, and Steele subsided. "Procedure is to have the bite marks looked at by a trained medical examiner," Ericsson went on. "Not some monster in your head."

Caleb gaped. He glanced at Steele, hoping for some backup, but Steele only wore the same disgusted expression on his face as Ericsson.

"The fuck?" he exclaimed. "Didn't you hear me? I can tell you right now if a demon did this, maybe even what kind. There's no need to waste a day waiting for forensics. The sooner we start tracking this thing, the less chance it has to kill someone else."

Gray roused. *These mortals do not wish for us to hunt the demon?*

No. Because they're fucking idiots.

Ericsson took a step toward him. Since he was shorter than Caleb, the agent wasn't able to loom, but he made up for it with a scowl whose anger bordered on hatred.

"I've been doing this job for a long time," he said, voice a savage growl. "Without the help of some damn demon. I'm not halfway to being a faust like Starkweather, accepting help from a monster just because it's easier than doing things the right way."

Caleb felt as though Ericsson had punched him in the gut. He knew the other agents looked at him sideways, especially after what had happened on Fort Sumter. But he'd never realized how working with him had affected their opinion of John.

When they'd met, John had been the district hotshot. On his way up the ladder with a bullet. Even the agents who hadn't liked him respected his ability.

The enormity of what they'd cost John struck him like a blast from one of the old cannons. Not just his chances at advancement, but the respect of the other agents. His reputation as a federal exorcist who bent the rules but never broke them. Who solved his cases through old-fashioned hard work and determination.

Now John was the guy who fucked an NHE and whose cases routinely went sideways. Who wasn't such a hot shot anymore. Whose coworkers obviously talked about him behind his back.

It wasn't fucking fair.

"John Starkweather is twice the agent you'll ever be," Caleb snarled.

Steele flushed puce. But Ericsson only said, "He used to be. Until he met you. Now his career is in the toilet, and no one will ever trust him to do more than shuffle papers." He stepped away from Caleb, shaking his head. "Steele and I might be stuck with you, but no way in hell am I going to let you destroy our careers the way you destroyed Starkweather's. So keep your demon shit to yourself, stay out of the way, and let us do our jobs."

Gray didn't like this, not at all. *Is he saying we have harmed John with our presence?*

Yeah. Caleb's hands clenched and unclenched. *It's not on us, though. It's on them. They're the ones who are choosing to treat him this way.*

"Mortal nonsense?"

Mortal nonsense. But it's okay. We're going to get through this.

Ericsson and Steele wanted to do things the hard way? Fine. Let them play their stupid games.

"I see," Caleb said aloud. "Well. I'll just stand aside and let you gentlemen get on with your investigation, shall I?"

Steele looked as though he suspected Caleb was being sarcastic, but wasn't quite sure. Ericsson only said, "Good. And be quiet."

They pushed their way through the low shrubs separating the marshy area from the maintained grounds. The two agents cursed the boggy earth as they made their way toward the remains. Caleb paused on the edge of solid ground, nostrils flared. The air brought him the scent of seawater and rotting marsh grasses…and something else.

A sort of cloying sweetness permeated the air, like a flower just on the verge of spoiling. Like fin rot and thick slime.

"*A demon.*" Gray's excitement thrummed through them. "*We must hunt it.*"

Caleb sighed and turned away. His skin itched with Gray's eagerness; they longed to track the scent, to find their prey. *Not yet.*

"*Because these mortals say we must not?*"

Because we've already cost John enough. They couldn't leave Charleston without him, and Caleb wasn't sure John was ready to cut ties and go on the run. He might never be ready. *Come on. Let's go sit in the car and wait for Agents Tweedledum and Tweedledee to finish.*

CHAPTER 3

"I'M SORRY ERICSSON and Steele are giving you such a hard time," John said as they stepped inside the condo. He'd spent the entire ride home listening to Caleb's complaints about his new partners. "I sympathize, babe. I do. But try not to let it get to you."

"I'm trying." Caleb stripped off his elk hide jacket and hurled it at the ugly orange couch he'd brought with him when he moved in. "Bad enough they don't want our help with the case, but they've ordered me to wear a suit, Starkweather. *A suit.*"

John winced. But at the same time, a little tendril of fear was starting to sprout in his gut. Maybe Ericsson and Steele were just being assholes. But there was another possibility. "I know it's tough. But Barillo is just looking for an excuse to make things even worse. I'm asking you not to give him one."

"I won't." Caleb ran his hand through his long hair. "We won't. Gray isn't happy about it, but he'll live."

At least Gray didn't actually need to eat demons to survive. But hunting was a pretty big part of Gray's existence. If Ericsson meant to make him just wait in the car while the two human agents took down NHEs...John didn't know how far Gray's patience would stretch.

Not knowing what else to do, John stepped up behind Caleb and slid his arms around his waist. "The good thing is, they won't be making you work overtime. So we'll have the evenings all to ourselves." It was a slim consolation, but the only thing he had to offer at the moment.

Caleb turned in John's arms and bent his head. Their lips met. A moment later, the background hum of Gray's energy suddenly spiked. The scent of rain-kissed sand and ancient incense flooded the room, and John's exorcist senses registered the brush of enormous power against his skin. It felt good, in a way he wasn't sure he could adequately explain to anyone who didn't have the same sixth sense.

It had been scary, the first time he'd felt it, face-to-face with Gray. With a creature that wasn't supposed to exist, as far beyond ordinary NHEs as a tiger was beyond a cow. But even then it had left him with a hard on.

"Hey, darling," he said softly.

Gray cocked his head, as if puzzled. His hair slithered around his shoulders, blowing in a wind that touched nothing else. "There is no need to greet me. I was already here."

"I know, I just...never mind." John sighed. "How are you holding up?"

Eyes black as wet obsidian regarded John. Little flashes of lightning sparked in their depths. "I do not like these new mortals," Gray said, not bothering to conceal his displeasure. "They are boring. They do not wish us to hunt." He paused. "But you are no longer angry at us, so I will do as Caleb says."

John winced. "Can I ask you something?"

"Of course."

He wasn't sure how Gray would take the question. Hell, he wasn't sure how Caleb would take it. "Before you ended up in a living body, did you know how to lie?"

Gray's brows drew together, and the lightning flashed more quickly in his eyes. "I hunted alone after coming to this world. I studied my prey. At times, I deceived it into thinking it was safe, when it was not."

Was Gray avoiding the question, or did he simply not understand the difference between an ambush and a lie? John bit his lip, trying to think what to say that wouldn't result in an argument. Because he truly didn't want to fight.

But being in a living body changed NHEs. And Caleb had remarked before that Gray was different than he had been at the start. They both were.

"That's not what I mean," he said at last. "You just always seem so direct. And I know *you* didn't lie to my face, but you kept something pretty big from me."

Gray's lips parted—then he vanished, and Caleb held up his hands. "Whoa, hey. Lay off Gray, all right? If you're pissed and have something to ask, ask me."

John didn't bother to hide his annoyance. "I think Gray can answer for himself."

Caleb crossed his arms over his chest. "Gray doesn't get why you keep bringing this up. I've spent all damn day trying to explain Ericsson and Steele's bullshit to him, and now, when he was hoping to get just a few minutes with you..." He shook his head, long hair whipping around him like a black cloak. "What do you want us to say? We're sorry. You're right—Gray didn't lie to you. I did, because I had to give you some excuse as to where we were in the evenings, and I'm sorry. We tried to explain to you why we didn't say anything, multiple times. I don't know what else you want from us."

Fuck. They were going to have an argument whether he wanted one or not, it seemed. "Our whole relationship is built on trust."

Caleb rolled his eyes. "I've been in relationships before."

"Not like this!" John dropped his hand. "I'm not afraid of Gray, because I *trust* him. I have to trust him not to get too rough in bed, because he could literally rip me limb from limb. I trust him not to go overboard when he asks to taste my blood, because those fangs are built for damage. If he gets too excited and bites me, the least I'm looking at is reconstructive surgery." John paused, letting his words sink in. "I trusted him—both of you—not to eat me when I walked up to you on Fort Sumter. Even though every instinct I had screamed at me to run the other way, I didn't, because I trusted you more than I feared you." John swallowed hard. "I feel like you just...acted like that trust was nothing."

Silence. Caleb's arms slowly unfolded. He took a deep breath, blinking rapidly. "Shit, John. We never meant—"

"I'm sorry—am I interrupting?" asked a voice faintly tinged with a Russian accent.

John spun, reaching for his Glock out of instinct. Yuri stood in the door leading to the back garden, which he could only have reached by climbing over the roof.

Like Caleb, he dressed all in black, including plenty of leather to keep away the claws and fangs of other NHEs. But his skin was pale as milk, and his long hair so blond it bordered on white. Blue eyes like arctic ice peered out from beneath a thick fringe of lashes.

The last time they'd come face-to-face, John had been too shocked by the very fact of another living drakul to notice just how damned gorgeous Yuri was.

And *this* was Gray's ex? Or, at least the body he'd been summoned into? Jealousy twined with anger low in John's belly. "This is a private conversation," he snapped, at the same time Caleb said, "Jesus, Yuri, have some fucking manners."

Yuri glanced at Caleb, brow arched. "I apologize. Should I use the front door next time?"

"What do you think? Were you raised in a damn barn?"

"You're quite right." Yuri held up his hands, but the edge of a smile continued to play over his lips. As though he found Caleb's admonishment more amusing than anything else. "Forgive me?"

"This time." Caleb glanced back and forth between them. "John, this is Yuri and Drugoy. Yuri, Dru, this is my boyfriend John."

Surprise flickered in Yuri's arctic eyes, there and gone so fast John wasn't entirely certain he'd seen it. "Ah, yes. The special agent who was almost eaten by the grendel."

John's face heated. "I had to try and stop it, before it hurt anyone else."

"Very brave of you." Yuri gave him a nod, then turned all his attention on Caleb. "We came to see how you were. And if Gray would like dinner." His grin showed off his teeth; clearly he meant the sort of meal that had to be chased down first. John's sense of his energy sharpened, Drugoy stirring somewhere under Yuri's smooth skin. The drakul were too powerful to hide completely, even when not manifesting.

"Always," Caleb muttered.

Yuri chuckled. "So I assumed. Perhaps we should get our dinner first, though. Most restaurants frown on bloodstained customers."

"Yeah. I need to ask you some things, anyway." Caleb thrust his hands into his pockets and glanced at John. "We'll talk when I get back, I promise."

John didn't want to start yet another argument, but he had no choice. "Yuri, I'm not sure how much you know about SPECTR, but if they find out another drakul is in Charleston, they'll do everything in their power to capture you."

"I'm very good at not getting caught," Yuri replied with a negligent wave of his hand.

"I'm sure you are, but...listen, were you on the Battery two weekends ago?"

A little frown line sprang up between Yuri's brows. "I don't recall. Why?"

"Because I already interviewed an exorcist who noticed *something* he couldn't explain." John glanced at Caleb. "Just a civilian—this time. But the last thing Caleb and Gray need right now is to raise suspicion they're acting outside of SPECTR's supervision."

"So no hunting on our off hours either?" Caleb guessed. "Yeah, Gray is...not okay with that."

"I know; I know." John reached out and put a hand on their arm. "I've agreed to keep Drugoy a secret from SPECTR. But if you're just going to tip them off yourselves, what was the point of lying to me in the first place?"

It was a low blow, but John saw it hit. "Yeah, yeah. Okay." Caleb sighed. "No hunting."

Yuri didn't say anything, only watched Caleb with slightly narrowed eyes. Hopefully, Caleb would take the opportunity to explain the situation to Yuri over their human dinner. "Thanks. You two have a good meal."

"We won't be too late." Caleb brushed a soft kiss across John's lips. "See you in a few hours."

He went to the front door, and Yuri sauntered after him. "It was nice to formally meet you, John," he said. Then the door shut behind them, and they were gone.

Less than an hour later, Caleb found himself sitting in the swankiest restaurant he'd ever been in. The sort of place where the menus didn't have prices, and even the water glasses were made out of crystal.

"I hope you've got the money to pay for this," Caleb murmured to Yuri. They sat across from one another in a discreet corner, away from the windows overlooking Charleston Harbor. "Because I might need to take out a mortgage on my nonexistent house to cover the bill."

Yuri arched one pale brow. "You're an immortal with immense strength and speed, Caleb. You don't need to worry about money any more than you need to worry about wrinkles."

Caleb glanced around nervously, but no one seemed to have overheard. "I'm...not sure what you mean," he hedged.

"Then allow me to put it a different way. There are many unscrupulous men in the world. Ones who deal with large amounts of cash, or jewels, so as not to have their activities traced. In the past, I have...relieved...some of them of the burden of their ill-gotten gains." Yuri shot him a wink. "Given enough time and a sizable enough deposit, one can live quite comfortably."

"Yeah, that's what I thought you meant." It was a good thing John wasn't with them. He certainly wouldn't be okay with stealing, no matter how evil the victim.

"You're still thinking like a mortal," Yuri chided gently.

Caleb looked away. "I'm still human."

"There are two ways of doing things, Caleb." Yuri took a sip from his water glass. "The mortal way. And the drakul way."

Gray perked up. *"The drakul way?"*

"You got Gray's attention there." Still, Caleb wasn't certain he liked dividing up the world, with him and Yuri on one side, and John and everyone else on the other.

The waiter approached and proffered a bottle of wine whose name Caleb had never heard of and couldn't pronounce. Yuri decreed it acceptable, and soon enough they each had a glass of dark red liquid in front of them. Caleb sipped his cautiously. "Wow, it's really good."

"Don't sound so surprised," Yuri said with a grin.

"Sorry. I don't know shit about wine." Caleb put his glass down, just as a small fleet of waiters appeared. They silently served the meal, then retreated. Caleb had ordered the only vegetarian option on the menu, billed as the "localvore vegetable plate." Yuri had cedar plank salmon.

"No blood," Caleb said, understanding dawning. "The fish, I mean. That is, obviously they have blood, but it's not gross like beef." Realizing what he'd said, he glanced around to make sure none of the staff or other customers had overheard. "Gray hates even looking at 'cold blood,' as he puts it. Makes dining out fun."

Yuri savored a bite of his salmon. "Drugoy as well. It sounds as though you have a story behind your remark, though."

"Our first nice dinner out concluded in a garlic-related incident."

"Oh dear." Yuri shuddered theatrically.

"It was a double date." Caleb found himself grinning, even though it hadn't been remotely funny at the time. "I spit pasta sauce all over some poor woman."

"No," Yuri broke into laughter.

"After I insulted her salad." Caleb took a bite of his roasted—and garlic-free—vegetables. The chunk of potato all but melted on his tongue. "Oh yum."

"I'm glad you're enjoying it." The finest of lines crinkled at the corners of Yuri's eyes when he smiled. "You said you had questions for me."

Caleb swallowed a chunk of carrot and nodded. "Yeah. When you met John the first time, after we killed the grendel, you said you hadn't realized he was one of ours. One of our what?"

"Your renfields, of course." When Caleb only looked at him blankly, Yuri paused, fork raised halfway to his mouth. "Gray doesn't have renfields?"

"I don't...think so?"

"But he's been here so long." Yuri lowered the fork to the plate, frowning now. "In all those years, he must have had mortals who served him. Perhaps he calls them something else?"

"I never cared about mortals until I had a living body. Unless they were possessed. Then I ate them."

Caleb shook his head. "Gray's not really into mortals. Except for John and Zahira, I guess, but he only met them after possessing me."

"I see." Yuri finally lifted his fork to his mouth, seeming to ponder as he chewed. "Let me explain. Demons have their fausts. We have our renfields." He smiled slightly. "I coined the term from the highly inaccurate novel, obviously."

Despite the delicious food, Caleb's appetite had deserted him. Whatever Yuri was getting at, Caleb wasn't sure he liked it. "I don't understand."

"Demons have fausts, whom they possess in exchange for...well, whatever it is that leads the mortal to risk possession. Strength or revenge or influence." Yuri shrugged dismissively. "But drakul—or Drugoy, at least—have mortals who serve them in return for enhanced paranormal abilities."

Caleb shifted uneasily. "That's not the case with John. I mean, he *does* get a, um, boost paranormally speaking when Gray...you know..."

"Lets John drink his blood?" Yuri asked.

It hadn't even occurred to Caleb. "Not blood. Other...fluids."

For a moment, Yuri was very still. Listening to Drugoy, probably. "I see," he said at last. "Was John your boyfriend before Gray?"

"No. We met because I was possessed." Caleb forced himself to eat a bite of sweet potato. "But Gray noticed him right way. I mean, we both did. I figured John would be freaked out if he found out Gray had fixated on him, so they didn't hook up until after John and I had been together for a while. Well, forty days, give or take."

"Ah." Yuri smiled, as if Caleb had confirmed something for him. "You say Gray fixated on John. And there is another mortal he notices in particular as well?"

"Zahira. Gray says they're both *ours,* which is kind of creepy. But we don't...I mean, Zahira is nice and all, but it's not the same. *Definitely* no sharing body fluids with her."

"Yes, yes. There are certain mortals drakul fixate on. I'm not certain if there's a pattern; perhaps in time, between the two of us, we may discover one." Yuri finished his salmon and paused while a silent waiter whisked it away. "As far as Drugoy is concerned, there is the common herd of mortals, to be disregarded unless they are posing an immediate inconvenience. And there are those worth his notice."

Caleb nodded eagerly. "Right! Same with Gray. He had to work with some of the SPECTR agents, when we were going after Forsyth, and he's pretty upset with our current boss, but it's not the same as with John and Zahira. He...likes them, I guess is the way I'd put it."

"The ones Gray notices—fixates on—are your renfields."

Caleb wiped his hands on the napkin in his lap. "I don't know. Gray loves John."

"Of course he does. Or were you under the impression drakul do anything halfway?" Yuri's expression turned rueful. "Their love—and hate—is immense. Gray doesn't care one way or the other about most mortals, but he would kill anything—anyone—that dared lay a hand on John or Zahira, wouldn't he?"

Gray roused. *"I would not allow them to be harmed."*

"Yeah, pretty much. When the vila enthralled Zahira, he was *furious*. He didn't just want to eat it—he wanted to rip its fucking head off. Then eat it, of course."

"Of course." Yuri paused. "Drugoy wishes to speak to Gray, once we leave here."

"About hunting?" Caleb guessed with a wince. "Look, Gray isn't happy about it either, but—"

Yuri held up a silencing hand. "Let them talk about it, Caleb. You and I have had our pleasant conversation. Allow them to do the same."

CHAPTER 4

"YOU DO NOT mean to obey the mortal," Drugoy states, the moment they have both manifested. "We will hunt now."

They perch atop one of the roofs of the old mansions near the harbor. The wind off the ocean is keen, and Gray breathes deep. There is no sign of a storm, which saddens him a bit.

"One day you're going to get us struck by lightning."

You are being foolish. Now allow me to talk to Drugoy.

"I would prefer to hunt," Gray says aloud. "I enjoyed our hunt of the werewolves, our hunt of the grendel. But John is right. If SPECTR discovers you, you will have to leave. And I do not wish for you to leave."

"You are thinking like a mortal." Drugoy's voice is a low rumble, like the shifting of the earth. His eyes glow redly in the night, as though a river of lava moves beneath black glass. "You are letting them cage you, trap you in their ways. But you have no need of them."

"I am not thinking like a mortal," Gray replies, stung. "I am not so foolish."

"Are you not? Mortals talk and talk and talk. They create their own chains, of rules and worry and nonsense." Drugoy's lips peel back, revealing fangs. "But we do not. Do you remember?"

"Remember?"

"Hunting together. Not here." Drugoy's hair blows in the wind, a pale wing that nearly touches Gray's shoulder. "You drove them down from the sky, and I up from below."

He does remember, but in the way Caleb remembers dreams. Fragmentary things, which grow more unfocused, rather than less, when examined. It was so very long ago. "Together, we feasted."

Drugoy watches him intently. "We can feast again."

He wants to. Badly. But there is John to think of.

"There was a demon, earlier today." Gray lets out a growl, remembering. "But the mortals with us would not allow us to hunt it. I do not understand. It is a demon. Why should we not at least track it to its lair?"

"Because they're assholes who are afraid of us. And they'll use that fear against John."

"Caleb says it is because they fear us. And if we make them fear more, they will turn against John." Gray is very close to hating these mortals, rather than simply finding them annoying. "Perhaps Zahira as well. I will not let John and Zahira be taken from us, and if it means I must not hunt...I will not hunt. For now."

Drugoy says nothing for a long moment. Then he tips his head back, face turned up to the moon. "You have truly had no renfields before? No mortals who were yours?"

"No." Gray extends the tips of his claws slightly, then retracts them again. "When I inhabited dead bodies, I did not truly feel. Pain was only a faint shadow, and there was no scent in the world save that of demons. Sometimes, I would lie in a crypt or deserted place during the daylight hours, and examine the memories I gleaned from the corpses I possessed. But they were dull, colorless things. They seemed to have nothing to do with me. Mere curiosities I replayed over and over again, unable to understand the passions driving them."

Drugoy turns to watch him, now. The wind tosses strands of white hair across his white skin. "Things were very different for you."

"Yes. It was not until after Caleb's heart began to beat again that I understood. Pain, pleasure. Love and fear. Taste and color and all the good things of this world." Gray looks out over the darkened water. Sometimes he is still astonished by how beautiful it all is. "I am glad to be with Caleb. With John. I wish we could go, could leave this place together, but it is not possible. So I must be content."

They sit quietly for a while. Even if they cannot hunt, it is good just to be together. Eventually, however, Drugoy stirs.

"You have walked this world far longer than I," he says. "And yet, when it comes to the existence you now find yourself in, in a living body, it would seem I am the elder."

"Yes. Caleb believes there is much we can learn from you."

"Indeed." Drugoy rises to his feet. "I will be patient, Gray. I will wait for you to realize."

Gray rises as well. "Realize?"

A smile lifts the corner of Drugoy's mouth, revealing the tip of a fang. "You have let the thinking of mortals bind you without need." He steps to the edge of the roof. "When you are tired of placating mortals, when you are ready to do things the drakul way instead, I will help you."

Then he steps over the edge and vanishes into the night.

"John?" Caleb called softly as he shut the door. "Are you still up?"

John had retreated to bed, sitting propped against the pillows, reading from his tablet. After the frantic pace of the last few weeks, it felt strange not to have a case to work on.

Well, technically, he did have a case. But as he couldn't conduct interviews dressed in his boxers, there wasn't much for him to do at night.

"I'm up," John called down. Caleb's footsteps sounded on the spiral stair leading to the second floor, and a moment later he appeared in the bedroom door. His long black hair was in disarray, either from the wind or from Gray manifesting, or both. At the sight of John, a smile broke over his face, lighting his brown eyes.

The smile soothed John's nerves. Not to say he had been precisely worried. But Yuri had the looks of a Russian model, and Dru was the only other one of Gray's kind, *and* there had been some connection between them on the etheric plane, which John still wasn't clear on. That was a lot for one underpaid federal agent to compete with.

"How was dinner with Yuri?" John asked, setting aside his tablet.

Caleb had already left his boots downstairs. He climbed into bed, sitting cross-legged at an angle so he more or less faced John. "Enlightening."

John cocked his head to one side. "How so?"

"You know Gray normally doesn't pay attention to unpossessed people, unless they force him to. But there are exceptions. You. Zahira."

John made an impatient gesture. "I know, Caleb."

"I guess it's normal? Of course, as Zahira would say, we have a sample size of two." Caleb shrugged. "It seems like drakul gravitate to certain people. For whatever reason." He paused, listening. "Gray says because you're interesting and he likes you. Well, Gray loves *you,* obviously. And I'm starting to figure out something I don't think Yuri really understands."

John leaned forward. "What?"

"He's lonely. He and Dru both." Caleb took one of John's hands and held it in his lap. "If I hadn't had you after Gray possessed me...I don't know what I would have done. I mean it. I would've been completely lost without you."

"I'm glad I could be there for you." Warmth flooded John's chest, and he tightened his fingers on Caleb's. "For both of you."

"Same here." Caleb smiled at him again. "I get the feeling Yuri and Dru didn't have that. There are people they interact with, but they keep them at a distance. *Renfields,* Yuri calls them. Dru shares his blood with them—they're all paranormally abled, so they get a boost."

"Wait." John frowned. "There are other people out there who know about drakul?"

"Not many, or at least that was my impression. Probably fewer than in the Vigilant."

"And Drugoy shares his blood with them?" A little sliver of unease lodged in his belly. "To make them stronger?"

"Mmm hmm." Caleb shifted to his knees, leaning in. The look he gave John could have set fire to the sheets. "I think our way of sharing is better, don't you?"

John's throat tightened, and his cock grew heavy with blood. He could feel the little teasing flare of Gray's energy, seething just under Caleb's skin. As for Caleb, he was just so damned gorgeous he took John's breath away. "I'd say so."

He ought to follow up on the whole renfield thing. But when Caleb kissed him, mouth hot and hungry, it suddenly didn't seem nearly so urgent.

When the kiss ended, Caleb dipped his head, brushing his lips along John's jaw. "I know we let you down. What can we do, to make things up to you? Blowjob? Or do you want Gray to fuck you? Or both of us to fuck you?"

Sex wouldn't make up for abusing John's trust...but it wouldn't hurt anything, for damned sure. "Both."

John had stripped to his boxers when getting into bed. Caleb ran his hand down and across John's bare stomach. There was a flash of claw tips, just enough to make John gasp, then Caleb's hand sliding underneath the waistband.

"You're getting good at that," John managed to say. Gray's energy vibrated in his senses, right on the edge of manifesting.

"We are," Caleb agreed, and pulled John's cock free.

John gripped the sheets as Caleb and Gray worked him over. A hot, wet mouth and suction, replaced by the scrape of a fang along his slit. Back and forth, trading off as necessary, and he wondered what he'd possibly done to deserve something this good.

They sat back before he came too close to the edge. Caleb stripped off their clothes, then stretched the length of their body against John's. A moment later, Gray kissed him—hard and hot and demanding. John opened his lips greedily, let Gray plunder his mouth, Caleb suck on his tongue.

"I should do something for you," he said, when he could speak again.

"You are," Gray purred.

John closed his eyes and reveled in sensation. Flashes of etheric energy washed over his skin, Gray and Caleb switching off smoothly. They bit at his nipples, sucked on his belly, teased the sensitive skin of his inner thighs with claws and nails. Taking their time to drive him wild, until he squirmed and whimpered.

They fucked him the same way, first Caleb, then Gray. Claws on the fingers gripping his hips, long hair brushing his aching cock as they bent over him. Etheric energy coming in pulses, until suddenly they stiffened, Caleb's cry shifting into a lower register. The energy hit John like a wave, and he gripped his cock, jacking himself frantically as he came.

They pulled free, and Caleb stretched out by John, pillowing his head on John's shoulder. "How was that?"

"Fantastic," John said honestly.

Caleb snickered. "We thought it would be fun to try trading places fast like that." He shifted to kiss John softly. "Listen, I just want to say… you're worth putting up with all the bullshit at SPECTR. With everything. You're the most important thing in the world to us, and we never wanted to make you feel otherwise."

"I love you, too." John reached to turn off the light. "And I get it. Yuri, Drugoy…they're the only one of your kind you've ever met. Are ever likely to meet."

"Yeah." Caleb sighed. His hand rested lightly on John's chest. "And they're going to have to leave, sooner or later. Otherwise, SPECTR is sure to find them. I need—we need—to learn everything we can from them before that happens. And maybe we can be there for them, while they're here."

"I get that," John said. And he did.

Maybe he shouldn't be thinking about digging into those old files. Whoever Yuri Azarov had been sixty years ago, being with Drugoy had surely changed him. At the least, he should tell Caleb he was doing it.

"Babe," he started, "I was thinking…"

He trailed off as Caleb let out a little snore. John lifted his head up and saw Caleb's eyes shut, his features relaxed in sleep.

"Never mind," he whispered, and kissed Caleb's brow.

The next morning, Caleb walked into SPECTR-HQ, his hair bound into a braid and his shoulders hunched beneath the weight of the three-piece suit he'd bought for the post-Fort Sumter hearings, when SPECTR had still been trying to figure out what to do with him. Not that the suit objectively weighed much, certainly not compared to his normal hundred pounds of elk hide and kevlar, but it seemed to press down on him nonetheless. Not to mention the tie strangling him.

John even had the audacity to compliment him. "Looking good, babe," he'd said when he came out of the bathroom to find Caleb struggling with the tie. "I know you're not a fan of suits now, but maybe after a while you'll come to like them."

Caleb had only rolled his eyes at the bit of wild optimism. That was John all over, though. Every cloud came with a silver lining.

Caleb had been assigned a new desk in the cube farm, not far from Zahira's. When she caught sight of him, her eyes widened. "Is everything all right?"

A little splinter of guilt niggled at Caleb. Zahira still didn't know about Yuri and Dru. If she realized there was another living drakul for her to interrogate, her head would probably explode from sheer delight.

"Right as it can be," he said, pausing by her chair. "How's ghoul squad?"

She tried to smile, but he wasn't buying it for a minute. "A necessary duty."

The sort of duty given to rookies and disgraced agents. Though technically, Zahira was a rookie. Still, she'd worked three big cases with them. Ghoul squad was definitely a big step down.

Ericsson and Steele seemed to think working with Caleb would permanently derail John's career. Would the same happen to Zahira?

Wish her good hunting. And to be careful. I would not have her hurt by demons.

"Gray says stay safe and good luck." Caleb shrugged. "We both do."

It brought a genuine smile to her face. "Inshallah, I will."

Caleb made his way over the industrial beige carpet to the cube he'd been assigned yesterday—then stopped. Foam stuffing spilled out of the slashed fabric of his chair. The pen holder was empty, pens snapped and ink leaking from them across the top of his desk. Someone had taken a permanent marker and defaced the plaque with his name on it, slashing through *Caleb Jansen* and writing *MONSTER* beneath it.

And to top it off, the distinctive scent of garlic wafted from the direction of the telephone. The vandals had wiped down the receiver with oil.

Gray reacted with displeasure. *Do not touch it. It is poison.*

The phone began to ring.

A snicker sounded behind them. Caleb turned slowly, and found a number of agents peering out of their cubes. Watching, because it was all a setup. Their expressions ranged from dull curiosity to cruel smirks.

Caleb's heart kicked against his ribs, and he flexed his hands. Fuckers. They'd done this to harass him. Just like the garlic oil on the doorknob to John's office, or the word *monster* written over the conference room where they'd met with Zahira.

The other agents wanted him gone. Hell, he wanted to go. Didn't they get he wasn't here of his own volition? They'd be better off petitioning the higher-ups to let him go than harassing him.

But he was here in front of them and lacked the power to sink their career, unlike those at the top of the SPECTR org chart. So he became their target instead.

"Better answer that," one of the agents said with a smirk. His suit jacket hung on a peg on his cube wall, his shirtsleeves rolled up to reveal muscular forearms. The nameplate just above his coat hook read *Oscar Quackenbush*. "You don't want to get in trouble."

Caleb crossed the space between them in two long strides. Quackenbush jerked back with a cry of alarm, his face going from smug to frightened in an instant.

For a moment, it almost made Caleb want to do more. To show them he wasn't going to put up with it. Wasn't going to keep doing things the mortal way.

Instead, he reached past the cowering man and ripped the jacket off its hanger. A quick tug, and the sleeve came free. Caleb tossed the rest of the jacket onto the floor and turned back to the ringing phone.

The garlic fumes would still sting his eyes and nose, but at least the sleeve protected his hand. He lifted the receiver gingerly, holding it as far out from his face as he could. "Hello?"

"Finally!" Steele snapped from the other end. "Get to the conference room. We have work to do."

CHAPTER 5

CALEB SAT AT the far end of the table from Ericsson and Steele, listening while they talked. They'd ignored him once he'd arrived, which was annoying but still an improvement over the assholes in the cube farm.

Assuming his new partners hadn't been the ones wrecking his desk and painting the phone with garlic oil.

He shouldn't have destroyed Quackenbush's jacket. If the agent reported him to Barillo, he'd be in deep shit. After everything he'd said last night to Yuri and Dru about not getting in trouble, he'd potentially fucked up less than twelve hours later.

"Forensics got back to us," Steele said. He pulled up something on his laptop Caleb couldn't see. "Definitely an NHE—the bite marks don't match human or animal. Something about the size of a human, but with a mouth stuffed full of needle teeth, had our victim for lunch."

"Do we have an ID on the victim?" Ericsson asked.

"Fortunately, the whole thing was caught on camera." Steele took out a tablet and pulled something up. "There are security cameras at various spots around Patriots Point, to keep an eye out for vandals. Don't want anti-war troublemakers wrecking the ships or aircraft."

"Yeah, imagine being against war," Caleb muttered under his breath. "Did they catch something?"

Ericsson cast him an unfriendly glower. "I thought we made it clear, you're to keep your mouth shut, demon."

Anger flooded out from Gray. *"I am no—"*
Christ, I know!

Hell with it. These fuckers weren't ever going to like them, no matter what Caleb did or said. "Gray isn't a demon." Caleb grinned, making sure his teeth showed. "He *eats* demons."

Ericsson's eyes widened, and Steele shivered. "Creepy fucker," Steele muttered.

"I don't care," Ericsson said, but it was all bluster, at least judging by how pale he'd gotten. "But if you're so interested, take a look."

Steele shoved the tablet halfway across the table, angling it so they could all see without Caleb having to come closer. Grainy footage began to play, shapes indistinct in the night. A figure exited from the covered area meant to give people waiting for the Fort Sumter Ferry a place to stand out of the sun or rain.

"That's one of the cruise ship workers. According to the supervisor, he stayed late to clean up the mess left behind by a group of drunk tourists," Steele said.

The figure in the video paused, before turning in the direction of the river bank. He took a step toward the river, then another.

A second figure appeared, almost out of frame. Even with the poor quality of the recording, Caleb could tell it wasn't human. But instead of running away screaming, the victim held out his arms and hurried toward the NHE. They both vanished out of frame—unless you counted the geyser of blood spouting from off camera a second later.

Caleb leaned forward. Ericsson and Steele both leaned away. "What the hell? He just went to his death? Is it an incubus? Succubus?"

"They don't eat their victims," Steele said. "They drain energy."

Oh. Right. Caleb had forgotten. There were too many damn demons to keep track of.

"That is why it is simpler to just eat them, rather than worry about type or kind."

Ericsson seemed too intent on his own thoughts to reprimand Caleb. "Siren. Got to be." He ticked off points on his fingers. "It hunted near the water edge. It lured the victim, made him think it had something he wanted. And it was after flesh."

"Shit." Steele leaned back and rubbed his face with his hands.

"I take it from Special Agent Steele's enthusiasm this isn't an easy NHE to track?" Caleb looked back and forth between them. "Is it because it lives in water, or…?"

"It's because they use their…their thrall…to hide their nature from humans," Ericsson answered. "They convince their target they're a long-lost sibling, or a talent agent, or are holding a book from the Library of fucking Alexandria." He took an antacid from his pocket and popped it into his mouth. "Whatever the target finds most irresistible."

Caleb almost said he was surprised to learn Ericsson had ever heard of the Library of Alexandria, but bit it back. They were letting him talk for the moment, but if he made another smart remark, they'd shut him down. "So it's not just sexual, like with an incubus," Caleb said. Even exorcists weren't immune to such a thrall. The incubus they'd fought had nearly gotten John, by pretending to be Gray.

That was the first time Gray had called John "ours." With the same possessive instinct he'd shown with Drugoy.

"John wished to go with the incubus. I could not allow it to take him. And I would not have him go with Drugoy, either."

"They aren't common, thankfully." Steele pulled the tablet back to him and closed it. "But they're incredibly dangerous. We might need to ask the chief for more help. Enough backup the siren can't charm us all at once."

Ericsson winced. "You know that's not going to happen. We're stretched thin as it is."

"Or, you could take the demon-sniffing vampire who's immune to the siren's thrall." Caleb sat back in his chair. "Just as, you know, a suggestion."

Ericsson scowled. But Steele looked hopeful. "Really? You can't be charmed?"

The incubus hadn't been able to affect them, anyway. *So a siren couldn't either, right?*

"Do not be foolish. I know a demon when I hunt it."

"Just one of the many services I offer," Caleb said, spreading his hands. "Point me in the right direction, gentlemen, and I'll take care of your problem. You can even have all the credit with Barillo."

John parked the sedan in front of a dry cleaner. They'd worked their way out from the college, passing from the nicer parts of town to those with cracked sidewalks and shuttered businesses. Though John doubted most college students owned clothes that had to be dry cleaned, Mike had been on a scholarship. Maybe he felt like he had to dress a little better to match the rich kids sitting next to him in class.

"What's the name again, Karl?" John asked.

Karl checked his phone for their list. "Jake Nixon, 37 years old, and owner of this fine establishment. Got into a lot of trouble with the law in his early twenties, mostly for drugs. One B&E. And it looks like he was pulled in by SPECTR once on suspicion of illegal summoning, but the charges were dropped."

"Huh." Had the charges been dropped because Nixon was cleared, or for lack of evidence? "Let's go in and have a chat with Mr. Nixon."

A shabby air clung to the interior of the building, as pervasive as the chemical scent of the cleaners. Scuffed linoleum covered the floor, and the fluorescent lights above let out a buzz that set John's teeth on edge. The woman behind the stained counter cast a disinterested eye at their badges, then shouted into the back.

The man who emerged was tall and weedy, his skin sallow, as though he didn't get into the sun often. When he saw their badges, an expression of fury flashed over his face, quickly tamped down. "My office," he snapped. "Now."

John didn't need to be an empath to know Nixon wasn't happy to see them. Antipathy toward law enforcement in general, or SPECTR in particular?

Nixon stormed into the back, and they followed. The office was tiny, its walls bare concrete and every available surface covered in receipts. The moment the door shut, Nixon rounded on them so sharply John had to stop himself from reaching for his Glock.

"What the fuck do you think you're doing?" Nixon demanded. "I ain't made of money. Your pals have already bled me dry."

John would have taken a step back, if the office had been big enough to let him. This wasn't how he'd expected this conversation to go. "I'm sorry? I don't know what you mean."

"Right." Nixon leaned a hip against his desk, arms crossed over his chest. "You're here to investigate a case. You're going to drag me away from my business, which I bust my ass to run, and let me stew in an interrogation room for a few hours. But oh look, there's an easy way to keep it from happening called 'emptying my wallet.'"

Heaviness settled into John's gut. He glanced at Karl, who looked equally shocked. "Mr. Nixon, are you saying SPECTR agents are shaking you down?"

"I ain't saying nothing." Nixon's lip curled in disgust. "You pigs need to communicate better, though, because I ain't got enough cash on hand to pay twice." He gestured at the water stained ceiling. "Does this place look like some kind of goldmine?"

Sekhmet, Most Strong, it couldn't be true. SPECTR was a great many things, but surely his fellow agents hadn't stooped to this level. They were supposed to protect people, not turn on the paranormally abled. Their own community.

Maybe it was a mistake. Or maybe Nixon was lying. John took a deep breath. "If you have a complaint to make against specific agents, please do so."

"Right. So your little empath there can say I'm lying about something, and I'll end up in a holding cell." Nixon shook his head. "Get out of here."

"We have some questions for you," John said, desperate to take control of the interview back. "Have you ever summoned a Non-Human Entity?"

"No." Nixon all but spat the word.

"Do you know anyone who has?"

"No."

John nodded. "Thank you for your time. We'll leave you to get back to work."

"Talk to the other fucking pigs next time!" Nixon called after them.

John managed to hold back until they were outside. Heat waves rose from the sidewalk, and the interior of the car felt like a furnace even after such a brief stop. He cranked the AC as high as possible and sat back. "Tell me he was lying, Karl."

"I wish I could." Karl's mouth was drawn tight, the corners of his eyes crinkled. "Nixon told the truth as he understood it. Including about being shaken down."

"Fuck." John slammed his palm against the steering wheel. "As if we didn't have enough problems." How far did this go? Was it a lone agent looking to make some easy money, or did it reach higher? "Do you think Barillo knows?"

"Even if he doesn't, if you take this to him, he won't listen. Not to you." Karl rubbed tiredly at his face. "He'll ask why we're harassing fellow agents instead of concentrating on our assignment. And without names or proof..." He trailed off.

Names. Maybe if they had names, Barillo would listen. Or someone higher up the ladder. "Did the list mention who arrested Nixon when SPECTR brought him in for questioning? It might not be the same person shaking him down, but it would at least give us a place to start."

"Start what?" Karl spread his hands apart. "We can't get a look at anyone's bank account without a warrant. If Kaniyar was still district chief..."

He didn't bother to finish the sentence. Kaniyar had gone on to head SPECTR after the former director, assistant director, and any number of SPECTR higher-ups were implicated during the investigation into Forsyth. She had better things to do than worry about whether an agent in a regional office had gone dirty.

"I don't know," John said at last. "But I can't let this go, Karl."

Karl sighed and sat back. "This is one of the times I wish I didn't know when you're telling the truth."

"Of course, we didn't find anything." Caleb shoveled the last of his hummus into his mouth with a slice of pita. "Ericsson and Steele were adamant—not a flash of fang or a glimpse of claw. I had to keep it to their pace and go where they went." He let out a frustrated sigh. "Which wouldn't be a problem if we'd just been talking streets, or the parks. But sirens don't stick to roads. What if there was a trace in the marshes, and we missed it?"

John sat across from him at the small restaurant they usually went to on date nights. Though with the outbreak, it had been a long time since they'd *had* a date night, come to think of it. Was that behind John's unexpected suggestion they eat out tonight? Or did it have something to do with the fact Yuri had taken Caleb out last night?

No, that was absurd. John wasn't the jealous type.

"At least it seems like they're starting to warm up to the idea of using your abilities," John said, because of course he had to find some positive angle. "Maybe working with them won't be so bad."

Caleb only shook his head. "Gray doesn't like them. At all. We want to be working with you and Zahira, the way it was before."

"I know." John's lips tightened, and Caleb felt a flash of guilt.

"Sorry. Here I am complaining, and you're not even in the field anymore." Caleb reached across the table and took John's hand in his. That was one of the reasons he liked coming here; no one so much as blinked at two guys holding hands. "Tell me about your day."

Their server approached the table. "Y'all doing all right over here?"

John ordered a second beer, and the server refilled Caleb's water glass. Caleb couldn't help but compare her to the waiters from last night —ready to help, but otherwise silent, efficient, and discreet. He'd tried not to compare the food as well, but that was harder. What was Yuri eating tonight?

"And is Drugoy hunting without us?"

Once she was gone, John shrugged. "Mostly Karl and I just

interviewed exorcists. And yes, I know how you feel about the registration list, so no need to get into it again."

"I wasn't going to," Caleb protested. "Any leads so far?"

John cast him a skeptical look, but only said, "One interviewee did have an interesting hypothesis about the uptick in NHE activity."

John recounted it while finishing his second beer and waiting for the check. "Is it possible?" Caleb asked, when he was done. "I mean, Brimm had a whole pack of ghouls he'd made just so he could order them around. Could someone else be doing the same thing?"

"It's not impossible," John said. "It hasn't come up in any interviews of those we've been able to exorcise. But there have been an awful lot of NHE possessions we've had to put down. The arrests turn violent, and the agents don't have a choice but to shoot." He shook his head. "There's something else. You can't tell anyone, but...I think an agent is dirty. Harassing people unless they pay up."

Fuck. No wonder John had seemed so glum. "Who?"

"I don't know. I also don't want to mention it to Barillo. Not until I've got some kind of proof."

"If there's any evidence, you'll find it," Caleb said with all the confidence he could muster.

"Maybe." John offered him a small smile, but it didn't quite reach his eyes. "Ready to get out of here?"

They'd barely taken two steps out the door when a startled shout came from the sidewalk ahead of them. Caleb looked up—and found himself staring into the terrified face of a woman he knew.

Haylee. Empath.

PASS member, who had called him a SPECTR plant when she found out his identity. Whose wrist was in a splint, because Gray had accidentally broken it when she tried to stab them with a bagel knife.

"She called us a demon."

Not interested right now. "Haylee," Caleb said, raising his hands. His heart pounded, and sweat slicked his spine. "Just calm down."

She backed away. People were stopping now, turning to see what was going on. "Run! Oh my God, get away from him! He's possessed!"

"Why does this mortal not understand? I told her we were no threat, yet she will not believe me."

All the blood drained from Caleb's extremities. He'd tried so hard not to think about what had happened at PASS. How the people he'd thought his friends had reacted when they found out about Gray.

A crowd began to gather, voices murmuring. Their gazes seemed to strip away Caleb's skin, leaving him flayed and bleeding. No one had made a move toward him yet, but if they did, it would become a mob. Images of being beaten in the street flashed through his mind. They had to protect John—if they grabbed him and ran, could they get away before things got ugly?

John took out his badge and held it up. "Calm down, ma'am. I'm a SPECTR exorcist. There's nothing to be afraid of here, I assure you."

His serene assurance, contrasted with Haylee's wild-eyed horror, shifted the mood of the crowd. The atmosphere went from potential panic and violence, to people watching a spectacle. Out of the corner of his eye, Caleb saw someone take out their phone and begin to record.

Fuck. If Barillo found out...

Haylee shook her head frantically. "Why are you lying? There's a demon in him!"

"I assure you, ma'am, there's not a *demon* in my friend." John glanced at the crowd. "I think you should move along now."

Haylee's frantic eyes darted around, but found no support. "Crazy mindfucker," a man called, having spotted her empath's armband.

She took one step back, then another. "Fine. Stay here. Let it kill you. But don't pretend you weren't warned."

She turned and ran, vanishing down the first side street. John sighed but didn't put away his badge. "Move along, everyone. Nothing to see here."

As the crowd began to disperse, he touched Caleb's arm. "Come on. Let's go home."

Caleb nodded and fell in by him. They walked in silence for a couple of blocks, before John said, "Are you okay, babe?"

No. No, Caleb wasn't okay. Because Haylee's fear brought it all rushing back. The way the other PASS members had either fled or attacked him. Nigel, Deacon, all of them. They'd wanted to kill Gray—to kill Caleb—even when Gray tried to explain he'd always been there. There wasn't any reason to be afraid.

They'd been his only friends outside of SPECTR. Besides John and Zahira, his only friends, period.

Grief dug like razor wire into his heart. He tipped his head back, forcing himself to breathe deep as realization swept over him.

He wasn't ever going to have friends again. No matter what happened with SPECTR, he'd always have to hide a part of himself away. No one could ever know about Gray, and the fact of it broke what little hope he'd had left.

Gray brushed against him comfortingly, like a great cat in the shared space of their mind. *"You will never be alone, Caleb. You will always have me."*

Yeah. He sent a surge of affection in Gray's direction. *I guess that's more than most people get.*

"And we have Yuri and Drugoy as well."

Also true. Caleb clung to the thought a moment, before nodding to John.

"Yeah," he said. "I'm fine."

CHAPTER 6

THE PHONE RANG about half an hour before their alarm was set to go off.

John rolled over, reaching blindly for his cell, only to find it silent and dark. A moment later, his brain caught up and realized the ring tone wasn't his. "Caleb?" He nudged the body beside him. "That's your phone."

"The fuck?" Caleb mumbled. He finally moved, fishing it out of the pocket of the jeans he'd left by the bed. "Christ, it's Steele."

John sat up as Caleb took the call. His nerves pulled taut, and he strained his ears, as if he could hear the other side of the conversation. Of course he couldn't.

"Hello?" Caleb said. "Okay. Shit." He sat up as well, nothing but a silhouette against the balcony windows. "Where should I meet you? Okay—be there as soon as I can."

Not long ago, it would have been John getting the unexpected call. John rushing out to whatever horrible crime scene had been discovered, with Caleb in tow.

Not anymore. Maybe never again.

Caleb turned in his direction with a wince. "Sorry, John—can you drive me?"

"Sure, babe." John switched on the light and reached for his underwear. "What's going on?"

"Like I said, that was Steele. We need to meet him and Ericsson at the Maritime Center." Caleb went to the closet and pulled out a fresh white shirt. When he looked back at John, his expression was grim. "The siren attacked a dinner cruise full of people."

John let Caleb off at the curb. "Want me to come with?" he asked, and Caleb couldn't have missed the note of longing in his voice if he'd tried.

"Hell, yeah…but you better not. If Ericsson gets territorial, it will only make everything worse." Caleb leaned over and kissed John. "I'll see you tonight after work. Sorry about making you drive us around."

"I don't mind," John said. "Good luck."

"Thanks." Caleb climbed out of the car and strode through the parking lot toward the docks, where Steele had directed him to come. Though a part of him hoped his separation from John at SPECTR was only temporary, maybe it would make sense to get his own vehicle. A car, maybe. Or a motorcycle like Yuri had.

Then I could drive.

I'm not letting you drive anything.

Why not? My reflexes are far better than those of a mortal driver.

Uh huh. And you'd follow all those mortal rules about speed limits, no u-turns, and red lights? When Gray didn't respond, Caleb snorted. *That's what I thought.*

The sun had barely broken the horizon, spreading golden light across the harbor and the churning Atlantic beyond. Gulls rode the wind, hanging motionless before swooping down to the sea below. The air already held the syrupy thickness promising another scorcher. Maybe they'd get lucky and a storm would break this afternoon.

Caleb found Ericsson and Steele waiting beside a police boat tied up at the dock. Ericsson spotted Caleb first. "There you are. Get in the boat."

We will hunt the siren? Gray asked hopefully.

No. Caleb tugged on the coat of his suit, hating it even more than usual. *You can't manifest, remember? We'll find the siren, keep anyone from getting their face eaten off, and let Ericsson bag it.*

Caleb chose a seat near the front of the boat, and the two agents took the rear. Within moments, they were off, cutting across the choppy water of the harbor. A few early boats were out, and a huge cruise ship loomed on the horizon, making its slow way to port.

More police boats bobbed alongside a dinner cruise vessel a few hundred yards off Shutes Folly. Caleb didn't know much about boats, but this one had two enclosed dining decks and an open air observation deck on top. An arm hung over the side, blood dripping into the waves below.

The ship itself appeared to be dead in the water, the only movement that of sea gulls swarming the deck. With a sick twist of his stomach, Caleb remembered they'd eat carrion given the opportunity.

Their boat pulled alongside one of the police watercraft. While Ericsson conferred with the cops, Caleb kept his attention on the dinner cruise ship. The wind brought him the scent of blood and body fluids, and something else. Rotting scales and dying flowers.

Demon.

"We hung back, as soon as we realized what was going on," a cop was telling Ericsson. "I don't know what tore those people apart, but no way was I going to wait around for it to do the same to us. I ordered everyone back to the boats."

"So there hasn't yet been a sweep of the vessel?" Steele asked.

"No." The cop shrugged. "Isn't that what you're here for?"

If this were John and Zahira, Caleb would have offered to go on board first. Let anything that might still be lurking deal with him. He had the feeling Ericsson wouldn't appreciate the suggestion, though, so he remained silent.

Their boat powered up, pulling alongside the vessel. The ladder the police had used to board still hung over the side.

"There's no power, so you'll need flashlights below decks," one of the cops said. Caleb didn't need one, but reminding Ericsson and Steele he was different—possessed—didn't seem like the best idea. He'd had enough of people staring at him in horror for a lifetime. So he took the flashlight and quietly followed them up the ladder.

Gulls scattered before them, shrieking their anger at the interrupted meal. Blood streaked the deck, a few of the larger pools still fresh enough to shift with the roll of the ship. Gnawed bits of what had been at least three or four people lay scattered about: an arm here, a loop of intestine there. The scent of demons saturated the air; Caleb's stomach cramped with hunger, and his teeth burned.

Steele stepped up to a door leading to the lower of the two enclosed dining decks and peered in through the window. An instant later, he staggered back, gagging.

Great. Might as well see what upset an experienced agent, who ought to be at least somewhat inured to horror. Caleb took a deep breath and stepped past him.

Morning light streamed through the glass enclosing the deck, illuminating the carnage inside with brutal clarity. Dinner had been in full swing when chaos descended on the dining room.

Unfortunately, dinner appeared to have been composed of human body parts, butchered and served up on china plates bearing the ship's logo.

Even worse, it appeared the guests had begun to dine on them.

"Holy shit." Ericsson's voice trembled. "The sirens enthralled them. They thought...they were preparing and eating normal food...and then the sirens showed them the truth...oh God..."

Ericsson turned and ran. A moment later, the sound of his stomach contents hitting the sea drifted through the open door.

Caleb moved farther in, his shoes sticking in the drying blood. *Sirens, Ericsson said. Plural.*

"He was right. For once. This is not the work of a single demon."

The guests had thrown up, torn at their mouths and throats with bloody fingernails. Tried to run.

But death had been waiting for them with sharp teeth and claws.

"Most of them aren't even eaten," Caleb said, and was vaguely surprised his voice didn't tremble. "They were killed for the fun of it."

"Cruelty for the sake of cruelty." Anger flowed into Gray's hunger. Caleb knew the scene wouldn't have bothered Gray before he had a living body. It did now. *"And they call us a monster."*

Steele and Ericsson joined them, though Ericsson was still a delicate shade of green. "We have to sweep the ship," he said. "Come on. Maybe these bitches left someone alive."

"There is no need. The demons will not have remained." Gray considered. *"Though some demons do build nests of their victim's bones. But they are not these."*

An old memory flickered across Caleb's inner eye: a nest of bone, glued together with blood and other fluids. At least it wasn't in color. *One horror at a time, please. And we still might find survivors. We have to look.*

Caleb and Steele both followed Ericsson in silence. They started on the upper deck, but there was nothing to be seen. Apparently, these diners had become dinner for those below.

Predictably, the kitchen was an abattoir. Who knew what illusions the sirens had fed the staff, for them to crudely butcher and prepare some of the guests. The staff had come to a bad end as well, though again vomit suggested not until after they'd been made aware of what they'd done.

"These creatures are evil," Gray growled in displeasure. *"They delight in*

suffering."

We'll stop them. One way or another.

"Yes. Even if these other mortals make it needlessly difficult."

Ericsson led the way further below decks. Steele's breath grew rougher, and Caleb hoped he didn't get so jumpy he shot one of them by accident. Ericsson's expression transitioned from sickly to angry.

Unlike the open luxury of the dining decks, space below the waterline was at a premium. Their flashlights cut through the darkness, revealing glimpses of pipes, valves, and fire extinguishers. With the power off, the only sound was the water against the hull.

No. Wait. Was that breathing?

There came a blur of motion, the flash of a blade. Caleb acted on instinct, shoving Steele behind him.

Six inches of kitchen knife buried itself in Caleb's chest.

Gray surges forward with a roar.

Their attacker screams and releases the knife, so it is still buried deep. Steel scrapes bone, pierces vessels, and blood floods into their lungs and the space around their heart.

The mortal who stabbed them is dressed in a uniform, which might once have been white, but is now rusty brown and red. He flings up his arms, scrambling back, until he trips and falls to the floor. There is no scent of demon, no promise of food. Only human sweat and terror, and dried human blood.

"Stand down!" One of the mortals—Steele—shouts behind him.

Gray turns to him. He grasps the knife and pulls it free of his chest with a sucking sound. Agony flares, then subsides as the wound begins to heal. "The mortal is no threa—"

Silver-jacketed lead rips through their shoulder, a blaze of unexpected pain. *"The fuck?"* Caleb shouts in their head. *"Why is he shooting us?"*

"Drop the knife!" Steele barks. His gun is still leveled at them, though his hands shake wildly. "Do it!"

Gray does as the mortal asks; the knife rings off the flooring. "You are being foolish," he says, taking a step forward.

More shots, the closed space making the sound agony for his sharp senses. He will grab this mortal by the scruff, tell him to stop at once, or

———

"No!" Panic spills out from Caleb. *"You're making things worse. Let me deal with this."*

Caleb's fear makes Gray even more reluctant to withdraw. But Caleb understands these mortals as he does not, so he retreats, hovering just under the surface, in case Caleb needs him again.

Caleb staggers, coughing. A fragment of bullet works up their throat and hits the floor. "Fuck, stop it, Steele. He wasn't threatening you. We saved your damn life!"

"You so much as show a fang, I shoot!" His eyes are wild, and Gray thinks he might pull the trigger again. "Those were my orders!"

"We—I mean, I—got stabbed in the fucking chest for you!" Caleb clutches the ruined fabric of the suit above the now-healed wound.

A new fear flickers in Steele's eyes. Perhaps he realizes he has made a mistake.

"You did good, Steele," Ericsson says.

Caleb's fury is like a thousand needles, goading Gray forward. His growl creeps into Caleb's voice when he says, "Excuse me?"

"You were warned, Jansen." There's no yielding in the mortal's stance. "You didn't follow orders—but Steele did." He points at the sobbing mortal in the white uniform, who has somehow managed to survive both sirens and flying bullets. "Steele, secure this guy. As for you, Jansen, take the rest of the day off. I don't want to see your freak face again until after I've had a chance to talk to Barillo."

Caleb wants to argue, Gray can tell. Instead, he squares their shoulders. "Yes, sir," he says, and walks until they are back in the free air, away from foolish mortals and their needless fears.

Zahira knocked lightly on John's open door. "John? You wanted to speak to me?"

He leaned back from the computer, where he'd been matching addresses against the map to choose the next round of interviewees. Only about 4% of the population had enough paranormal ability to register, and less than a quarter of them were exorcists. But that still left almost a thousand people in the Charleston area. Without any new information to point them in the right direction, that was a lot of interviews to get through.

"If you have the time." He gestured to the empty desk where Caleb had sat. "How are things on the ghoul squad?"

"Busy." She made a face. "I'm getting quite the tour of abandoned houses."

"I'll bet." John paused and glanced at the door. Lowering his voice, he said, "I have a favor to ask. It might sound strange, but I can't really explain why I need it at the moment. And if you don't have time, or just don't want to, I completely understand."

She leaned closer. "What is it?"

He took a deep breath. He didn't have to do this. Or if he was going to, he should have brought it up this morning on the way to the docks with Caleb. But it had slipped his mind.

"You haven't made any secret of your interest in drakul," he said. "So it won't look suspicious if you use your clearance to dig into any files on the Lake Baikal vampire."

"The Lake Baikal vampire?" she asked, as though doubting she'd heard him right. "The one the Russians supposedly summoned in the 1950s?"

"They did," John confirmed. "I know the files exist—I've seen them myself. At the time, the details weren't important, so I didn't pay much attention. I'd like the chance to look them over again, but Barillo is watching my every move."

Zahira's dark brows drew together. "Why do you want the files?"

It was a question John had been asking himself. Surely there were better ways to find out about his boyfriends' new best friends. A barbecue on the patio, or a few rounds of drinks at a bar, anything. If what Caleb said was true, and Yuri and Drugoy had slipped away from the Soviet army, then some or most of what was in the files would be pure fiction, written by a commander desperate to keep himself from the firing squad.

He didn't even know what he expected to find. But drakul were exceptionally powerful beings, and the idea of having one he didn't know much about loose in Charleston got his hackles up. If he could learn more about them, find out something of what Yuri had been like before possession, maybe it would ease some of his concerns.

He couldn't stop recalling how Drugoy had looked at the blood on his face. As though tempted.

"I'm interested in the human who was possessed," he said, not exactly answering the question. "Why did they choose him? Who was he?"

Zahira's frown deepened. "Are you worried about Caleb?"

Sekhmet save him, that was the last impression he wanted to give. "No!" Realizing he'd answered a bit more loudly than he'd intended, John lowered his voice again. "No. I can't really say why I need to know at the moment. I'm asking you to do a lot on trust."

Zahira considered for a moment. "But you'll tell me when you can?"

"Yes. I promise." She'd lose her mind when she realized there was another drakul for her to question.

"And it *will* give me the chance to read more about drakul. I'll request as many other files as I can, so no one will get suspicious." She perked up. "If I can't work alongside Gray for the moment, at least I have more access to material on drakul than I did in the Academy. Maybe I can get a paper out of it."

"That would be great." John smiled at her. "Thanks, Zahira. If you ever need a favor, don't hesitate to ask."

"I will. Ask, I mean." She stood up and went to the door. "I'm glad we're friends, John."

"So am I." He watched her leave. "So am I."

CHAPTER 7

CALEB FOUND YURI on the Battery, watching the sun go down.

He hadn't gone back to SPECTR, just as Ericsson had ordered. He'd stopped at the condo, taken down his braid, changed into his leather coat, and debated leaving a note for John. Probably he should have texted John to tell him what had happened, but he hadn't been able to bring himself to do it. At least John could truthfully claim not to know anything about the situation, if Barillo hauled him in.

Barillo might keep it under wraps, especially if he meant to make a real move against Caleb. For all his bluster, he'd need authorization from a lot higher up the food chain to lock Caleb away at some black ops site. There was still time to figure out what to do about SPECTR.

So Caleb had taken the opportunity to walk and think. Replayed the moment Steele shot him in a panic, and Ericsson's praise after.

If the asshole had just let Caleb help from day one, maybe all those people on the dinner cruise wouldn't have died. Maybe they could have caught the sirens, or at least put enough fear in them to lay low. But he'd hamstrung Caleb, and encouraged his partner to fucking shoot Gray, and Caleb was finally out of patience.

He'd tried. Given it his best shot. Not even John could say otherwise.

The air hung close and oppressive. The evening felt charged, all the energy of the long, hot day building and building, until the pressure was about to explode. Gray stirred, his eagerness burning in Caleb's fingertips and teeth. *"Nightfall will bring the storm."*

Good.

Tourists still crowded the waterfront, and gulls swooped and dived after dropped ice cream cones and french fries. The smell of hot grease wafted from restaurants, and the clop of hooves proclaimed a bridal carriage making its way along the street. Young boys sold sweetgrass roses to passersby. An old man chatted in Gullah on his cell phone, the rich words tinged with laughter.

Caleb leaned on the rail beside Yuri and stared out over the water without speaking. Dolphins hunted fish parallel to the shore, their fins occasionally breaking the surface, then vanishing again. The sun's last rays cast a red hue over the water, as though it were tainted with blood.

"This world is so beautiful."

It made Caleb smile, for the first time that day. *Even after months of color, of sensation, you still feel wonder.*

"Of course." Gray seemed to mull it over for a moment. *"Mortals rush ahead, one instant to the next. They dismiss the past and yearn for the future. And in doing so, they do not appreciate the now. But the now is all we ever have."*

Yeah. I guess so. He was as guilty of it as anyone. *You're right. It is beautiful.*

"Hello, Caleb," Yuri said, when the sun slipped fully below the horizon. "It's good to see you again. Your text said you need Drugoy's help?"

Gray's upgrade to Caleb's vision revealed a thousand different colors in the heaving water. "Yes. There's a nest of sirens in Charleston. They attacked a dinner cruise and killed almost everyone on board." And if the survivor ever got his head straight again, Caleb would be surprised. "I can't just sit here on my hands while NHEs run around loose, killing people. Not when I could do something about it, but SPECTR won't let me, because they're too scared of Gray."

Yuri arched a perfect brow. "What are you saying, Caleb?"

He straightened and turned to Yuri. "I've had it with doing things the mortal way. We're ready to do it the drakul way."

A slow grin slid over Yuri's face, exposing his teeth. "Follow me."

"You want to look for them on jet skis?" Caleb asked in disbelief as Yuri pulled his big, black motorcycle into the parking lot of an outdoor rental place. The drive over had been nothing like Yuri's wild tear through the city a few days ago, when they'd been trying to stop the grendel before it killed again. No running red lights or terrorizing pedestrians.

"I preferred the other ride," Gray interjected.

I bet you did. Crazy drakul.

Yuri cast him a bemused look. "They're sirens, Caleb. Where do you think you will find them?"

Heat rose to Caleb's face. "Ericsson and Steele had me walking the waterfront, trying to pick up their scent."

"Foolish mortals," Yuri sighed. "There are three things sirens love above all else. Water, luxury, and cruelty."

"We saw the cruelty part close up." Caleb glanced out over the water. Storm clouds rolled in from the west, blotting out the few stars visible through the glare of city lights. Far on the horizon, lightning danced, and Caleb felt an answering spark deep within. "So you're thinking, what, some kind of party boat? Luxury yacht?"

"The latter, yes." Yuri waved a hand. "Wait here. I believe the proprietor is about to close the shop. Fortunately, I always carry cash."

A few minutes later, Yuri returned with the keys to one of the jet skis held high. "Amazing how a handful of large bills can make one's life so much easier."

"I'll bet," Caleb said wryly. "So what's the plan? We aren't just going to jet around all night, looking for fancy yachts and hoping to catch the scent?"

"They have struck twice in a relatively small area. Demons are creatures of habit. That is where we should start looking for them."

"Gray thinks we should start looking at the previous kill sites and work out from there," Caleb reported.

Lightning flickered again on the horizon, close enough for a growl of thunder to register in Caleb's bones. Yuri glanced at the clouds. "There's a fourth thing sirens love. Storms."

Now that was something. "So we look for boats where people are still partying on the deck, even if it's coming down in buckets." Caleb found himself grinning, his blood starting to surge with eagerness. "Let's get started."

Yuri hesitated, and a surprising flush spread over his pale skin. "It pains us to admit it, but…Drugoy is not fond of water."

If Gray was the storm, Drugoy was the earthquake. "Makes sense," Caleb said.

"We'll help you, of course—Drugoy wouldn't miss such a feast." Yuri held out the keys. "But…do you know how to drive a jet ski?"

He and John had taken a pair out, on one of their days off, before everything had gone to hell. Anticipation rose in Caleb—they were finally doing something, unencumbered by all of SPECTR's stupid rules. Let Barillo and Ericsson and the rest flail around, bound by unreasoning fear. Caleb was going to act. To stop the sirens. To save lives and make the world a better place.

To hunt.

"Yeah," he said taking the keys. "But I think Gray would like to drive."

Gray leans low over the handlebars of the jet ski, Drugoy clinging to his waist. His heart pounds with elation, resonating with the roar of thunder as the storm breaks over the city. Wind, rain, and foam sting his face. The waves grow rougher, slapping against the craft with the urgent rhythm of a lover.

Most of the boats crowding the harbor during the day have already berthed, and more retreat before the storm. The lights of the city reflect against the low clouds, and lightning erupts again. Joy flickers along his nerves in response, and he growls in time with the thunder.

They pass the hunting grounds of the sirens—the point where the first body was found, the course traveled by the dinner cruise before it began to drift. They turn upriver, and ahead of them the Cooper River Bridge blazes with light. Lightning dances, striking one of the great towers.

A yacht rolls in the shadow of the bridge. Lights strobe on one of its uncovered decks, and figures dance in time to the faint pulse of music, despite the rain pounding down from above. Gray's eyes narrow, and he breathes deep, wanting to be certain.

Yes. Even with the churn of wind and rain, there are too many of them in one place to hide their scent.

"The sirens are here," he says.

Drugoy had ducked slightly behind him, but now raises his head. "Yes. I smell them."

"We have to get onboard," Caleb says, as though Gray somehow did not know this. *"There ought to be a ladder around the back of the yacht, for getting in and out of the water."*

Gray revs the jet ski's engine. *No. They will not know we are coming for them until it is too late.*

"What are you doing? Have you lost your mind, you damn maniac?"

"Get ready to jump," Gray advises Drugoy. He opens up the throttle and pushes the jet ski to its fullest speed.

It shoots like an arrow over the water, all but airborne, only his preternaturally fast reflexes keeping them from wiping out. The yacht looms closer and closer, a target made of light and moving bodies and the delicious scent of demons.

"You're going to get us killed! I'm never letting you drive again!"

"Jump!" Drugoy cries, and Gray does. Caleb's telekinesis gives Gray an extra boost, and they are nearly flying through the air, arcing up and over the side of the yacht, to the uppermost deck.

The sirens are gathered on the deck, dancing and singing. Microphones and instruments are scattered about, and a banner emblazoned with Twisted Rapid flaps madly in the wind where it is tied to the railing.

The sleek, fish-flat faces of the sirens on the deck turn to him, their toothy mouths gaping.

Gray's boots hit the deck at the same moment the jet ski slams into the side of the yacht. The craft yaws violently to one side, and drinks, deck chairs, and half eaten human body parts go flying.

Gray roars, a sound that rattles the entire boat. Two of the five sirens flee, leaping onto the lower deck. An instant later, their shrieks fill the air; Drugoy is down there waiting for them.

Gray springs at the nearest siren. She goes down beneath him, biting furiously, but her needle teeth snap on his coat. Her sisters come to her aid, clawing and biting at Gray, their voices lifted in song meant to enthrall him. He ignores them, sinking his fangs deep into the first one's throat.

Arteries rip and her trachea collapses beneath the bite. Blood, rich with power, floods into him. Every cell seems to cry out in thirst for her etheric energy, and Gray drinks and drinks, until there is no more to be had.

The other sirens let out shrieks of fury, their song abandoned. Teeth sink into the back of Gray's neck, above the protective collar of his coat, and tear out a mouthful of flesh. He roars in response, flinging them off —then grabbing the nearest one. She claws at his face, but he bites her arm and feeds.

And feeds.

Power burns in his blood. The final siren tries to run, but he is too fast. He catches her at the railing, wrenches her head back hard enough to crack bone, and bites again.

Power. Power and blood and feeding, and the raw, primal pleasure of it all.

Her body slips from his hands, even as Drugoy climbs onto the upper deck to join him. Drugoy's face is stained and smeared with blood, and the reddish light within his glass-like eyes blazes.

"Good hunting," he says.

The hatch from inside the yacht swings open. Hissing and snarling, more sirens fill the doorway, their eyes burning with hate and the need for revenge.

Gray and Drugoy exchange a single, joyous glance. Then, with twin roars, they rush the demons flooding out.

Two hours later, Caleb flung back his head, body gyrating in time to the club's pounding music.

Euphoria washed through him, a wild high from the battle against the sirens that hadn't yet faded. The two drakul had gorged themselves, until lightning crackled in Gray's hair, threatening to discharge. They'd left behind the sinking boat, leaping to a tower of the Cooper River Bridge and climbing it to return to land.

Once they were back on solid ground, Yuri had grinned and grabbed Gray's hand. "Now it's time for Caleb and I to have some fun, don't you think?"

So here they were, in a club too exclusive for Caleb to have ever set foot in before. Surrounded by bodies and heat and leather, and the only thing that could have made the moment more perfect would be to have shared it with John.

Yuri danced with anyone who approached, his body lithe, untiring. No need to stop moving, to worry about staying hydrated, when you were possessed by a drakul.

A cute guy approached Caleb wearing a suggestive grin. Caleb grinned back, but shook his head. He didn't want to give the wrong impression, and besides, this wasn't about socializing. Not really.

This was about the effortless joy of moving, the ecstasy of breath and bone. This was about feeling *alive* and free. Unchained, and not worrying about anything in the world, at least for a little while.

A flash of red hair out of the corner of his eye caught Caleb's attention. He stopped dancing. A familiar shape slipped out of the club.

Deacon?

Maybe not. He'd only seen the guy from the back, for a fraction of a second. And if it was him, he'd probably left after glimpsing Caleb.

At least he hadn't started screaming like Haylee.

"Caleb!" Yuri's hand closed around Caleb's wrist. "Having a good time?"

Fuck Deacon. Caleb had a new friend now. A *real* friend, who he didn't have to pretend around. "Yeah," he said. "I am."

"Good." Yuri tugged him away from the dance floor. "I have someone I'd like you to meet."

Yuri led the way out of the club and down the block, ducking into a short side alley. Caleb was surprised to see his motorcycle parked there, along with two others. A dark-skinned woman dressed in silver and purple motorcycle gear leaned against a matching bike, her arms folded over her chest. When she saw them, however, she straightened and let her arms fall. "Yuri." Her brown eyes sparked in the dimness. "And this must be Caleb."

Caleb reached out to shake her hand. A faint growl escaped Yuri. Startled, Caleb turned to him.

"Sorry. That was Drugoy." Yuri held up his hands, as if disavowing Drugoy's reactions. "Isabelle is one of ours."

Which sounded...really fucking creepy spoken aloud.

"We do not wish Drugoy to touch John. We should not touch Isabelle," Gray offered. Because apparently drakul had their own crazy etiquette.

"Nice to meet you," Caleb said, tucking his hands into his pockets quickly. He nodded at Yuri's motorcycle. "You made Isabelle bring your bike?"

"As if." She pointed at the motorcycle parked next to it. The bike's purple and silver paint job matched her jacket. "I rode my own."

"Another friend was kind enough to bring it for me," Yuri said.

Friend. Did he mean another renfield? "So who does the third one belong to?"

Isabelle tossed a set of keys at him. "Take a guess."

Yuri grinned at Caleb. "I thought you'd like one of your own, instead of having to ride behind me."

Shock washed through Caleb. The bike had to cost several grand, at the absolute least. Maybe more. It had a custom paint job like Isabelle's. Dark gray, with blue-white lightning across the tank. "You can't just... just *give* me a bike."

"Why not?" Yuri smiled. "What is money for, if not to make life more pleasant for oneself and one's friends?"

"I cut him a good deal on it," Isabelle added, with a glance at Yuri. "My family owns the shop. I did the paint job myself a while back—just been waiting for the right person to come along." Her gaze dipped, then lifted again to Yuri's face. "Speaking of which, you owe me one last payment, I think?"

"Greedy," Yuri said, but the word was fond. Then he was gone, and Drugoy's energy filled the little alley with the scent of warm earth and heated rock.

Isabelle's lips parted slightly. "Isabelle is an exorcist," Drugoy said, in a voice like breaking stone. "She can sense many things."

He rolled back one sleeve and set a claw to his own wrist. The scent of blood joined the other smells in the alley, and Caleb was suddenly aware of Gray watching intently through their eyes. Drugoy held out his wrist, and Isabelle latched onto it, her mouth on the wound.

Drinking his blood.

That does not look pleasant, Gray opined. *I prefer our way with John.*

Yeah, no, I'm not up to watching anyone screw in an alley, thanks. Caleb looked away, feeling as though he'd witnessed something just as intimate.

A few seconds later, Drugoy vanished. Yuri stepped back, tugging his sleeve down over an unmarked wrist. "Payment complete?"

"Yes." Isabelle's eyes all but glowed, and there was a swagger in her posture Caleb hadn't noticed before. "I'll leave you two to the rest of your night."

Right. The motorcycle. "The bike is beautiful," Caleb said. And it was: a sleek machine made for speed. Nothing loud, nothing attention seeking, outside of the paint job. "But I can't accept a gift like this."

You are being foolish, Gray said.

Yuri stepped closer and put a hand on Caleb's shoulder. "At least take it for a test drive," he cajoled.

I will drive.

Oh hell, no. You've already wrecked one expensive toy tonight. Caleb reached out and ran his hand appreciatively along the tank. Longing seized him… maybe just for a short ride…

"All right," he said.

"Look at it, Caleb," Yuri said, hours later.

Dawn couldn't have been more than an hour or two off. They'd ridden around the city for hours, tearing up and down the peninsula at speeds far in excess of anyone's idea of safety.

But neither of them could die. At least, not in anything so simple as a motorcycle crash. And if at first Caleb had held back a little, Yuri's example had awakened Gray's competitive instincts. Fear melted away, and soon they were racing over bridges and up interstates like a pair of blades splitting the night. There had been nothing but the wind tearing at his hair, and the growl of the bike beneath him, and the sheer joy of speed.

Of being alive, and reveling in it.

Eventually, Yuri slowed and exited off the interstates, weaving through narrow streets for once empty of tourist traffic. Caleb spotted a familiar spire and took the lead, pulling up outside the church steeple Gray liked to climb.

Gray and Dru scrambled up and settled in, watching the distant lights of ships on the horizon. Until Dru was gone, and Yuri in his place.

Gray retreated as well. Caleb glanced up at Yuri, who had risen to his feet. But Yuri stared out over the city, the blaze of light and darkness spread out beneath them.

"What exactly am I looking at?" he asked.

A smile curved Yuri's mouth. "Everything. This city. This is all ours, Caleb." He spread his arms, as if he had summoned Charleston into being just for them. "You and I are in paradise, right this very moment. We hunt as we please. Feed as we please. We're strong, and fast, and nothing can touch us."

Elation surged through Caleb. It was subtler than the high of dancing and riding, but no less strong. He stood up as well, gazing out over the familiar streets as though he were seeing them for the first time.

In a way, he was.

He'd wasted so much time being afraid. Afraid of SPECTR, of weak men like Barillo and Ericsson. He'd let their fear infect him, and for what?

Barillo couldn't kill him. Couldn't contain him, no matter what delusions Barillo harbored thanks to Forsyth. Caleb and Gray had *let* themselves be taken by Forsyth, because they were afraid for John.

"We are strong enough to protect John now."

Yes. Yes, they were. Only Caleb had let Barillo convince him otherwise.

Thanks to Yuri and Dru, the scales had finally fallen from his eyes. They didn't have to do things the mortal way. They could do them the drakul way.

And nothing could stop them.

"You're right. Nothing can touch us." A wild joy bloomed in his heart. He drew a deep breath and shouted out across the city: "Do you hear us? We're not afraid anymore!"

Energy flooded his senses as Drugoy manifested. The drakul threw his head back and roared like a lion proclaiming its dominion over its hunting ground.

Gray joined him. Together, they stood atop the steeple, the sound of their roars echoing over the city.

CHAPTER 8

GRAY MANIFESTS AS they shut the door to the condo behind them. His hair is a wild tangle, heart still pumping as though they had run all the way after leaving Yuri and Drugoy, instead of riding the motorcycle.

He runs up the iron stair easily, taking the spiral three steps at a time. There is no light in the condo, but the ability to see in the dark had been the first adjustment he'd made to their eyes.

John stirs when they enter the bedroom, not doubt alerted by Gray's energy. "Hey," he said, sitting up. "I got Caleb's text this evening. Is everything all right?"

Caleb had simply told John they needed to talk more to Yuri and Drugoy. Which had not been a lie.

"We'll tell him everything after we get things straightened out with Barillo tomorrow." Relief spills from Caleb. *"But I'm guessing he didn't hear about what went down with Steele and Ericsson. They must be keeping it under wraps for now."*

Gray does not wish to think of Barillo, or Steele, or Ericsson. He does not wish to think of anything but John, who smells of musk and human sweat. Whose blood tastes better than anything else in the world.

"Yes," he says, leaving behind a trail of clothing from door to bed. "Yuri has friends. We met one."

John laughs. "I would think Yuri does have friends, yes. What was he like?"

"She was not as interesting as you," Gray says, and pounces, shoving

John back into the pillows.

John laughs again, his hands gripping their tangled hair. "Missed me?"

"You will come with us, next time." John's absence was the only dark spot on what had been a perfect evening.

"Maybe not for the crashing-a-jet-ski-into-a-boat part of the night. But yeah."

"I'd like that," John says, and drags them down for a kiss.

He is everything. Yuri and Drugoy are their friends, but John is their heart. He kept them anchored to themselves, the night on Fort Sumter. Kept Caleb from feeling so alone, after Gray first possessed him. Showed Gray what it was like to love, to care, to want and need.

"What do you wish?" Gray asks, when the kiss is done. "We would do anything for you."

John runs a tongue across Gray's throat, then bites the lobe of his ear. "I'm thinking sixty-nine."

Gray strips off John's boxers; he is already hard beneath. "Let me taste you," he says, even though there is still a healing scratch on John's wrist.

"Yes," John says, and slides down the bed so his mouth is level with their cock.

Gray slides his arms around John's legs, holding him. Careful of his fangs, he licks and sucks, until he has John moaning. Then he extends a single claw.

Does Drugoy ever taste Isabelle? Or does the blood flow in only one direction?

If so, Drugoy does not know what he is missing. Gray will have to inform him.

"Please, stop thinking," Caleb begs.

Easily accomplished. Gray drags his claw along the inside of John's thigh, careful, so careful, not to go too deep. John's mouth is wet heat around their cock, and he fastens his mouth on the cut.

Ecstasy. The shallow cut barely bleeds, but the flavor is so different from that of demons. So rich and compelling.

But they are being greedy. Gray falls back, so Caleb can use their mouth without fear of fangs. John moans his appreciation, and his grip on their hips tighten. Soon enough, salty heat coats their tongue. Caleb swallows, throws his head back. *"Come on. We can do better than Drugoy."*

It is not a competition…but Gray will not disagree, changing places with Caleb. He growls, scrapes a fang across John's thigh, and is rewarded with a moan around their cock. Everything is heat and love and pleasure shared, and he lets it crest and crest, until they come hard.

"Mmm," John murmurs, smacking his lips.

Much better than Drugoy's method.

Caleb laughs in the shared space of their mind. *"Hell fucking yeah it is."*

Gray rights himself in the bed, then draws John closer, nuzzling against his neck. "We love you," he says, because it feels important. "And we will never let anyone harm you. Ever."

John relaxes into their embrace. "Love you two, too." He snorts. "That sounded dumb. You know what I mean."

"We do."

John drifts off shortly after. Gray holds him, watching the dawn creep through the windows.

Today, Barillo will finally understand. All of them will understand. John and Zahira are not to be threatened.

And if Barillo does not cooperate, they will simply have to do things the drakul way.

"Fuck yeah," Caleb agrees.

"Yuri bought me a motorcycle," Caleb said over breakfast the next morning. "So you don't need to worry about giving me a ride into HQ, if it'd be easier to pick Karl up and go straight to your first interview."

John froze in the act of putting his cereal bowl into the sink. Caleb had been in a spectacular mood all morning, bounding out of bed and into the shower without any of his usual grumbling. He'd also left off the suit, and was back in leather pants and a plain t-shirt. No braid for his hair, either; it spilled loose over his shoulders and down his back.

"Yuri bought you a motorcycle," John said carefully. "Why?"

Caleb shrugged. "He's got the cash, trust me. I guess he wanted to give us a present."

It didn't sit well with John, though he wasn't entirely certain why. Despite the sex, he felt as though Caleb was pulling away from him. They never saw each other at work, and evenings were apparently dedicated to Yuri now.

He'd told himself it was natural for Caleb to want to spend time with Yuri. Gray with Drugoy. They were the only ones of their kind. Of course they'd want to get to know each other.

But he was starting to wonder if it was possible for a human man to compete. At least, one who didn't have pocketfuls of easy cash.

He turned to Caleb and leaned against the sink. "Is everything all right?" he asked, though whether he meant them, or work, or all of the above, he didn't know.

Caleb shrugged easily. "Had some trouble with Ericsson and Steele yesterday on the siren case. Don't worry. I'm going to talk to Barillo about it this morning."

"That's a reason *to* worry, I'd say." John's heart slipped toward his feet. "Do you want me to come in with you?"

"Nah." Caleb stood up and brought his empty bowl to the sink. He slipped his arms around John's waist, tugging him closer. "I've got it under control."

John peered searchingly into Caleb's brown eyes. "Are you sure?"

"Positive." Caleb grinned. "For the first time since...I can't even remember when, I feel like I know where I stand. What I need to do. Who I am."

Acid churned in John's gut. "Which is...?"

"From SPECTR's point of view, an asset Barillo would be an idiot to throw away. Don't worry," Caleb said again, pressing a kiss to his brow. "You're going to have Karl fretting, and you know he can't ask you what's wrong unless you bring it up first." He gave John a last squeeze. "We'll see you tonight. How about a quiet evening in, just the three of us?"

"Sure." John watched Caleb grab his leather jacket off the hook and pull it on. "I love you," he called as Caleb went to the door.

Caleb paused and looked back. "We love you, too. Later."

John went to the window and peered out. Caleb swung up on the bike parked out front. John didn't know anything about motorcycles, but it looked expensive and had a custom paint job. The engine revved, and Caleb took off, black coat and hair flying out behind him.

Under any other circumstances, it would have been hot: a bad boy on a bad bike. But the sense of unease refused to leave John.

Caleb was acting different. That part wasn't his imagination.

Should he go into HQ? Try to head off or diffuse the situation— whatever the situation even was? Or would Caleb take it as a sign John didn't trust him?

He was losing them.

John took a deep breath. He didn't know that for sure. Right now, maybe the best thing would be to trust Caleb and do as he'd suggested. He went to the coffee table, where he'd left his tablet, and pulled up the list of interviewees. As he perused it, he phoned Karl.

"John?" Karl sounded surprised to hear him. The sound of Karl's daughter shouting came from the background, only to be hushed by his husband.

"Caleb didn't need a ride in, so I wondered if you'd like me to swing by and pick you up?" John asked. "We can get an early start."

"Sure thing. What was next on our list? The waiter at the breakfast place?"

A business name on the list caught John's attention. He paused, then reread the entire entry.

There couldn't be a connection. He was being paranoid. Or jealous, which was even worse.

They needed to stick to the script. They'd agreed to work their way out from the college. There was no reason to switch things up.

"John? You still there?"

"Yeah." John swallowed. "Change of plan. There's someone else I'd like to interview first."

John and Karl stepped into the showroom of Aiken and Daughters Custom Motorcycles. The air smelled of grease and leather. Carefully placed lighting gleamed off chrome and paint. Helmets lined one wall, and parts and a small selection of leathers took up the others.

"Nice," Karl said, eyeing one of the motorcycles.

The door behind the counter opened, and a smiling woman came out. "Good morning, gentlemen. Can I help you with something?"

John took out his badge. "Special Agent Starkweather, Agent Rand, SPECTR. Is Isabelle Aiken here?"

The woman frowned. "She's my sister. I mean, yeah, she's in the back working. What is this about?"

"We just need to ask a few routine questions," John said in his most reassuring voice. "Is there a place we could talk to her privately?"

"The break room, I guess." The woman beckoned to them. "Follow me. I'll get her for you."

She left them in a break room whose scuffed appearance was at odds with the shining perfection of the showroom. A calendar displaying half-naked firemen hung on the wall, above a coffee maker emitting the scent of burned grounds. A scarred table took up most of the small room, accompanied by four plastic chairs.

Karl seated himself with an expression of distaste. As John pulled out another seat for himself, a woman stepped in. She wore coveralls stained with paint and grease, and a wary expression. "What do you want?" she asked from the doorway.

"Isabelle Aiken?" John gave her his best smile and introduced himself and Karl again. "We just have a few questions for you."

She glared at them both. "And if I don't want to answer?"

John tried not to read too much into her hostility. There was probably no connection whatsoever between Caleb's new motorcycle and this shop. And even if there was, it certainly didn't mean anything, other than Yuri had bought it here. He had to buy it from *somewhere*, after all.

If Caleb found out, he'd think John was being a jealous idiot. And he'd be right.

"We can have this conversation at SPECTR-HQ instead," John said. "I don't think we need to do that—I would prefer we didn't, as a matter of fact."

"Fine." Her jaw tightened. "Go ahead, Spec. Ask your questions and get out."

She reminded him a bit of Caleb: angry and defiant, distrusting anything that smacked of authority. "Have you summoned a Non-Human Entity in the last two months?"

"No," she spat.

"Do you know anyone else who has?"

"No." She stepped back. "Now, if we're done here, can I get back to work?"

John glanced at Karl, who maintained a neutral expression. "One more thing, if you will. Do you know Yuri Azarov? He might have been a customer here."

It was a stupid question, and John regretted it the moment it was out of his mouth.

Except she flinched. Not much, be enough for him to notice.

"Never heard of him," she said. "Now get out of my shop."

"Who is Yuri Azarov?" Karl asked, as soon as they were back in the car.

What to say without lying? "A friend of Caleb's. He's into motorcycles, and...well, there's something about him that bothers me."

"You have good instincts, then." Karl cast John a grim look. "All of Ms. Aiken's answers were lies."

John felt as though ice water trickled down his back. "She's been summoning NHEs? And knows someone else who has?"

"And knows Yuri Azarov. Are you going to bring her in? Or both of them?"

Isabelle Aiken was an exorcist. Not a strong one, according to her records, but it was almost impossible for her not to have sensed Drugoy at close quarters.

Most exorcists would call SPECTR if they came across a possessed person. If Aiken had already been summoning NHEs herself, she might not have wanted to draw SPECTR's attention, even with an anonymous tip.

Or she might have started summoning if Drugoy had enhanced her abilities, the same way Gray had boosted John's through the roof.

Sekhmet save him, this was getting too complicated. If Aiken knew what Yuri was, and John brought her in, would she start talking about drakul? Or would loyalty to Drugoy, or her own distrust of authority, keep her silent?

He needed to talk to Caleb about all this before making a decision. No way around it.

"Aiken didn't strike me as someone likely to give up any information to SPECTR if she could help it." John started the car and backed out of the space. "Remember, she also failed on the question as to whether she knew anyone else summoning NHEs. If we take her in, any cohorts might panic and run."

"She's probably calling them now," Karl said. "Are you going to have her phone records pulled?"

"Yes. But I'm thinking about more direct action."

Karl turned to stare back at the shop vanishing behind them. "Good old-fashioned stakeout?"

John nodded. "Good old-fashioned stakeout."

Caleb strode into SPECTR-HQ, his leather coat flaring and flapping behind him. The fluorescent lights gleamed off the buckles on his boots, and he walked with his head up and shoulders back. Agents in the hall moved out of his way, worried looks on their faces. The hall emptied into the cube farm, and a knot of murmuring agents looked up. Ericsson and Steele were among them.

Ericsson's face darkened at the sight of Caleb's clothing. But he only said, "Barillo wants to talk to you."

"Good, because I want to talk to him." Caleb didn't slow, but he tossed over his shoulder, "Oh, and your siren problem is taken care of. You're welcome."

Barillo's secretary either wasn't in yet, or was off fetching coffee. Caleb strolled past the empty desk and threw open the door to Barillo's office.

Barillo sat at his desk, glaring at his computer. When Caleb stepped in, he surged to his feet. "Leave the door open, Jansen."

It was the first time they'd been alone in the office together since Gray had inadvertently frightened Barillo. Since then, Caleb had done everything he could—bent over backwards—worn a fucking *suit*—to make the district chief happy.

But nothing he did would ever be enough. That was all right, though. He was done with caring about whether or not Barillo was happy. That was the mortal way. They were doing things the drakul way now.

Caleb turned and very deliberately shut the door.

"Didn't you hear me?" Barillo barked. A droplet of sweat stood out on his brow, and his eyes glanced at his holstered gun, which he'd hung up on a hook next to his desk.

"Oh, I heard you. But I wanted to save you some embarrassment." Caleb grinned. "We need to talk."

"You're damned right we do." Barillo was reaching for bravado now. "Special Agent Ericsson reports the thing in your head made an appearance yesterday, during the sweep of the boat. Steele had to discharge his gun several times to make the drakul back off."

"I should have let the mortal die."

Probably. "I assume Ericsson didn't bother to mention the traumatized victim with a knife, who would have stabbed him if Gray hadn't intervened?"

"This isn't about that. It's about the fact you just can't seem to follow orders, no matter how many chances I give you." Barillo shook his head. "You're a menace, Jansen."

Caleb crossed his arms over his chest. "You seem to be operating under a misapprehension, chief. So let us clear things up for you right now."

Caleb fell back, and Gray surged forward, dropping his arms. "If I wanted any of you mortals dead," Gray said, "you would already *be* dead."

CHAPTER 9

BARILLO BROKE FOR the gun. But Gray was far too fast for him, and Barillo's hand closed only on air.

Gray held up the weapon in its holster. Then, very deliberately, he bent it in half.

Barillo's eyes were wide, his lips parted. His brown skin took on a grayish hue. Gray folded back up inside, leaving Caleb on the surface once again. Caleb held out the weapon for several seconds, before dropping it to the carpeted floor.

"We've put up with your bullshit for far too long," he said. "It ends today. From now on, things are going to be different. But that's good news for you, Barillo."

Barillo's throat worked as he swallowed. "H-How?"

Caleb leaned against his desk. "Because I'm going to solve all your biggest problems. Maybe not by the book—but I'm not an agent, am I? I'm just a contractor. So from now on, you're going to take the cases with the biggest, baddest, NHEs and give them to me. And I'm going to make them go away for you. You don't ask how, you don't question my methods, you just leave me to it."

Several moments of silence passed. Then Barillo said, "Why should I agree?"

"Because I'm guessing the higher ups are breathing down your neck right about now. Charleston is out of control, isn't it? You took over, and all the sudden there are demons popping up all over the place. It can't look good on your record." Caleb reached out and took one of Barillo's candies from the jar on his desk without asking. "The office's solve rate is dismal, because agents are too overwhelmed to keep up. Perps aren't caught in time to be exorcised, which means more cases end in a hail of bullets, which also isn't making your bosses happy with you. I can fix that for you."

"And in return?" Barillo asked tightly.

Caleb shrugged. "What else do I need? Oh, right. You quit harassing John and Zahira. Give them back their old jobs. And if I need to work with agents, *they're* the ones I'll work with."

"You're asking me to let an NHE—you—run loose in this city, without supervision?"

"I'm glad you understand. You're not as dumb as I thought." Caleb straightened. "Your other option is that I simply leave. Whatever delusions you're under about keeping us here, are just that. And if your bosses aren't happy about an outbreak of possession under your watch, they're definitely not going to be happy about you losing Gray. Director Kaniyar in particular."

He let it sink in for a moment. Barillo clearly struggled for some way to object. To go back to bellowing at Caleb.

But Caleb was right. Barillo's position had to be in jeopardy after this summer. It had been one disaster after another for the last two months, and the problem was only getting worse, not better.

So the question was, did his sense of self-preservation outweigh his hatred of Caleb and Gray?

"All right," Barillo grated out. "Do it."

Caleb grinned. "I knew you'd make the right decision."

They left Barillo's office. *"So we can hunt as we wish from now on?"* Gray asked.

Caleb barely suppressed a laugh of triumph. *We can.*

He went to the cube farm straight away. The agents watched him uneasily; maybe they expected him to return from the chief's office cowed. Beaten. Afraid.

If so, they'd been as wrong as Barillo.

"Head's up!" he called. The few agents still pretending to work stopped. "Who has the case with the most dangerous NHE at the moment?"

Silence was his only response. Caleb sighed and snapped his fingers. "Come on. I don't have all day."

"We've got a therianthrope?" said a man whose name Caleb never managed to remember. "Boar, so it's got major tusks and is pretty huge?"

Gray's interest sharpened. *"We will hunt it."*

Hell yeah we will.

"Great. Give me the file." Caleb snatched the folder from the agent's hand. "It's mine now. Find something less likely to eat your spine and go after it instead."

Caleb turned to address the sea of staring faces. "That goes for the rest of you. We took out the sirens—plural—last night. If you've got something especially dangerous, Gray and I are here to help you." He paused. "And if you don't like it…I suggest you get the fuck out of our way."

Zahira met John a few blocks from Aiken's bike shop. She pulled up beside him, and they both rolled down their windows, letting in a blast of hot air.

"Thanks for meeting me here," he said. He'd swung by Karl's house so Karl could get his own sedan. Karl went to HQ to grab the gear they needed for surveillance, while John kept an eye on the bike shop and made notes on the case. Two sets, in fact—one for the record, and a second to share with Caleb this evening.

When Zahira called, he risked leaving the bike shop unobserved long enough to meet her nearby. Their federal-issued sedans were bland enough not to attract attention on their own, but two might catch Aiken's eye, especially if she was feeling paranoid.

"Have you heard the news?" she asked, dark eyes shining. "I wasn't at HQ this morning, but apparently Barillo is letting Caleb work cases on his own now."

John's mouth fell open. "What?"

"And I'm off ghoul squad as of this afternoon, mashallah." She was beaming now. "I bet Barillo will take you off the interviews, too. Maybe we'll be partners again!"

John's thoughts jostled together. Interviews were grunt work, but he didn't dare let someone else take over Aiken's questioning, until he knew more.

And, more importantly, what the hell had Caleb done to get Barillo to change his mind about…everything?

"Oh," he said faintly. "That's…that's great."

"I know!" Zahira's grin stretched practically from ear to ear. "Anyway, here are the files you wanted." She passed them through the open window. "I got copies of everything SPECTR has on the Lake Baikal vampire. There isn't a lot, but hopefully you'll find whatever it is you're looking for."

"I'm not sure what I'm looking for," he confessed. He tucked the file, along with his private set of notes, into the glove compartment. "Thanks, Zahira."

Karl pulled in on the other side of John and waved at Zahira. She waved back cheerfully.

"I'll let you get back to your stakeout," Zahira said. "But I'll see you tomorrow! Inshallah, we'll be working together again!"

She drove away. Karl grabbed a camera bag from his car, locked it, and climbed into John's passenger seat. "I take it Zahira told you the news."

"Yeah." John started the car and pulled into traffic. "How's the mood at headquarters? I'm not asking for specifics," he added hastily. "I know you can't give me those. Just, you know, in general."

Karl was silent for a long moment. "Uneasy," he said at last. "No one's quite sure what's going on. I think some people are relieved. And a few are the opposite."

"Makes sense." John could probably have figured that out on his own.

"I do have something you'll be interested in." Karl tugged on the seatbelt so it lay more comfortably over his chest. "I did a quick records check. Nixon, our friend at the dry cleaners, was taken in by Special Agent Ericsson."

"Ericsson?" Interesting. Of course it didn't mean the agent was dirty —someone else might have taken advantage of Nixon's scare to start shaking him down. "Caleb's been working with him. I could ask if he saw anything suspicious."

John scanned the street outside of the motorcycle shop. When he spotted an open parking space along the curb within visual distance, but hopefully not close enough to attract attention, he took it. "Thanks for keeping me company, by the way."

Karl shrugged and took a couple of thermoses out of the bag he'd brought from HQ. "I've never had the opportunity to do a stakeout before. Coffee?"

"You're a lifesaver." John took a sip from his thermos while Karl emptied the rest of the bag. Two pairs of binoculars, a camera with high-powered zoom, and a pair of night vision goggles.

"Hopefully we won't have to use these," Karl said, indicating the goggles. "It's light pretty late. But at least we have them if we need them."

"Agreed." John set aside the coffee. "I owe your husband an apology for dragging you into this."

Karl snorted. "He owes you a favor. Tonight is game night. He and Mikki will spend the evening with butts planted in front of the TV, trying to out-score one another in whatever shooter game they're into this week. Usually I'm yelling at them to keep it down, and for God's sake eat something besides cheese balls and soda for dinner."

John had texted Caleb something vague about having to work late. He didn't want to bring up what might turn into a bad situation until he had more to go on. Caleb hadn't gotten back to him yet, but given what Zahira had said about him returning to the field as a free agent, he and Gray were probably out mauling something.

He and Karl lapsed into silence. They took turns watching the shop through their binoculars, while the other scanned the surrounding area. The bike shop closed for the evening, and soon employees drifted out. Aiken's sister, who had greeted them initially, left for the night. John had checked the public registry, but Isabelle was the only Aiken on it, so whomever she was summoning demons with, they weren't family.

Shortly thereafter, a familiar car pulled past them and turned into the bike shop's parking lot. Karl had been on watch, so John grabbed his binoculars too. "Wait a minute. Is that…?"

He had to be wrong. Misremembering a vehicle he'd seen once or twice before, and then only out the window of the condo, when the driver had dropped Caleb off after a PASS meeting.

The car door swung open, and a red haired man climbed out. He paused and turned as he shut the door behind him, giving John a clear look at his face.

Deacon. Caleb's former friend from PASS.

"What the hell?" John murmured.

Karl leaned forward. "Who is he?"

"A friend of Caleb's. Ex-friend, after Gray vamped out at PASS. But he's a telekinetic, not an exorcist."

"It could be a coincidence," Karl said. "Maybe he's a custom bike enthusiast?"

"Maybe." But John didn't believe it.

A big, black motorcycle growled up. The rider wasn't wearing a helmet, and John's stomach clenched at the sight of white-blond hair, streaming in the wind. "That's Yuri Azarov."

"You said he was Caleb's friend, too," Karl said. "What are you holding back, Starkweather?"

Instead of responding, John switched out his binoculars for the camera and began snapping pictures. Deacon paused at the door to the shop, clearly waiting for Yuri. The bike pulled up into an empty space, and Yuri dismounted.

Whatever was happening here, John knew it couldn't possibly be good.

Deacon had been friends with Mike, the empath who was possessed by the grendel. Mike had needed an exorcist to summon the grendel. And now here Deacon was, at Isabelle's—an exorcist's—shop.

Deacon had tried to kill Gray when he revealed himself at PASS. But here he was smiling and greeting Yuri like an old friend.

He might not know about Drugoy, the way he hadn't known about Gray. But what if he did?

None of this made sense. John had to tell Caleb. Show him the pictures and the notes he'd made.

"They're going inside. Do you think the other exorcist is going to show up?" Karl asked. "Why are you so worried? Does Caleb have something to do with this?"

John turned the key. He didn't have any answers, but leaving here, talking to Caleb, was the best way to get them.

At the sound of the engine coming to life, Yuri turned sharply. Across the distance, John fancied their eyes met.

Sekhmet save him.

He stomped on the gas, tires squealing as he pulled a u-turn. Within a few minutes, the shop was fading into the distance behind them.

"Are you going to answer me?" Karl asked impatiently.

"I don't have any answers." John's fingers ached from gripping the steering wheel too tightly, but he couldn't force himself to relax. "I don't know what's going on, or what it has to do with Caleb. But I'm going to find out."

John paced back and forth across the living room of the condo, hands clasped behind his back. Caleb had finally responded to his first text with a short: *Can't talk. Hunting. Home soon.*

John had fired back. *Need to discuss some things with you ASAP.*

Caleb hadn't answered.

He hoped to all the goddesses Caleb came home soon. That he had some plausible explanation about why Yuri, Aiken, and Deacon would be meeting up. Or at least be genuinely surprised a connection between them existed at all.

John came to an abrupt halt. He could see his reflection in the half-window in the front of the living room, which had been part of the carriageway when the condos had been a warehouse. He stared at his own shadowed face, trying to deny he'd even had the thought.

But he had.

He'd trusted Caleb and Gray, not just with his life, but with the lives of everyone around them. They'd abused that trust, lying to him about Yuri and Drugoy. And even though they'd apologized, John couldn't help but feel they'd been drawn into the other drakul's orbit. Away from him.

Caleb was a good guy, though. Truly horrified at the things they'd seen. He'd have no part in creating them. Neither would Gray. They wouldn't…what was John even thinking? Conspire with Yuri and Drugoy to cause a demon outbreak?

Right. Because the last thing a drakul would want would be to turn Charleston into an all-you-can-eat buffet.

Oh crap. Sekhmet, Powerful of Heart, please, *please* let him be wrong.

Something moved in the darkness past his reflection. Light flickered off metal.

Instinct had him dropping to his belly before his brain even caught up. A bullet tore through the glass of the window, whizzed past John's scalp, and slammed into the matching window at the back of the room.

His heart hammering, John lifted his head just slightly off the floor, listening intently. His holstered Glock hung on a hook inside the door, where he'd left his coat. The ugly orange couch Caleb had brought with him when he moved in provided a bit of cover, but he'd be exposed for the last several feet. If the shooter was still out there.

Oh fuck. Had he locked the door?

He dove backward, toward the kitchen, at the same instant the front door flew open. The light fell across a face he recognized far too well.

Ericsson.

John hurled himself behind the kitchen island, even as bullets struck the floor, island, and pots and pans hanging from a rack above. Several of them crashed to the floor or top of the island, knocked from their hooks by the impact.

John pressed his back to the island, heart slamming in his chest.

Ericsson was trying to kill him. Had he talked to Nixon, or found out they were digging into Nixon's arrest record?

Had he panicked? And if so, could John talk him down?

"I know you're dirty, Ericsson," John called. "But murdering a fellow agent? You've gone from losing your job to serious prison time. You don't want that, do you?"

Glass crunched beneath Ericsson's shoes—he must have taken out some of John's display cases. John closed his eyes and visualized Ericsson's progress through the condo. "Nixon? That idiot squealed? Doesn't matter."

What the hell? John opened his eyes again and scanned the kitchen. His muscles tensed, but if he moved too soon, he'd just end up making himself a target. "Then what is this about? What has you trying to kill a fellow agent?" Maybe if he kept emphasizing that, it would give Ericsson second thoughts.

"You got in the way of the wrong person, you sick fuck." Closer. He was nearly at the kitchen, moving slow so he'd have a good shot if John broke cover.

"I'm not the sick one," John said, wrapping his hand around an iron skillet, which had fallen to the floor beside him.

"I'm an exorcist, too. You think I can't feel all that power, just pouring out of them? Blood is one thing, but taking it up the ass? You're just twisted."

He must be talking about Gray. Had whatever happened at headquarters today pushed Ericsson over some invisible edge? What was going on here? John felt as though he had a puzzle with too many pieces.

But he'd never solve it if he died here on the kitchen floor.

Ericsson swung around the side of the island, even as John lunged upward with the skillet in front of him. The bullet tore through the skillet, and a line of stinging pain burned across the outer edge of John's arm. Adrenaline roared through him, dulling the pain and leaving the taste of metal in his mouth.

The iron skillet slammed into Ericsson's face, all of John's weight behind it. He shouted and went back, giving John enough space to sprint to the knife block. He wrenched out a blade, spun, and threw it, even as Ericsson raised the gun again.

The shot went wide, but the knife didn't. Ericsson shouted and dropped the gun, clutching at the blade buried in his upper arm.

The distant sound of alarms came through the open door, drawing nearer. Ericsson visibly wavered—then bolted.

John went for his gun. As soon as it was in his hand, he started after Ericsson. But before he made it to the door, a wave of dizziness passed over him. He caught himself on the wall, looked down, and discovered his left sleeve soaked in blood.

"Fuck," he mumbled. And sat down hard on the floor to wait for the ambulance to arrive.

CHAPTER 10

CALEB SLOWED THE motorcycle as he approached the sleepy street they lived on. Today had been fucking amazing. After waltzing out of HQ, they'd spent the afternoon tracking down the boar therianthrope. He'd always heard pigs were smart, and boars fucking terrifying—there was a reason for the cross guard on medieval boar spears. The wereboar lived up to the tales: huge, smart, and fearless.

But they'd done it. Even better, they'd rescued a woman who was about to become a snack. From the blood on the boar's tusks, it had already been chowing down on people. The woman ran off, and they had a good, hard fight.

Admittedly, getting gored hadn't been fun. But it would have been a lot more permanent an injury for the human agents originally assigned the case.

Red lights flashed off the old brick of the condo's building. Caleb came around the corner, slowed the bike further—then brought it to a sharp halt.

The front door to their condo stood open. And someone was being loaded into the ambulance parked out front.

"John."

Caleb didn't remember getting off the motorcycle. Heart hammering, he ran, pushing past onlookers and police, ignoring shouts. Gray rose to just beneath his skin, riding the fine line of manifesting, desperate and afraid.

A bloody bandage encircled John's upper left arm, and his skin was a few shades paler than usual. The EMTs had cut his shirtsleeve to reach the wound, and the remaining cloth was stiff with drying blood. "John!" Caleb shouted as he was loaded into the ambulance.

"Caleb?" John licked his lips. "It's okay—just got to go to the hospital, get stitched up. Protocol says I have to get checked out."

"Sir," one of the EMTs said, "we need to get going. You can meet Mr. Starkweather at the hospital."

"John, what happened?" Caleb asked, grabbing the door to prevent the EMT from shutting it. "Was there an accident?"

John shook his head. "Ericsson shot me."

The ground fell out beneath Caleb. "Ericsson? Tried to kill you?"

He'd known Ericsson was an asshole. But attempting to murder another agent? He'd never imagined Ericsson would go so far.

"I thought it was because I'd found out he was dirty," John said in a rush. "But he said we were twisted. That blood was—"

"We can't sit here," the EMT snapped. "As soon as we deliver the agent, we're needed on another call."

Caleb's numb fingers slipped from the door. As it slammed shut, John called, "Just wait for me—"

The rest of his words were cut off. The ambulance pulled away, lights flashing.

"Ericsson." Fury washed from Gray to Caleb, echoing, building on itself as they passed it back and forth. *"He tried to kill John. Tried to take him from us."*

One of the cops came up behind Caleb. "Sir? Are you a friend of the victim?"

Victim. John.

Fucking Ericsson.

"I'm his boyfriend," Caleb said, feeling a thousand miles distant. "We live together."

"I'm afraid you'll have to wait for forensics to finish before you can go inside."

Cops were crawling all over the condo. SPECTR would probably descend soon enough, given two of their own were involved, and the whole thing would degenerate into a pissing contest between the police and the agency. But for now, yellow police tape made a barricade across the walk. Beyond, Caleb could make out a bullet hole through the front window. What sort of destruction awaited inside?

Ericsson had come into their home. Tried to kill John.

John said he was dirty. I heard that, didn't I?

"Yes." Gray's thoughts were a low growl. *"And he called us twisted."*

Twisted.

What had Steele said the first day Caleb was forced to ride along with them? *"You ever manage to score with that chick? The one in the band with the dumb ass name? Twisted Rapid or some shit?"*

Gray offered a second memory. One from the sirens' boat, the band equipment on the deck. The banner fluttering from the rail: Twisted Rapid.

The cop was saying something, but Caleb didn't care. Ericsson was dirty. There was a connection between him and the sirens.

And he'd tried to kill John.

Caleb turned his back on the cop and strode to the motorcycle. John wanted them to come to the hospital, talk things over, and then turn the whole thing over to Barillo.

"The mortal way," Gray snarled.

Ericsson had been an asshole to Caleb from day one. Talked shit about women. Had some connection to the sirens.

And he'd tried to kill John. *Their* John.

Fuck it. Ericsson was going to answer to them, before anyone else. And they were done with the mortal way.

Gray crouches on the roof of an old brick building, converted to office space sometime in the past. The building beneath him is silent, the mortals inside gone home hours ago. Across from his perch is an Irish pub Steele once spoke of visiting. And almost directly below him is Steele's sedan.

"He'll know where to find Ericsson." Caleb pauses. *"And if he knew what was going down…"*

He will regret his involvement.

The front door to the pub swings open. A blast of music and light follow a familiar figure out onto the sidewalk.

Steele.

Their prey.

He reaches the car. But before he can open the door, Gray drops onto the roof. The metal buckles beneath the impact, and he shows Steele his fangs.

"Where is Ericsson?" he growls.

Terror fills Steele's eyes. He falls back, reaching for his holster, then cursing when he finds nothing.

"Dumbass left his gun in the car. Bad move if your partner is a homicidal maniac."

Steele breaks and flees. A narrow, tree-lined alley runs between the brick building and an adjacent parking garage. It seems to offer the perfect escape, and Steele takes it. As though he truly believes he can outrun them.

They catch him just before he reaches a dead end. The trees and brick pavement give way to cracked asphalt at the back of an older building converted into a bank. Any rear exit is long bricked up; there is only wall and a few high windows. Steele sees he is in a trap and stumbles to a halt. "Stay back!"

Gray doesn't. Steele swings at him but Gray bats his arm aside and grabs him by the front of his shirt. Lifting him with one arm, he slams Steele against the wall.

"Ericsson tried to kill John," Gray says. "To shoot him, in our own home. You will tell me where he is, now."

All the color drains from Steele's face. "I don't know what you're talking about."

Gray tightens his hold, rage thrumming along his veins, mirrored and amplified by Caleb's. *"Let me talk to him,"* Caleb says.

Gray is doubtful, but falls back. Caleb gives Steele a hard shake. "Let's get one thing straight," he says. "I'm done dicking around with you. Either give us a straight answer, or I let Gray tear your spine out through your ear."

I do not believe that is possible. Gray considers. *But I am willing to try.*

"I swear!" Steele whimpers, and the smell of urine joins asphalt and garbage. "Please, oh please, oh please, don't kill me."

"Convince me not to. John said Ericsson was dirty. What's his connection with the sirens?"

Steele blinks. "The sirens?"

"Twisted Rapid. Ericsson was dating one of them, and then the whole band turns up possessed?" Caleb leans in closer. "What did he do?"

"I don't know!" Steele appears shocked. "I didn't even know there was a connection between the sirens and the band! Ericsson was the one who went to inspect the wreck pulled out of the harbor. He told me to stay at HQ and do paperwork."

Could he be telling the truth?

"Maybe." Caleb lowers Steele just slightly, enough so the toes of his

shoes brush the asphalt. "You always do what Ericsson tells you?"

Sweat drips down the sides of Steele's face, carrying the tang of fear. "Doing what he told me was…lucrative," he confesses. "But I don't know anything about the sirens, or why he'd try to kill Starkweather! Even if Starkweather had some dirt on him, you go away for murder a lot longer than for corruption." Steele swallows convulsively. "I don't think he could have anything to do with the sirens. He only met the chick a couple of weeks ago. Less than forty days. She couldn't have been possessed then—he would have known it."

"Tell that to all the people she killed," Caleb snaps, because Steele's words are foolishness. The sirens they fought were fully transformed, secure in the skins of the mortals they possessed. "Where is Ericsson?"

"What are you going to do when you find him?"

He has become too comfortable in his fear. Gray surges forward, eliciting a scream of startled terror.

"What we will not do to you, if you answer Caleb's question," he growls. "Tell us. Crawl home. And pull the covers over your head. Because if you lie, we will come back for you."

"Y-yeah." Steele shakes so hard his heels drum against the wall behind him. "I-I'll tell you."

John walked into the emergency room, his upper arm numb from the local anesthetic. He'd refused the offer of other painkillers, though he'd accepted a prescription for later. Barillo would want to take his statement as soon as possible, and he needed to be clear headed.

He still couldn't believe Ericsson had shot him. Meant to kill him. Agents might have disagreements, and rivalries, and even hate each other on a personal level. But in the field, they had each other's backs, no matter what.

Shooting a fellow agent crossed a line that couldn't be uncrossed. Even if John wasn't the most popular man in the office right now, ambushing him at home was something no other SPECTR agent would ever forgive.

Of course, Ericsson hadn't meant for anyone to find out. He'd meant John to die, and he surely hadn't used his government-issued Glock with its silver-jacketed lead to do the job. Had he meant it to look like a break in? A revenge killing on the part of someone John had helped put behind bars?

John had hoped Caleb would convince the nurses to let him in the back, so they could talk about it. What Ericsson had said, about blood…

When he entered the waiting room, his expectant gaze didn't find Caleb waiting anxiously for him. Instead, Zahira sat on one of the worn chairs, reading a magazine that was probably old enough to vote.

"John!" She rose to her feet, relief stamped over her features. "Are you all right? I mean, of course you aren't, but how are you feeling?"

Tension pulled John's shoulders tight. "Where's Caleb?"

"I don't know. I haven't seen him." Zahira looked around, as if either of them might have somehow missed a tall, possessed man in a black coat. "Barillo called me and told me to bring you to HQ. He said you were shot by Special Agent Ericsson?"

An unexpected pain squeezed John's chest. Maybe he'd worried about Caleb drifting away, but he'd thought Caleb would at least care enough to come to the hospital and make sure he was okay. That Gray would have.

"Right," he said, struggling to keep his feelings off his face. "I'd found evidence he *might* be dirty. But I hadn't even had the chance to look closer, let alone gather anything to take to internal affairs."

Zahira frowned. "Trying to kill you seems like an overreaction."

"Unless he's hiding something else." John led the way to the exit. "He denied it had anything to do with Nixon—the exorcist who claimed SPECTR agents were shaking him down. Something more is going on."

He couldn't shake what Ericsson had said, about blood being one thing and sex another. About all that power, and how exorcists could feel it.

Damn it, he needed to talk to Caleb and Gray.

The thought stopped him cold. He'd left his notes and the files Zahira had given him right out on the coffee table. The cops probably wouldn't bother with them, but if Barillo sent agents to the condo and they took a closer look…

"John?" Zahira asked from behind him.

"Nothing. Sorry." There was no reason for Barillo to do that. The police would handle the forensics. "We should get to HQ."

Zahira's phone rang. "It's Barillo," she said, before answering. "I have Special Agent Starkweather, sir. I—" She paused, frowning as she listened. "Yes, sir. I'm on it."

"What is it?"

"Come on." She led the way outside, hurrying to her sedan. "Agents went to Ericsson's apartment and found his cousin living there. The cousin claims Ericsson sublet to him and has been living in a nice house on James Island. The kind he shouldn't be able to afford on his salary."

"Not looking very innocent, is he?"

"No." Zahira snapped her seatbelt closed and hit the flashing lights. "We're the closest agents, so Barillo is asking us to head over there. Backup is on the way. Can you go in with me, or are you on painkillers?"

"I didn't take any, since I knew Barillo and internal affairs would want to grill me." John hung onto the door as Zahira pulled onto Calhoun Street with a squeal of tires. He stared out the window at the dark expanse of the Ashley River as they took the bridge for James Island.

With any luck, they'd find Ericsson there. But where the hell was Caleb?

Gray moves like a shadow across the wide, manicured lawn toward the house. It is large, in the midst of a sprawling subdivision of nearly identical houses, the entrance into the complex guarded by a gate. Ericsson's government-issued sedan sits in the driveway, beside a cherry red convertible.

"Alfa Romeo. Guess Steele was right about the lucrative part."

Gray pauses in the shadows cast by the landscaping, eyes fixed on the house. Every light is ablaze, as if Ericsson believes that will keep him safe.

Mortal nonsense.

A shadow moves on the other side of drawn blinds. Topmost floor.

Gray scales the wall easily. Caleb shatters the window inward with his TK, and they are through in a shower of glass, blinds tangling around them. Ericsson stands by the bed, packing clothing into an open suitcase. A towel tied roughly around his upper arm suggests John was not the only one injured in their fight.

Ericsson drops the clothes and pulls out his gun, even as they charge him. A bullet slams into their hip, spinning them around. Ericsson puts the bed between them, gun leveled at their head. "Stop!" he shouts.

Gray gathers himself to simply leap over the bed. *"No,"* Caleb says. *"I want to hear what he has to say first. About the sirens."*

Gray does not care about the sirens. He and Drugoy ate them; does it matter how they came to be? But Caleb does care, so instead of attacking Ericsson, he begins to circle the bed. Ericsson hastily backs away. "Stop right there."

"You wished John dead," Gray says. "Why should I stop?"

Ericsson's skin has taken on a greenish-white hue. "It wasn't personal. I was doing a favor for a friend."

"You are a liar."

"It's true!" Ericsson swallows thickly. "Fuck. This is all that bitch Cindy's fault."

"She was one of the sirens?" Gray asks. He drifts closer, and Ericsson puts distance between them again.

"Stuck up bitch. Thought she was too good for me. She was planning on going to the police." Ericsson tries an unconvincing smile. "You know how it is, right, Caleb? I mean, maybe *you* don't, but take my word for it. You go out with a chick, spend some money on her, then next thing you know the slut changes her mind and is threatening to tell the police you assaulted her."

Disgust rolls out from Caleb like a tide of bile. *"He sexually assaulted her. Christ."*

"I had to shut her up," Ericsson babbles on. "But she'd told her friends in the band, and if she disappeared, it would look bad for me. So I came up with an idea."

The horror of the dinner cruise, the dead served as meals, the sheer cruelty saturating the murders, fills Gray again, as fresh as if the remains of butchered mortals still lay around him. All of that suffering, all of that malice.

"And all because this fucker couldn't take 'no' for an answer. God damn him."

Gray moves, catching Ericsson off guard. He slaps away the gun before it can take aim again, and the snap of finger bones sends a savage thrill of satisfaction through them. He grabs Ericsson's shirt, slamming him into the wall.

"You murdered dozens to cover up for your own crimes." White-hot fury fills every fiber, every cell, of their body. "No wonder you were so eager to kill John."

"It wasn't my fault!" Ericsson shrieks, twisting in their grasp. "If she'd just kept her mouth shut, none of this would have happened!"

Gray lets out a wordless roar of rage and bashes Ericsson into the wall again. Perhaps he shall continue to do so, over and over, until nothing is left. Perhaps—

The lights gleam off of Ericsson's athame, which he must have had sheathed at his hip. The point slams into their temple with a crunch of bone, then into their brain.

Light flashes across their vision. Thoughts scramble, and everything seems to go sideways as severed arteries pour blood into their brain, further damaging delicate tissue. Caleb's consciousness flickers, and they let go of Ericsson, stumbling back. Gray forces a hand up, grips the athame, and wrenches it back out. Blood is reabsorbed, neurons regrowing.

"The fucker stabbed us in the head!"

Gray blinks; they are on their knees, covered in blood. Ericsson crosses to them, the athame in his hand again. He must have picked it up from wherever Gray had dropped it.

"They say you can't exorcise a drakul." Ericsson stops in front of them. "But if I put all my power through the athame while it's buried in the top of your head, I wonder if we won't get somewhere after all." He lifts it high, both hands wrapped around the hilt, even the one with broken and swollen fingers. "With you out of the way, Starkweather won't have a chance. And that bitch Zahira is next on the list."

Gray comes off the floor with a roar. Ericsson will not hurt John again. He will not hurt Zahira.

They will not allow it.

Their fangs bury deep into Ericsson's throat.

Veins tear and cartilage crunches. Blood explodes into their mouth, a thousand times sweeter than that of demons. Mortal blood is not food, but it is so very, very good.

Ericsson's body spasms, dying, but Gray grips him to keep him from pulling away. They sink to the floor with Ericsson's suddenly heavy body, and feed and feed, until the beating of his heart is stilled.

CHAPTER 11

AS THEY PULLED onto the street where Ericsson's new house was located, the headlights swept over a familiar motorcycle, parked a few doors down from the address Barillo had given them. "That's Caleb's bike!"

"Caleb has a motorcycle?" Zahira asked. "When did that happen?"

Hell. Oh hell.

John had been hurt when Caleb didn't bother to show up at the hospital. But maybe Caleb hadn't come because he'd been more interested in tracking down Ericsson.

"And, more importantly," Zahira went on, "how did he know to come here? From your surprised look, I assume you didn't text him."

Pieces were coming together in a pattern. John couldn't quite make it out, but he had a bad feeling once he did, he'd find a pale-haired vampire in the center of it.

"Blood is one thing," Ericsson had said. It had bothered John, even in the middle of a fight for his life, but he hadn't been able to put his finger on why.

The only legitimate way Ericsson could know drakul blood boosted the abilities of the paranormally-abled was for Caleb to have told him. Given their adversarial relationship, Caleb wouldn't have done that.

"You think I can't feel all that power, just pouring out of them?" Them. John had assumed he meant Caleb and Gray, but what if he meant another

drakul? It sounded crazy, but instincts honed from his years as an agent insisted he was on to something.

Everything was crashing down around him. Only, he wasn't sure what he could have done differently. If he'd trusted Barillo enough to tell him...

"How far behind us is the backup?" John asked.

Zahira parked the sedan and checked her phone. "About five minutes. Should we wait?"

"You wait here. I'm going inside." He took out his Glock, wincing as the wound on his arm pulled.

She shook her head. "No. I'm coming in with you."

"Zahira, please." His throat felt dry, and the anesthetic was wearing off. "I'm not asking you as a senior agent, but as a friend. Let me go in alone. If I'm not out by the time backup arrives, come in and get me."

Their eyes met. After a long, searching look, Zahira nodded. "All right. You have five minutes. Make it four now."

John didn't waste any time. His pulse pounded in the base of his throat as he cut across manicured lawns to reach the house. He scanned it as he approached; one of the upper story windows was broken out.

Gray had surely entered the building through it. Was Drugoy with him?

The front door was unlocked. John eased inside, gun at the ready. Every light was on, and the downstairs seemed undisturbed. Offering up a prayer, John started up the stairs.

He skipped the second floor and went straight to the third. A door just off the landing stood open. Holding his gun at the ready, John stepped into the doorway.

Ericsson lay sprawled on his back near the bed, eyes seeming to stare in John's direction. Gray knelt over him, black coat flared around him, hair hiding his face from John's sight.

The light from the hallway cast John's shadow over them. Gray jerked up, lips drawn back in a growl.

Blood smeared his mouth, dripped down his chin. Ericsson's blood. Human blood.

There was no air left in the world. John fought to draw a breath, then another. He felt as though the house had tilted off its foundations, or the island slid into the river, or the globe gone spinning off its axis.

Gray blinked at him, and the snarl disappeared. "John?"

John didn't answer. Couldn't answer. Ericsson had tried to kill him, and Gray had killed Ericsson, and somehow Yuri was tangled up in it all.

The Vigilant had warned him, right from the start. Drakul couldn't be trusted not to drink human blood. The temptation would get the better of them in the end.

And like a fool, John insisted he knew better. Swore up and down Gray was different. Betrayed his oaths to SPECTR, risked his life and others, because he'd been so sure they were wrong and he was right.

"John?" Gray repeated. He rose to his feet, hand outstretched.

"Stay back." It was all John could do to keep the Glock from trembling in his grasp. He needed to think, needed—

A crash came from downstairs. "SPECTR agents! Weapons down and hands up!"

Gray's eyes widened. He stepped toward the door.

Oh shit. This had the potential to become a bloodbath. "Get out." John's voice shook on the words.

Gray didn't move.

"I said get out of here!" His heart felt like a pane of glass, cracked side to side. "Go! Get out! Don't come back!"

"John—"

"I don't ever want to see you again!"

Gray lowered his arm slowly. Boots sounded on the stairs behind them, Zahira and the other agents drawing closer and closer.

Gray spun and dove for the window. The blinds clattered wildly, then fell back into place.

"John! Report!" Zahira called from the stairwell.

"All clear," he said past the thickness in his voice. "And...I found what's left of Ericsson."

She gasped when she saw the carnage. Ericsson's ruined throat. The silver athame coated in blood and long, black hairs. "What...what happened here?"

John's arms ached as he put his Glock back in the holster. "The thing everyone warned me about."

John does not ever want to see them again.

Gray stumbles across the lawn, arms and legs feeling suddenly alien, as though they no longer belong to him. John saw them feeding on Ericsson. And now he is afraid.

"Of course he fucking is." Horror bleeds through from Caleb, mingling with shock. *"Oh God. Christ. We shouldn't have done that. Oh God oh God oh God."*

Gray falls to his hands and knees. His stomach heaves. Blood and bile make a slick black pool in the silvery moonlight.

He can't stop seeing John's face. The fear in his blue eyes. The way he flinched, yelled at them to stay back. To keep away from him.

To go, and never, ever come back.

"Gray?"

Drugoy stands a few feet away, head cocked in concern. Gray stumbles up, and Drugoy catches his arm. Supports his weight.

"What are you doing here?" Gray asks numbly.

"Looking for you. We went to your home, but the police were there and you were not." Drugoy frowns. "We worried."

"Something has happened." Gray closes his eyes, but he only sees John's face again, so he forces them open. "We made a mistake. And now John hates us."

Drugoy's hand tightens on their arm. "Come with me."

They go, because they do not know what else to do. This motorcycle ride is so different from the one...was it just last night? Drugoy leads them back across the river, away from James Island. Away from Ericsson's body, and from John. It is late enough that the streets are beginning to empty, and the parks are nearly deserted.

Drugoy chooses one of the parks, leading the way until they are deep in the shadows beneath the live oaks. "Tell us what happened."

Gray does. Drugoy sits beside them, both propped against the trunk of one of the old oaks, his shoulder touching theirs.

"You are unhappy for no reason," he says, when Gray at last runs out of words. "We have eaten many mortals in our time. It means nothing."

"The Vigilant feared us. They said—"

"Mortal nonsense," Drugoy snaps. "They fear us, so they sought to bind you with wild tales. We are drakul, and it is our nature to feed."

"Mortals are not food," Gray insists.

"This Ericsson is no more dead than he would have been if you had snapped his neck. Why not take some pleasure from the act?"

Gray shakes his head. Why can Drugoy not understand? "Because John hates us now."

Drugoy lets out a low growl. He turns to face Gray, the shadows of the trees casting shapes on his pale skin. "Forget the mortal. Come with us. We will leave this city together and go somewhere new."

"We don't have a choice." Despair wells up from Caleb. *"We're going to have to go on the run with Yuri and Dru, and hope SPECTR doesn't find us."*

Gray wished to leave. Has always wished for freedom. But not without John.

"Listen to me." Drugoy places one hand on Gray's shoulder, claws sliding out just enough to make certain of his attention. "These mortals mean nothing. This John of yours, with his short life, has tried to bind a god to his will. For no other reason than he is small, and afraid of that which is greater than him."

Gray opens his mouth to protest, but Drugoy's claws dig in deeper. "Forget him," Drugoy insists. "I searched for you. I searched for you so long, and now I have found you. I am no mortal, trembling like a mouse before the cat." He leans in closer. "I understand you, as no one else ever can. And I will never leave you."

The touch of his lips on Gray's is a shock. Gray pulls away, stumbles confused to his feet. "What are you doing?"

Drugoy rolls to his knees and stares up at Gray. His eyes gleam, red fires through black glass. "Your love for the mortal is misplaced. Come with us. We will disappear like smoke. Travel the world. See and do things no mere mortal could imagine. Together."

How have things gone so wrong so quickly? "I do not want this," Gray says. "You are my friend. But I love John. I am sorry."

"I *searched* for you," Drugoy says. "We were together, five-thousand years ago, on the etheric plane. We were together, and we hunted, and then you were gone. I saw it happen. A rift opened in the world, and you were taken from me."

Drugoy tries to seize his hand, but Gray steps back. "I was summoned into this world. Yes."

"You were *gone,*" Drugoy repeats. "I searched for you. Other rifts opened, but they were too small for me to go through. Demons could fit, but not me. Never me." The red fire in his eyes brightens. "Until finally I found one large enough, and I felt the tugging, and I came through."

"Into Yuri."

"Not Yuri." Drugoy tips his head back. "Another. And this world was so bright. So *beautiful*. I knew pleasures such as I had never known before. Fed as I had never fed before. But too soon, I was sent back."

A sense of stunned horror from Caleb grows stronger with every word Drugoy speaks. *"Fuck. I don't like this."*

Drugoy smiles, exposing fangs. "I came through, each time I saw an opportunity. Again and again and again. I fed and I destroyed and I was sent back. And still I could not find you." He holds out his hand pleadingly. "Then I was sent into Yuri. Yuri said we would look for you together. It took a long time, but we found you, at last." Drugoy's mouth flattens in a furious line. "And I will not allow some stupid mortal to come between us!"

"Gray, I really, really don't like this."

Nor do I.

"I am sorry you suffered." Gray takes one step back, then another. "But it does not give you the right to say who I may love."

Drugoy's face crumples. "You cannot leave. Come back."

It hurts to walk away. Because Drugoy is the only one of his kind Gray has ever known on this side of the veil. The only one who can understand, even a little. And he has already lost so much, this last thing feels as though it will break him.

"Goodbye, Drugoy," he says. "I hope someday I will see you again, and we will be friends."

He turns and leaves, walking as quickly as he can. For a long moment, there is nothing but silence behind him. Then Yuri calls out. "You can't survive long without us, Caleb. You know SPECTR will hunt you. We'll wait for you at the big dockyard off East Bay Street. You can find us there when you come to your senses."

John sat in an interrogation room at HQ, his head pounding and nausea clawing at his gut. His arm hurt, and of course he didn't have anything stronger than an aspirin to take for it.

Right now, he desperately wished he hadn't refused the painkillers after all. Anything to put a soft haze between him and the world. Anything to make the memory of Gray with Ericsson's blood on his face less real.

"I warned the director," Barillo said. He sat across from John, his arms folded over his chest. "I warned anyone who would listen that *thing* was a menace. We'll be lucky if it doesn't eat half of Charleston by dawn."

Zahira sat beside John. "Sir, I think we should wait and hear Gray's side of the story. Ericsson tried to murder Special Agent Starkweather. His athame was found with blood and black hairs stuck to it, suggesting he attacked Caleb and Gray as well. We shouldn't be so quick to rule out self-defense."

John wanted to agree with her, more than anything. But he couldn't. The words wouldn't even form in his head.

Barillo had no such problems. "He drank Ericsson's blood. How the hell is that self-defense?"

"Gray is a predator. Biting may naturally trigger certain behaviors—"

"Enough!" Barillo slammed his fist down on the table. "The drakul is dangerous and out of control. People are going to *die* if we can't get him in a cage, and fast."

Zahira's chin jutted out. "He's not going to go on some killing spree."

"You want to bet your life on that? Fine. But I'm not betting the lives of the people of Charleston," Barillo said.

The door opened, and Steele entered, accompanied by a guard. Steele's skin had taken on the hue of spoiled milk.

"Is it true?" Steele asked immediately. "Ericsson's dead?"

"Yes." Barillo leaned back and eyed Steele. "What we've got here is a cluster fuck. Your partner was living in a house he shouldn't have been able to afford. Starkweather says he might have been shaking down the paranormally abled. And worst of all, he did his utmost to murder a fellow agent. If you know anything about what Ericsson was up to, now would be the time to say something. Because with Ericsson dead, your ass is the only one internal affairs has left to chew."

Steele sat down slowly. "What about the sirens?"

A chill ran down John's spine. "Sirens?"

Steele glanced at him. "After you were shot, your boy came looking for answers. Seemed to think Ericsson was involved with the sirens. And I mean, sure, he saw Cindy once, but he couldn't have anything to do with her whole band getting possessed, right?"

"According to Karl, Isabelle Aiken lied when she said she didn't know anyone who had been summoning NHEs," John said. "Did she and Ericsson know each other?"

"The name doesn't sound familiar...but I don't know, man." Steele shook his head. He seemed to have aged a decade in mere hours. "Look, I'll cooperate. Ericsson and I were receiving payments in exchange for leaving exorcists alone. But a couple of months ago...something changed about him. He started hanging around with some guy and his friends. Maybe this Aiken chick was one of them."

Alarm bells were going off in John's head. "What guy?"

"Some Russian dude." Steele squinted his eyes in thought. "Yuri, that was the name. Yuri Azarov."

CHAPTER 12

CALEB SLIPPED IN through the balcony door to the condo. He'd parked
the motorcycle a few blocks away, before using every trick Gray knew to
move silent and undetected. As he'd suspected, police were stationed
outside the condo, along with a car with a few too many antennas to be
anything but an unmarked vehicle. Probably SPECTR agents, waiting on
the off-hand chance he was stupid enough to come back here after killing
one of their own.

He shoved down the memory of Ericsson's blood in his mouth and
made his way along the roofs, keeping low. From there it had been an
easy climb to the balcony. The door was locked, but it snapped easily
under his strength.

Caleb leaned against the bedroom wall, legs shaking. He wanted to
collapse to the floor and never move again. But that wasn't in the cards.

What Drugoy had said played over and over again in his head,
alternating with John saying he never wanted to see them again. Yuri
hadn't been Drugoy's first host. He'd come through before, devoured
people, run mad, and been banished. Again and again.

Christ.

"Because of me." The weight of it flattened Gray's words. *"It is my fault
we lost John."*

I was right there with you. I'm every bit as guilty. He'd wanted nothing
more than to kill that son of a bitch Ericsson. After all the atrocities he'd

caused, he'd threatened not only them, but John and Zahira?

He took a deep breath, meaning it to be calming. But the familiar smell of their bedroom, of John's aftershave mingled with Caleb's favorite shampoo, was a stake to the heart.

But he had to come back here, one last time. John deserved better than to just have them disappear into the night, never to be seen again. He'd scribble a quick note—apologize, tell John he loved him. They loved him. They'd never meant for it to end like this.

More: he needed to tell John about the sirens. Because Caleb still didn't know how the fuck Ericsson had managed to make the siren possessions permanent before the forty days were up. It shouldn't have been possible, at least not that Caleb had ever heard. If there was some new way of summoning NHEs, John ought to at least know.

John would figure it out. He was a good guy.

"The best."

Yeah. And fuck, he didn't have time to cry now. He had to get this done, then leave Charleston behind. The custom bike was too recognizable; he'd have to ditch it. And his coat. Cut his hair.

Caleb forced himself up off the floor and to the stairs. At least with his night vision there was no need to risk giving himself away with a light. As he went, he tried to memorize the condo where they'd all been happy, if only for a little while. His paintings on the walls, John's diplomas in the office area, the couch where they'd watched TV, and the kitchen where they'd eaten so many meals.

There was blood on the floor of the kitchen. Bullet holes and wreckage.

This was what they'd done to John. Come into his life, and left nothing behind but a mess to clean up.

John's tablet lay on the coffee table, along with a notepad and a file folder. Caleb picked it up, intending to flip to a blank page, when his own name caught his attention.

It looked as though John had been making notes on the exorcist interviews he and Karl had been doing. But as Caleb scanned through them, dread pooled in his belly.

Isabelle Aiken: works at a custom motorcycle shop. Lied about not summoning NHEs. Lied about not knowing anyone who had.
Lied about knowing Yuri Azarov.

Of course Isabelle would have been on John's list of exorcists. No shock there. And it made sense she might lie about Yuri, not realizing John knew about drakul. But she'd lied about summoning NHEs?

About summoning demons with someone?

Yuri Azarov gave Caleb a custom motorcycle.
Caleb's friend (?) Deacon knows Yuri and Aiken.
Deacon was a friend of Michael Langen, who was possessed by a grendel. Needed an exorcist to summon it.

Deacon couldn't have been involved. He'd been horrified when Gray had emerged. If he knew Yuri, it had to be a coincidence. He couldn't know Yuri was a drakul.

Did Aiken summon the grendel? Someone else?
YURI?!

Yuri? What did John mean?

Caleb dropped the notebook and snatched up John's tablet. After he entered the passcode, a new folder on the desktop greeted him: *Aiken Surveillance*.

Hand shaking, Caleb opened the folder. It was filled with image files —photos from a stakeout, to go by the label.

Isabelle. Yuri. And unmistakably Deacon.

Caleb had thought he glimpsed Deacon in the club, the night he and Yuri had gone dancing after hunting the sirens. Yuri had alluded to a second renfield who had brought his motorcycle. But it *couldn't* be Deacon.

Unless Deacon had known about drakul all along. Unless his horror upon seeing Gray had been some kind of act. But why?

Gray stirred uneasily. *"If Deacon belongs to Drugoy, and Drugoy does not wish mortals to come between us..."*

No. No, that's too convoluted. Drugoy would have to be some kind of mastermind. And, no offense, but drakul strike me as doers rather than thinkers.

"But there is not just Drugoy. There is Yuri."

The file folder. Caleb set aside the tablet and opened it to photocopies of a file he'd seen before. The Lake Baikal vampire. Yuri and Dru.

The first page was the account they'd read last spring, when they were trying to figure out why Forsyth was warehousing demons. The account Yuri claimed was mostly fiction. Caleb flipped the page.

A grainy photo of Yuri stared out, his hair cropped short, dressed in what Caleb assumed was a Soviet-era uniform. *Yuri Azarov,* someone had labeled it in English. *Exorcist. Soviet intelligence.*

Exorcist.

Soviet intelligence.

The file slipped from Caleb's numb fingers. When Yuri had never mentioned a paranormal ability, Caleb had simply assumed he didn't have one. After all, Gray had cheerfully shared the fact Caleb was a telekinetic; it had been the perfect opening for Drugoy or Yuri to mention the exorcist abilities.

Having Gray in his head had amped up Caleb's TK from barely able to move a sheet of paper, to strong enough to propel his own body a good distance. If Yuri had started out as a strong exorcist, what effect might Dru have had on his ability?

Could he, for instance, install demons in such a way that their hosts didn't have forty days to get rid of them? Permanent possession from the get-go?

Bile rose in his throat. No. No, Yuri and Drugoy couldn't be involved. They'd helped hunt the sirens, after all.

Ericsson had called his attempt on John's life *"a favor for a friend."* And Drugoy had shown up outside Ericsson's house, as though he knew Caleb and Gray would be there.

Drugoy, who swore he wouldn't let some stupid mortal come between Gray and him.

Yuri Azarov had been an intelligence officer before his possession. Ericsson's revulsion toward Gray and Caleb might have been real, but Yuri surely knew how to play off whatever weaknesses Ericsson had. To offer power, favors, for an inside scoop on SPECTR.

Ericsson to watch Caleb and Gray at work, and Deacon to watch them after hours. Yuri had ringed them in with his renfields, then used them to slowly cut Caleb out of the network of human ties he'd made since coming to Charleston. Ericsson had probably been behind every whisper of frightened gossip, every drop of garlic oil, every bit of vandalism aimed at them. Deacon had been the one to urge the other PASS members to attack Gray.

They'd cut him off until all he had left was John and Zahira. So Yuri sent Ericsson to take care of them, too.

"Yuri and Drugoy knew John and Zahira were ours." Gray's stunned disbelief and pain began to give way to anger. *"They wished to destroy everything we had, so we would have nothing but them."*

Caleb grasped the anger gratefully. On the one hand, nothing about their situation had changed. They'd still lost John. They'd still have to flee Charleston.

"But not until we have made certain Yuri and Drugoy can never harm John or Zahira again."

Grim purpose filled Caleb. He hadn't wanted to text John the information about the sirens, because he thought he had too much to say. But, as it turned out, that wasn't the case after all.

Yuri and Ericsson were behind the siren attacks. Yuri can make a possession permanent from the start. Ericsson was working with him the whole time. In return for the sirens, Ericsson agreed to kill you, and possibly Zahira.

We're going to put a stop to them.

Caleb hesitated, but what the hell. This was his last chance.

We're sorry. Just know, no matter what happens, we'll always love you.

He sent the text. Then he squeezed the phone, and it shattered into pieces in his hand.

"Let's go," he said out loud. "There's nothing left for us here."

Caleb rode his bike to the enormous dockyard off East Bay Street, against the Cooper River.

Dawn wasn't far off. He left the motorcycle on the street and scrambled over the chain link fence surrounding the yard. The dockyard was truly enormous, stretching blocks in either direction. Rows of train tracks crisscrossed the area near the fence. Beyond them, a vast lot of cars waited to be loaded onto ships for transport. Cargo cranes towered against the sky, and a few low buildings dotted the concrete expanse.

At the moment, everything at the southern end of the yards was quiet, though the shouts and calls of workers sounded from the north. Hopefully they either wouldn't realize anything was wrong, or would have enough sense to run the other way if they did.

Yuri stood at the base of one of the cranes, staring out over the water. His pale hair glowed orange beneath the sodium lamps as he gazed out over the heaving river. An unexpected sliver of pain lodged in Caleb's heart.

Because he'd liked Yuri. He'd thought Yuri understood.

Everything could have been different. They could have had another drakul at their side. A friendship that would see them through life's ups and downs for decades to come.

But apparently that hadn't been enough for Yuri and Drugoy.

"I know everything, Yuri," Caleb said as he approached.

"Oh, I sincerely doubt it." Yuri turned to them. "You came."

"You sent Ericsson to kill John. You forced demons into innocent victims." Caleb swallowed. "You're behind the outbreak of possessions, aren't you?"

"Not all of them." Yuri shrugged. "Isabelle did quite well for herself, offering temporary possession to those who wished a boost of strength, or the ability to seduce a lover, or all the other reasons mortals find to enter such agreements. A few even had the willpower to return and have the demons removed before their time was up." Yuri paused. "Of course I ate them instead."

Christ. "Why?" Caleb flung his arms out. "You could have done anything in the world. You have money, youth, fucking near immortality. Why this *horror?*"

"Horror?" Anger flashed in Yuri's eyes. "We made this city into a paradise! Filled to bursting with demons to hunt. You and I could have sampled all of its pleasures, and Gray and Drugoy fed until even their vast thirst was slaked." His hand balled into a fist. "This was our *gift* to you. And you threw it back in our face. After all we did for you. After all we *suffered.*"

Heat boiled in Caleb's chest. He flexed burning fingertips, claws so close to manifesting. "Your sirens used illusions to convince innocent people to eat other innocent people for dinner. What the fuck do you know about suffering?"

"More than you ever will." Yuri's slender body trembled. "Sixty years ago, I was chosen to host the drakul. I had proved my loyalty, my cunning, and so was deemed the perfect subject. Drugoy came through, and he was so much more than my so-called superiors had promised. The moment we were joined, I knew it was meant to be. Together we were strong, and fast, and could summon anything short of another drakul just by thinking about it." His lips curled. "But they were frightened, just as your precious John was frightened. They wanted to exorcise Drugoy. Send him back and once again take away his chance of finding Gray. So we ate them."

"We ate him," Caleb had said when Yuri asked what happened to Forsyth. And had been so fucking relieved to have someone else who could understand.

Yuri turned away from them. Crossing his hands at the small of his back, he stared out over the river. "I lied, before. When you asked what happened. I said they hadn't caught us." He drew in a deep, shuddering breath. "But I want you to know. *Drugoy* wants you to know. It was true, what the official reports said. Our forty days weren't yet up, but we were too strong for them. They feared us. And so they betrayed us."

He kept his back to them, but his hands slowly tightened. Blood began to drip from one palm, where his nails pierced the flesh.

"They trapped us." His voice dove in register, Drugoy speaking along with him. "Encased us in iron and concrete, and dropped us into the lake. Down in the crushing dark, beneath the water, where our power was dampened. Year after year after year. No light. No food. No reprieve, even for a second. Suffocated in our prison, pulped by the pressure of a mile of water. Constant, endless, suffering."

Caleb's lips parted, but no words came out. He'd never quite grasped what being immortal, or nearly so, truly meant until that moment.

Hell, he probably didn't grasp it even now. That level of horror was beyond his power to imagine.

He didn't want to feel sorry for Yuri and Dru, not after what they'd done. But he couldn't help it. "Christ. But you…you escaped."

"Our power was dampened, not entirely banished." Yuri's shoulders straightened. "The lake taught us patience. It taught us how to be still. To think. To plan. Year after year, we chipped away at our prison. Fifteen years went by, but in the end, we were free."

How they could have managed something like that without feeding, Caleb couldn't begin to imagine. For the first time since deciding to confront Yuri and Dru, he started to wonder if he should be afraid.

Yuri half-turned at last to look at them. "We have walked this world ever since. I've been the one to keep us safe—*me*." A lopsided smile touched his lips. "As you know, Caleb, drakul aren't the great thinkers among etheric entities. We traveled, and gathered resources, and scoured the world. Looking, always looking."

"For Gray."

"We searched for so long—first in Russia, then across Europe, and finally here. My skills in intelligence paid off in more ways than my mentors ever imagined. When we saw you on the television…" Yuri closed his eyes briefly, then opened them again. "It made the rest of it worthwhile. All the years of madness and pain for Drugoy, when he came through the veil only to be cast back out. All the time we spent drowning in the lake."

He let out a long breath. "Drugoy wanted to rush in immediately. I managed to convince him to let me plan this, as I'd planned everything from the moment we emerged from the lake. Bursting through the thick winter ice, back into the sun. We came here and watched from afar, using renfields we cultivated. We were so, so patient. Learning everything we could about you. How best to court you." Yuri spun to face Caleb fully, and red flashed in the depths of his eyes. "And it would have worked, if not for that stupid mortal."

Caleb's teeth burned as well as his fingertips, Gray lashing just under their skin. "If you knew so much about us, you should have known we'd never forgive you for killing John."

"He's a mortal! What are they compared to us?" Yuri stepped closer. "Their lives are so brief. Like fireflies blinking in and out over the marsh. Yet you insist on clinging to the trappings of mortality, to the limitations they impose on you. I wanted to free you from your chains!"

Darkness spilled across Yuri's eyes, lit from within by red. "Gray, you carry five millennia of their memories within you. You know even better than I how brief their lives are. How inconsequential."

Gray went still. Something almost like pity emanated from him, surprising Caleb.

"They have misunderstood everything," Gray said. *"And they do not even know it."*

Caleb fell back, letting Gray take over. "You are wrong," Gray told Drugoy. "Five-thousand years have taught me every life is of consequence. You say mortals live short lives. You pretend our love for John must be less because his days will come to an end. But there is never any moment but now. This moment, this second, this breath, matters as much as any other in all of history. What we choose to do with it matters as much as any other choice."

For a long moment, Drugoy didn't move. Then his face slowly twisted into a snarl. "If you love mortals so much, you will die like one."

CHAPTER 13

GRAY LEAPS AT Drugoy, at the same moment Drugoy leaps for him. They crash into one another, snarling and biting. Claws rake across Gray's face, and his own snag in flesh through a gap in Drugoy's coat.

They fall back, circling slowly. Taking one another's measure. Gray has watched Drugoy hunt and fight, but this is different. His blood drips from Drugoy's claws, and red darkens Drugoy's fine shirt.

Gray rushes him, but they are matched in speed. Drugoy dodges, then kicks, boot slamming into Gray's hip. He twists, staggers, but keeps his feet.

"I would have given you everything," Drugoy rumbles. The concrete beneath his boots begins to fracture. "Done anything for you, if you had only taken what I offered."

Gray's lips are tight against his gums, displaying his fangs to the fullest. "You have nothing I want."

Drugoy roars and charges. But this time, Gray is ready. He twists aside, grabbing Drugoy's arm as he does so. With a roar of his own, he uses a combination of momentum and Caleb's TK, and hurls Drugoy through the air.

The other drakul smashes down amidst the rows of parked cars. A windshield explodes beneath his weight, roof and part of the hood crumpling with impact. The car's alarm begins to shrill.

'Fuck, we have to end this fast. No way is that noise not going to bring security

guards."

Drugoy leaves behind bloodstains as he sits up. He grasps the passenger door of the car, which has popped out from the bent frame. With a squeal of abused metal, he rips the door free—and hurls it at Gray.

It strikes edge-on, biting flesh and snapping the bones of their chest. Gray hits the concrete, skidding some distance, leaving behind skin and ripped leather.

Drugoy rises to his feet and strides across the cars, stepping from roof to roof. Each crumples beneath his boots, and more alarms shrill, beating against Gray's sensitive hearing. Bone snaps back into place in Gray's chest with an agonizing grind, and he rolls to his feet even as Drugoy springs from the last car.

Caleb's TK gives them a boost, and they are almost flying through the air. They crash into Drugoy in mid-air with an impact Gray feels in his teeth. They twist, clawing and biting at one another—until they hurtle into one of the massive cranes at the edge of the river.

Gray makes certain Drugoy takes the brunt of the force when they collide with the crane. It would be enough to kill most demons.

But Drugoy is no demon.

The metal buckles under the impact, the entire crane shuddering. Blood paints Drugoy's pale hair red, and shards of bone protrude through his shirt and jeans. But the massive injuries fail to even slow him. One arm still works, and he manages to seize Gray by the hair. Then, using his immense strength, he smashes Gray's face into the metal crane.

Bone snaps, and teeth shatter. For a moment, wild colors spangle their vision, their brain slamming into their fractured skull.

Gray releases Drugoy, stumbling drunkenly while he heals. Thoughts unscramble, and sight clears, the wall of pain receding, though not fast enough.

Caleb shudders. *"Christ, what is it with people wanting to scramble our brain tonight?"*

"Stop!" shouts a human voice. "Stop, or we'll shoot!"

"Damn it, no. We have to get them out of here, Gray." Panic rises from Caleb. *"Enough people have died already."*

Four or five men in private security uniforms stand facing them, guns drawn and leveled. The men's eyes widen as they realize they are dealing with something more than human vandals.

"Run," Gray orders, putting all the power he can into the word, hoping to frighten them. "Run or die."

"Well, well," Drugoy says. He climbs from the wrecked crane. One leg straightens with an audible *crack*. An ugly grin twists his expression. "This does make things more interesting."

The guards open fire. Drugoy laughs, even as the bullets impact them both.

That at least seems to decide the mortals. They try to flee, but the rows of vehicles block their paths. With a low growl, Drugoy leaps in pursuit.

"What the hell? What is he doing?"

Gray doesn't know—and it does not matter. The mortals run between two of the low, concrete buildings, fleeing blindly. On the other side of the buildings, away from the vehicles, is a patch of bare earth dotted with piles of rubble and recovered steel, as though another structure has just been demolished. Chains, perhaps meant for binding the beams for transport later on, snake across the bare earth.

A chain link fence boxes in the demolition site on three sides. The only way out is the way they came in the first place. The humans are trapped.

Drugoy reaches them first, but Gray is on his heels. A pile of recovered steel beams lies just behind one of the buildings. Gray seizes a beam by one end and swings it. The opposite end catches Drugoy's skull with a decisive *crunch*.

Drugoy collapses. Some mortals scream and clutch at one another, while the others try to climb over the fence. Gray ignores them all as he strides toward Drugoy.

Blood and brains soak into the dry earth. But Drugoy's half-crushed face begins to reform even as Gray approaches. One black glass eye blinks at him—then Drugoy's hand shoots out.

Gray senses a surge of etheric energy. Drugoy's own energy seems to expand, and his healing accelerates. But it is still a moment before Gray understands.

He is using Yuri's ability to summon demons directly from the etheric plane.

A prickle of fear from Caleb. *"He can just…eat them like that? The way you can when John rips NHEs out of a possessed person?"*

So it would seem.

"Oh fuck."

Gray shares the sentiment. Because the longer they fight, the more blood they lose, the slower they heal. If Drugoy can feed throughout the fight, he faces no such limitation.

"That must be how they survived the lake. Any time Yuri could regain just

enough strength—or hell, sanity for all I know—to use his talent, they fed, and Drugoy put another crack in their prison."

I do not think that is important right now.

The ground rumbles, and cracks spread out from Drugoy. Cranes sway, and one of the piles of rubble collapses. Drugoy surges to his feet, his eyes glowing hotter than ever from the etheric energy now roaring through him.

Then he holds out a hand and once again uses Yuri's exorcist abilities.

The mortals begin to scream—but the screams quickly become howls. The guards' bodies twist, clothing rips, and faces mutate. The delicious scent of mange-clotted fur and old blood pours out of them.

Werewolves. A whole pack.

Drugoy grins. "Get him," he orders. And the werewolves charge.

Gray does not understand how this is possible. Demons recognize drakul as predators; they should flee in terror. Instead, they obey Drugoy and hurl themselves en masse at Gray.

"No—we've seen this before. Remember Brimm? He controlled the ghouls with some sort of bonds of etheric energy. John severed them with a silver knife."

But they have neither John nor a silver athame. So Gray can only fling himself into the midst of the pack, disrupting their charge.

Claws and teeth rip at him from every side. He ignores the damage and fastens his fangs into the throat of one. Charged blood floods into him, healing wounds. He tosses the werewolf aside and seizes another.

A loop of heavy chain wraps around his arm, yanking him to the side. Drugoy holds the other end, using it to drag Gray off his feet, while the werewolves continue to maul him. He cannot fight both them and Drugoy.

Even as they savage him, Gray ignores the werewolves. Drugoy is the greater threat. Bracing his boots against the earth, Gray uses all his strength to pull back against the chain Drugoy has wrapped around him.

The werewolves change tactics, knocking his feet from under him. He bites wildly, gets a mouthful of etheric energy, and makes it to his feet again.

Only to have Drugoy jerk at the chain and pull him to the ground before he can brace himself.

The pack takes advantage, swarming Gray. Agony spikes through their head as one of the werewolves tears off his left ear, while two others rip chunks from his legs. Their blood seeps into the thirsty earth, and their wounds close more and more sluggishly.

"We have to get out of here!" Fear coats Caleb's words, and Gray can taste it in their mouth. He manages to get his fangs into one of the werewolves, drinks it down, before Drugoy realizes what's happening.

Drugoy roars and jerks on the chain again with all his strength. Agony flares through them, arm dislocating at the shoulder—then they are flying through the air, to crash into one of the light posts. Gray hits the ground; before he can get to his feet, the chain draws tight across his chest, pinning them to the lamppost.

"Move!"

Gray tries to fling himself forward, but Drugoy is too fast. The links of the massive chain bind them to the lamppost.

Ordinarily, it would be no trouble to break free. But they are weak. Drained by the fight with the werewolves, and with Drugoy before that. Gray snarls as he struggles against the binding. Despite their depleted state, one of the links begins to stretch and bend.

"Not so fast," Drugoy says. He stands poised a few feet away, a length of steel rebar in his hand. "You will break my heart and Yuri's? Then we will stake yours."

Drugoy hurls the rebar like a javelin, with tremendous force and precise aim. It slams into Gray's chest, piercing his heart, before burying itself in the steel post behind him.

Agony blooms, but he is trapped by chains and iron. Staked. Pinned in place, helpless.

"No," Caleb moans. *"No, no, no…"*

Concrete shatters beneath Drugoy's every step. The werewolves are gone—released for later hunting, perhaps.

Drugoy crouches in front of them. One hand caresses Gray's bloodied face, before sliding around to grip his hair. "To think, all these years, I searched for you," Drugoy says. "Only to have you betray me."

Before Gray can snarl a response, that it is Drugoy who betrayed them, the other drakul lunges forward.

Fangs bury themselves in Gray's throat, tearing through muscle and cartilage. He roars and tries to fight, but his body is chained and staked, and Drugoy's hand in his hair wrenches his head back.

Drugoy begins to feed.

Raw terror radiates out from Caleb, mingling with agony. Their heart struggles to beat around the rebar, fibrillating madly as their blood gushes into Drugoy's mouth. A low, animal growl rises from Drugoy as he drinks.

And drinks.

And drinks.

Their heart quivers faster and faster, desperate to get blood to starving tissue. But there is not enough blood left even if the iron bar hadn't shredded needed muscle. All the strength drains from Gray's limbs, and the light at the top of the lamppost seems to dim. Memories flicker wildly, like static across a screen.

"I love you," John says. And it is wonderful in a way Gray didn't know things could be wonderful.

Feeding on the sirens: strong, powerful, unstoppable.

The rush of wind in their face, the motorcycle roaring beneath them.

John's face, twisted with fear. "I don't ever want to see you again!"

Their heart slows. Grows weaker. Barely quivers at all.

The fangs withdraw. Through a haze, Gray sees Drugoy stand up, wiping blood from his mouth with one hand. "One more chance," Drugoy says. "After all this time, I still cannot bear to let you go. Not until I know there is no hope left."

The werewolves are howling in the distance. Screams mix in with the howls; the pack has found the mortal workers on the north end of the dockyard.

Drugoy vanishes, and Yuri holds up his arms, as though showing something off. "I will yet make this city a paradise on earth," he says with an ugly smile. "By the time I'm done, every last mortal will be possessed or dead. Your precious exorcist will be torn apart by the horde. We will rule the day and the night, glutted on the blood of a thousand demons, and no one can stop us."

He turns and walks away. Gray's vision grows dimmer and dimmer, until Yuri's hair is only a pale smear against the darkness.

Then it is gone, along with everything else.

There came a wild pounding on the door of the interrogation room. Barillo scowled. "What?"

Karl stuck his head inside, an uncharacteristic expression of fear on his face. "We've got trouble."

"Spit it out, Agent Rand! We're in the middle of an important interrogation here."

"There's been a massive outbreak of NHEs on the east side of the peninsula." Karl blurted. His voice trembled, and he cleared his throat. "I saw fire on my way in, and…things were running across the road. Our emergency line is jammed."

No. Sekhmet, Devouring One, this couldn't be happening.

Barillo's face took on a grayish hue. "Wh-what? How could that be?"

"Jim has as many traffic cameras as he can find pulled up," Karl said. "Come see for yourself."

They all followed him, even Steele. An agent in the cube farm sat in front of his monitor, staring fixedly at the scene. He jumped when Barillo barked, "Report."

Rather than say anything, the agent rolled his chair back, giving them an unfettered view of the traffic cams. He'd fit seven on the screen, and each one told its own story of mayhem.

A pack of werewolves loped down East Bay Street. Ghouls descended on a wrecked car on Cumberland, savaging first responders. A fire burned uncontrolled at a yacht club, while hellhounds encircled the fire trucks come to put it out.

The centermost image, bracketed by horror and mayhem, showed a familiar figure walking down Calhoun Street. The asphalt shattered each time Drugoy's feet touched the earth. His white-blond hair blew in the hot wind gusting from a building fire. One of the cops responding to the fire approached, gun at the ready. Drugoy held out his hand.

The cop's body went through an agonizing series of contortions. Fangs erupted from his mouth, his face stretched into a muzzle, and he dropped to all fours. With a shake of its head, the new werewolf turned on the firefighters.

Drugoy's step never wavered.

John's mouth turned dry, his tongue thick. All the feeling seemed to have left his fingers and toes. Even in his wildest imaginings, he'd never pictured *this*.

"Dear God in heaven," Barillo said shakily. "What the fuck is that?"

John took a deep breath, struggling against the bands constricting his chest. But he could only force out one word. One single, damning word.

"Drakul."

SHAKER
OF
EARTH

CHAPTER 1

A MEMORY, FRAGMENTED as a dream seen through a sheer curtain, hazy and strange.

Hunting. The prey scatters, sensing him above it. They flee down, only to be ambushed by the other drakul who waits below.

Together they feast. It is not the same as drinking blood in the mortal world, but there is satisfaction in the act. When it is done, they retreat and curl up around one another in silence. Waiting and watching, until more prey is spotted and they hunt again.

The hunt is good. But it is also good not to be alone.

Then a split opens in the world, and he is dragged through. The other drakul clutches at him, tries to keep them together, but cannot.

After, there is mortal flesh, with strange and alien memories crowding out his own. There is the hunt, and it is good, and that is enough. It must be enough.

He is alone for a very, very long time.

"Caleb? Hey? You still in there?"

Caleb's eyes fluttered open, the lids scraping over dry corneas.

Pain filled the world from side to side, clouding his vision with red and black, and he wished he hadn't woken up after all. His head felt like it might explode, his throat ached with dryness, and muscles he didn't even know he had screamed as though he'd wrenched each one. But none of it compared to the agony centered in his chest.

His heart strove to beat normally, but the steel rebar through it made that impossible. Instead, it quivered without rhythm, striving to pump blood to his lungs and failing. He tried to catch a breath, but nothing seemed to be working right.

He'd never felt this bad, not even when that asshole Sean had shot him through the head. What had happened?

Memories sparked and stuttered, like an engine struggling to fire. John's face, twisted with fear and horror. *"Go! Get out! Don't come back!"*

Drugoy's lips on theirs, his hurt look when Gray pulled away.

Yuri's eyes, full of rage, giving way to Drugoy as he snarled: *"If you love mortals so much, you will die like one."*

Fuck.

Caleb tried to swear aloud, but it came out as a groan. "Shit," said the voice that had brought him back to consciousness in the first place. "Okay. Hold on and let me see if I can take care of the rebar."

Caleb's eyes focused lethargically. A figure crouched anxiously beside him. Red hair. Green eyes. Cute face.

"Deacon," he managed to say, before speech failed him. *You're one of Drugoy's renfields. You pretended to be my friend, and the whole time you were watching and reporting back to Yuri.*

"Yeah, it's me." Deacon's pale skin had gone the color of curdled milk. "Hold still. I'm going to use my TK."

Deacon stood up and held out his hands. Taking a deep breath, he locked his gaze on the steel rod.

Drugoy had thrown it with enough force to penetrate the steel lamp post Caleb was chained to. There came a tortured squeal of metal. The sensation of the rusty metal twisting and shifting inside his body drew a weak scream from Caleb's throat. The world collapsed into a point of agony, and he wanted to beg Deacon to stop, to leave him be, to—

The steel rebar tore free and flew ten feet, to clang against the shattered concrete.

Caleb dragged in great, heaving breaths. Ordinarily, Gray would heal him, if not instantly then within minutes. His heart ought to be stitching back together, broken bones popping into alignment.

But Drugoy had fed on them to the point they had almost no blood left. He felt a splinter of sternum work its way free, but even that seemed to take great effort on Gray's part.

Not good. He wanted to check in with Gray, but distracting him when he was the only thing keeping them barely alive seemed like a terrible idea.

Though the heavy chain had been wrapped around them multiple times, the ends weren't secured. Deacon grabbed one end and trotted around them in a circle, unwinding it. It made a hellish amount of noise, and he winced.

"Damn it. Going to attract the attention of those werewolves."

Caleb became aware of the sound of distant screams and howls. The sun was coming up over the Atlantic, but a red glow lit the sky to the west as well. Fire?

"I might be able to knock them away with my TK," Deacon went on. "And maybe if they smell Gray, they'll stay clear. I hope so, because you're in no shape to fight them."

Caleb wanted to ask why the hell Deacon was letting him go. Had Yuri and Drugoy sent him, just to make sure Gray didn't die until they were done with him? *"One more chance,"* Drugoy had said. Like he seriously thought Gray was going to change his mind after everything.

"No," Caleb grated. The links of the chain loosened around him, and he slumped to the side. "Louder. More." He grabbed at the chain and shook it weakly.

Deacon didn't look at all certain. "You can't fight, Caleb. You can't even stand up. And what about Gray? Is he still in there?"

A clot of anger lodged in Caleb's veins. It was partially Deacon's fault this had happened in the first place. But he couldn't spare the strength to be pissed. "Make noise!"

Deacon shook his head, then turned to a pile of steel scrap. A moment later, the pieces lifted into the air and scattered over the concrete, sending up a hellish clanging.

Caleb gripped the lamp post in both hands and dragged himself to his feet. The world spun, and he had to shut his eyes. "Yell."

"Oh no!" Deacon shouted. "I'm trapped under this big pile of steel. I sure hope no werewolves come try to eat me while I'm lying here all helpless!"

In other circumstances, Caleb would have laughed, or at least cracked a grin. But Deacon had betrayed him, and he wasn't at all sure the werewolves *weren't* going to be the end of him and Gray. They didn't have any blood to spare.

A growl sounded from nearby, and he glimpsed shadows slinking through the wreckage the fight with Drugoy had left behind. The pack coming back for another round.

He'd lost track of time, but it couldn't have been more than an hour ago when the werewolves had been human security guards responding to the commotion. Before Yuri's exorcist ability infected them with demons, bypassing the usual forty days required for the NHE to take over completely.

Deacon backed away from the loping figures. "They're here. Three of them, it looks like. Now what?"

"The rebar." Caleb's words slurred drunkenly, his tongue heavy in his dry mouth. "Impale one with it. We'll do the rest."

Deacon shook his head but didn't have time to comment. Two of the werewolves charged.

The rebar crashed into one, taking it through the shoulder. Blood gushed, and Caleb caught its scent.

Rational thought evaporated in the face of a hunger more powerful than anything he'd experienced before. It felt as though something tried to claw its way out of his belly, screaming and howling with need. The world shrank, vision tunneling. He heard a yelp from the other werewolf, but it seemed far away, inconsequential.

He hung on for a split second, waiting for Gray to rise and transform their teeth into fangs and nails into claws. But they didn't even have enough energy for Gray to manifest.

Shit. This was going to be unpleasant.

He surrendered to hunger and lurched away from the lamppost at the werewolf. It let out a screech of pain as it ripped the length of steel bar from its shoulder. More blood gushed, the great artery in the arm torn, but it would only be a matter of seconds before it began to heal.

The fresh edge of sheered metal caught Caleb's eye. A fragment of siding, ripped apart in the fight or as part of the demolition that had left behind the rubble, he didn't know. Caleb picked it up and swung it as hard as he could at the werewolf's neck.

The edge bit deep, slicing through hide and into a jugular. Before it could react, Caleb let go of the metal, grappled it from behind, and thrust his face in the wound.

The thing's stench nearly suffocated him: mange clotted fur and rotting meat. His human fingers slipped in its coarse fur, but he sealed his mouth to the wound and caught as much of the foul blood on his tongue as he could.

Energy crackled through him, like a jolt of lightning. He swallowed once, twice—

The werewolf wrenched free of his weak grip and turned on him, claws flashing as it raised its paw-like hand.

The other werewolf slammed into it, hurled by Deacon's telekinesis. "Run!" Deacon shouted. All the color had drained from his face, and he visibly shook as he raised his hands. He was running out of juice fast. "I can't hold them off any longer!"

The etheric energy Caleb consumed in the demon's blood spread through him. Not much, not nearly enough to start healing.

But enough for his teeth to sharpen and claws to erupt from his fingers.

There was no finesse. He fell onto the werewolves and bit blindly, sinking his teeth as deep into meat as he could.

Blood burst into his mouth, channeled by the grooves on the backs of his teeth, and a moan of ecstasy escaped him. The werewolf struggled to get away, but Caleb's leather coat foiled its claws. Energy flooded through his body, and the holes in his heart finally sealed. Its beat steadied, the shattered bits of sternum snapping back out and into place. Lungs inflated.

And he sensed something coalescing, rising up from where it had spent every second, every moment, keeping them from slipping away into death.

Gray.

Yuri and Ericsson were behind the siren attacks. Yuri can make a possession permanent from the start. Ericsson was working with him the whole time. In return for the sirens, Ericsson agreed to kill you, and possibly Zahira.

We're going to put a stop to them.

We're sorry. Just know, no matter what happens, we'll always love you.

John's phone lay in the center of the conference room table, Caleb's texts displayed. He'd shut off his phone while Barillo grilled him about Ericsson's death. About Gray bent over Ericsson's body, teeth fastened in the dead agent's neck, draining his blood.

He hadn't thought to check the phone until he saw the scenes of mayhem relayed by traffic cams all around Charleston. Pandemonium reigned in each one, demons loose in the streets, fire raging, and in the center of it all, Yuri strolling down Calhoun Street as though he hadn't a care in the world.

We're going to put a stop to them.

He'd been so afraid Gray and Caleb were working with Yuri and Drugoy to make Charleston an all-you-can-eat drakul buffet. But it sounded as though the ex-Soviet intelligence officer had played them just as he had everyone else.

Karl sat to one side of John, Zahira to the other. Steele hovered uncomfortably at the end of the table. Barillo stood directly across from them, arms folded over his chest.

"I tried calling, but Caleb isn't answering his phone," John said, glad his voice didn't shake. "It's possible Gray fried the electronics accidentally."

He didn't speak the other possibility aloud, that Caleb had caught up with Yuri and Drugoy, and the fight had gone badly for them.

"You knew about this other drakul, Starkweather," Barillo said flatly. "And yet you didn't tell anyone."

"Ericsson knew, too," Steele said. He'd been uncharacteristically quiet, no doubt reeling from his partner's betrayal. "They did the sirens...I didn't think it had been long enough, but if Jansen is right and this other drakul can make a possession permanent from the beginning... fuck."

"I wasn't asking about Ericsson," Barillo said. "I was asking Starkweather."

"Sir, we don't have time for this," Karl said, directing the words to Barillo. "We need every hand on deck, now. We can sort out blame later."

"When I want your opinion, I'll give it to you, Rand," Barillo said.

John's pulse sped. "With all due respect—"

"Don't give me that bullshit," Barillo snapped. "You don't have any respect for the job or the organization. You only care about that *thing* you're fucking." His lip curled. "You know what I think? I think maybe you were fucking this second drakul, too. Is that why Azarov sent Ericsson after you, Starkweather? Lovers' quarrel gone bad?"

John ground his teeth together until he feared they might crack. He'd had enough of Barillo's insinuations. Yes, he'd screwed up about as much as it was possible to do as an agent, but—

No. Wait. Barillo might be an asshole, but he might inadvertently be onto something after all.

"Gray knew Drugoy from before he was summoned into this world," John said slowly. "They hunted together."

Zahira let out a gasp. "Drugoy was the other drakul Gray mentioned, the day I interviewed him?"

"It's a weird coincidence, I admit." John shrugged. "But Yuri and Drugoy wanted me dead, and they didn't want Caleb and Gray to know who ordered the trigger pulled."

John remembered all the little pangs of jealousy he'd had over the last few days. He'd been so sure he was losing Caleb and Gray to the other drakul. Not just because of the fact Dru was Gray's former... something...but because of the time they spent together now. The lavish gift of the custom motorcycle from Isabelle Aiken's shop. Fine dining for Caleb, and a feast of blood for Gray. Goddess only knew what else.

And John was just a mortal exorcist. He didn't have Yuri's money, or Drugoy's previous connection. How could he possibly compete?

Except he hadn't needed to. Gray and Caleb loved him. It had been Yuri and Dru who had tried to compete, and failed.

It sounded crazy, but he felt the truth of it in his bones.

"But Ericsson wasn't supposed to kill only me," he went on, feeling as though he were trying to find the shape of something in the dark. "Caleb's text says Zahira might have been on his list as well. Gray doesn't care about most mortals. He's typically indifferent, unless they make themselves an annoyance. But there are two he cares about."

"Gray is my friend, as well as my coworker," Zahira said with a nod.

"Our relationships with him are different, obviously," John hastened to add. "Yet we're the ones Yuri and Dru wanted out of the way."

There came a sharp knock on the door. "What?" Barillo barked.

One of the techs stuck her head inside. "We've gone through Ericsson's phone, sir. He was using his birthdate as the lock code, so it wasn't hard to open."

"Well?" Barillo asked. "Did you find anything useful?"

The tech looked oddly nervous. "We did. I...you might want to take a look for yourself."

Gray roars.

The sound is one of fury and warning, as he flings aside the dead werewolf and hooks his claws into the second. Of defiance.

Of challenge.

Because Drugoy and Yuri have *dared* do this to him.

They hurt Caleb and tried to kill John. They loosed havoc in *his* city, and threatened *his* mortals, and he will not have it.

He bites the second werewolf, drinks it down as fast as he can, strength returning with every gulp. The third is circling Deacon, but when it spots Gray coming toward it, it tries to run.

Not fast enough.

He chases it down before it gets twenty feet, claws sinking into head and shoulder, yanking its skull back so hard something snaps in its neck before he drives in his fangs. His heart pounds now, whole again, and he welcomes the steady beat almost as much as Caleb's overwhelming sense of relief.

The werewolf gives one last convulsion and dies, all of its etheric energy absorbed. Gray tosses its body aside and turns his gaze to the west.

The dawn light tints a rising column of smoke. The blare of alarms accompanies that of sirens, and the distant screams of mortals.

He holds still for a moment, letting memory spread through him, like a drop of blood through a pool of water.

Yuri and Drugoy betrayed them. Used them. Because Drugoy is as mad as any demon.

"Because he was summoned into a living body," Caleb says, subdued now. *"It isn't his fault. Not really."*

It explains him. It does not excuse him. Or Yuri. Yuri, who wove this web for Drugoy's sake, hoping to catch Gray and bind him and Caleb to them.

"Agreed."

A shoe scuffs against concrete behind them. "Are...are you all right?" Deacon asks uncertainly. "Gray, isn't it?"

He turns. The mortal stands behind him, looking up apprehensively.

This mortal broke Caleb's heart, pretending to be afraid of Gray. All on Yuri's orders.

Gray seizes him by the throat. Deacon's eyes go wide, and he claws at Gray's hand, but his attempts to free himself are pathetic.

"You are one of Drugoy's renfields," Gray growls. "Tell me why I should not simply kill you now."

CHAPTER 2

JOHN CROWDED INTO the tech worker's cubicle along with Karl, Steele, Zahira, and Barillo. *Heather Lee* read the nameplate; John recognized the name from IT emails, though he hadn't met the woman in person before. She connected Ericsson's phone to a cord, and the monitor in front of her began to mirror its screen. "We looked for relevant names in the contact list," she explained. "I thought we'd have to dig for deleted texts, but he either didn't bother, or didn't have time, to get rid of any of them."

Ericsson never imagined he'd get caught. Just as with the shakedowns and the fancy house. He'd felt invulnerable. Was that Yuri's influence? If Ericsson was a renfield, he would have been powered up on Drugoy's blood.

Caleb and Gray had been acting invulnerable as well. As though there could be no possible consequences for their actions, right up until the moment there were. Yuri and Drugoy had a way with people, it seemed.

"So, the first thing we came across that seems incriminating are a series of texts to and from a woman named Cindy Newman."

"That was the singer Ericsson hooked up with," Steele offered. "Jansen said her band got turned into the sirens." He bit his lip. "I still can't believe...you should've seen that dinner cruise. What they did to those people. Fuck, Ericsson threw up over the side when he saw it. He couldn't have anything to do with them."

"Maybe he didn't realize how bad things would get," Zahira said grimly. "What do the texts say?"

Lee brought them up and began to scroll. "I'll let you read for yourself, but the gist is Cindy Newman and Darrel Ericsson went on a date, and…well, a few days later we get this exchange."

Darrel Ericsson: Got some free time this weekend. Let's do it again.

Cindy: Are you out of your mind?

DE: What? You had a good time, once you loosened up a little.

Cindy: You mean after you roofied me.

DE: What are you telling people?

Cindy: The truth. The rest of the band knows. They told me to go to the police. But I just want to be left alone. I don't want to hear from you again.

DE: You keep your fucking mouth shut. I can ruin you. I'm a federal agent.

Cindy: Please, just leave me alone.

DE: Too late for that, bitch.

DE: You're going to be sorry.

DE: I have ways of taking care of bitches like you.

DE: Cunt.

Bile rose in John's throat. "He raped her," he said faintly. "And then he forced NHEs into her and her bandmates. The dinner cruise, everyone the sirens killed, it was all just to cover his own ass."

Zahira's lips moved soundlessly in prayer. Steele's face took on a greenish hue. "I didn't know," he said. "I swear to God, I didn't know. I would've turned him in myself, and to hell with the consequences."

A clearer picture was forming in John's mind of what must have happened in Ericsson's bedroom before he got there. Caleb and Gray had arrived, whether to confront Ericsson or kill him outright, John couldn't guess. They'd already suspected about the sirens; possibly Ericsson said something to confirm it. Then they fought, and Ericsson stabbed them through the skull. Had he threatened Zahira then, or before?

Had he tried to exorcise Gray? It wasn't supposed to be possible after forty days, but as far as John knew, no one had tried with a knife actually embedded in the host body's brain. Hard to save the victim after stabbing four inches of silver into their head.

Maybe it had been—or at least felt—more like a life-or-death fight for Gray than John had imagined. And not just Caleb's life—Zahira's and John's.

If Gray meant to feed on Ericsson from the start, he could have done it without breaking a sweat. Waited for Ericsson to leave and jumped down off the roof. Ericsson wouldn't have had a chance to fight back.

Caleb, at least, had wanted answers.

"Is that all?" Barillo asked. "You could've just told us in the conference room, Lee."

"No, sir." Her hands trembled slightly as she swiped to another text chain. "This one is between Azarov and Ericsson."

Yuri Azarov: How are things in SPECTR? Anything new to report?

Darrel Ericsson: Not yet. Keeping up the pressure on Jansen. I wrote "monster" on the door of the conference room they use, where everyone could see it.

YA: Good, good. I have a little something for you. Your chief continues to complain about his "problem employees" to Isabelle. She planted the suggestion he separate them from one another, then see if performance improves.

DE: I bet he loved that.

YA: Predictably so. I leave the details up to you, but I would like you to become Gray and Caleb's new partner.

DE: You're kidding me.

YA: I assure you, I am not. Don't worry, I don't expect you to make friends. Quite the opposite, in fact.

DE: All right. Shouldn't be too hard. Hell, Barillo will probably think he was the one who came up with the idea.

YA: Perfect. Keep me informed.

"There are some more texts, later," Lee said. "Azarov ordered Ericsson to assassinate Special Agent Starkweather ASAP. Ericsson wanted time to set something up, but Azarov shut him down, said it had to be in the next few hours. Once Ericsson killed Starkweather, he was to murder Special Agent Noorzai as well."

She trailed off, carefully not looking at Barillo. The chief shifted uneasily from foot to foot. "I don't know any Isabelle," he growled at last. "This is—is some kind of setup. They wanted to discredit me." He rounded on Karl. "Tell everyone I'm not lying!"

"You don't know anyone named Isabelle, to your knowledge," Karl replied. And stopped there.

Fuck. How could this be happening? "Is there anyone—*anyone*—here not following Yuri's orders?"

John didn't want to look at Zahira, but couldn't help it. She'd been the only agent willing to work with them. Learning as much as possible about drakul, about Gray, had been her driving goal from day one. But what if…

"Of course I'm not, John!" she exclaimed, glaring at him. "Ericsson was supposed to kill me next, remember?"

He scrubbed a hand over his face. Goddess, he was tired. "Yeah, I… sorry."

"She's telling the truth," Karl said, unprompted.

"I wasn't taking orders from any damned NHE," Barillo snapped. "I'm telling you, it's a setup!"

"You haven't talked about SPECTR at all to anyone outside the office?" John challenged. "Not complained about any employees to a female acquaintance?" Too bad he didn't have the photos from the stakeout on his phone. "African-American, about five-six, hair in braids, loves motorcycles?"

Barillo's lips parted slightly, and something like recognition flickered through his eyes. But he only said, "Stop trying to make this about me, Starkweather. If you'd come forward with information about the second drakul, none of this would have happened."

"Or it might have happened sooner," Zahira said. "From what I'm hearing, Azarov had too many plans in place. He must have had a Plan

B."

She wasn't wrong. But Barillo wasn't in the mood to be argued with. "I ought to lock you up and throw away the key, Starkweather."

If Barillo had done Yuri's dirty work, at least it seemed to have been inadvertent. Right now, keeping him happy seemed the best option. "I admit, I acted inappropriately for an agent of SPECTR. I broke the law by failing to report an NHE to the proper authorities."

"Technically, you *are* the proper authority," Karl pointed out.

"What I did was wrong." John lifted his chin slightly, not looking away from Barillo. "Whether I broke the letter of the law or not, I certainly broke its spirit. Let me help stop Yuri and Dru, and I swear—I *swear*—I will turn myself in for whatever punishment SPECTR, or the court system, believes fits my crimes."

"He's telling the truth," Karl said. "Chief, please. We need all the help we can get."

Barillo scowled at them all, and for a moment John was certain he was going to order Zahira to cuff him. Instead, he said, "So how do we stop this thing? And where the fuck is Jansen?" A thoughtful look replaced the scowl. "Wait. The text was probably to throw us off the trail. I bet Jansen is working with Azarov."

It took John a moment to find words through his shock. "That doesn't even make sense!"

"Doesn't it, though?" Barillo snorted. "All this has been to get me out of the way. I wouldn't put up with any of Jansen's bullshit, so he called his friend Azarov in to help smear my name. Subverted Ericsson to make me look bad." The sneer returned. "And now they're having a spat over their mutual fuck buddy."

John clung to his rage, because it let him forget about his fear. "Go to hell."

"Please, both of you!" Karl exclaimed. "Chief, my husband and daughter are out there. Hopefully safe at home, but our house isn't a fortress."

Crap. John had been so worried about Caleb and Gray, he'd forgotten other people—his own friends—had the same concerns about their families. "I'm sorry, Karl. I'm sure they're fine."

Karl waved impatiently. "My point is, we have NHEs to fight, and instead we're standing here fighting each other. We need all hands on deck, as soon as possible."

Another agent trotted up behind them, his pale cheeks flushed with exertion and fear. "Chief! There you are."

"What is it, Quackenbush?"

"Bad news," Quackenbush said. "The cell towers are overloaded, but our agents who have been able to get through report they're losing ground by the minute. Demons are pouring out all over the place."

Barillo swore.

"And, just to add to the trouble, there's been an earthquake. A small one—we didn't even feel it down here—but strong enough at the surface to knock things off the shelves. Which means even more people are trying to make panicked calls."

Zahira's dark eyes widened in dismay, and she glanced at John. "Do you remember what Gray said about the other drakul he hunted with in the etheric plane? About what it was?"

"What it was?" Steele asked. "It's a drakul—what else is there?"

But John knew what she meant. "The drakul aren't just demons. A wendigo might embody hunger, or a werewolf rage, but drakul are forces of nature. The leader of the Vigilant called them gods upon the earth, and after what I saw at Fort Sumter, I don't think she was wrong." He met Zahira's worried gaze. "Gray is the storm. And Drugoy...Drugoy is the earthquake."

Silence followed his pronouncement. Then Barillo muttered a curse. "Fine. You're in, Starkweather. Everyone gear up and meet me up top in five."

Christ, Gray, he can't tell us anything if you're strangling him! Caleb exclaimed. *Let go. I'll handle this.*

He could sense Gray's reluctance, and hell, Deacon wasn't exactly Caleb's favorite person at the moment, either. But if Deacon hadn't let them go, they'd still be staked to the lamppost, just waiting for Drugoy to come back and finish the job.

"Very well," Gray replied after a moment. *"But I do not like him."*

Gray fell back, and Caleb instantly let go of Deacon's throat. Deacon scrambled away, coughing and massaging his neck.

"Sorry," Caleb said, holding up his hands. "Gray isn't very happy with you right now. But you did save us." He paused. "The question is, why? Did Yuri send you?" But that didn't make any sense.

"Sort of." Deacon cleared his throat and took another step back, green eyes wary. "He sent me to keep an eye on you. Make sure the werewolves didn't decide to add drakul to the menu. And that no one showed up to free you."

"So why let us go?" A dreadful thought occurred. "Or is this some new trick of Yuri's?"

"No!" At Caleb's skeptical look, Deacon's shoulders slumped. "I know you don't have any reason to believe me. Hell, I probably wouldn't believe me either, in your place."

Caleb folded his arms over his chest. His leather coat was ragged and streaked with blood; it would be a miracle if the thing survived. "Convince me."

"I never had much paranormal ability." Deacon looked away, his expression wretched. "I mean, I guess I did compared to some people. I could move small things with my mind, just enough to be aware of what my potential would be if I had real power. Then I met Yuri and Drugoy. And I thought…" He swallowed convulsively and winced again. "I don't know what I thought. You know what it's like. The money, the lavish gifts. The blood."

"And in return you, what, stalked us?" Caleb demanded.

"I was supposed to befriend you." Deacon licked dry lips. "I talked Nigel into counter-protesting outside of SPECTR, in the hopes you'd be intrigued. If that hadn't worked, I would have found another way, but it did. By that time, I'd already introduced Mike to Yuri and Isabelle."

"Why? You had to know what they were going to do to him." Mike had ended up possessed by a grendel, in exchange for revenge against the bigots who beat him up. Things hadn't turned out well.

"It was nothing he didn't want!" Deacon protested. "I would've felt the same in his shoes. Things were coming to a head—Mike's forty days were about up—and Yuri and Drugoy had already made contact with you. Yuri told us to stage the incident at the PASS meeting—that was supposed to be the fee for having Isabelle exorcise Mike."

Caleb felt sick. "I'm guessing Mike didn't realize Drugoy planned on eating him."

"No. At least, I don't think so. I didn't realize it, either. Or maybe I did, and I just didn't want to believe it." Deacon stared miserably at the cracked concrete. "I'm sorry, Caleb. When Yuri first told me to make friends with you, it was just a favor I was doing for him. But then it got…it got real. At least for me. I didn't want to hurt you, but I didn't think I had a choice."

Asshole.

Gray stirred. *"I do not like him. I do not like Isabelle. Drugoy's renfields are a reflection of his twisted heart."*

Maybe it said something, that Gray had fixated on good people like John and Zahira.

Or it might have, if they hadn't fucked everything up so badly that John didn't ever want to see them again. Zahira would probably feel the same way.

"So you were supposed to make friends with me, just so you could turn PASS against me," Caleb said.

Deacon nodded. "Yuri wanted you to feel isolated, so you wouldn't have anyone but him and Dru."

Isolated socially, and isolated at work. "He had Ericsson watching me at SPECTR. Doing shit like putting garlic oil on my phone."

"Yeah. Ericsson was another renfield. He got off on the power, you know? And of course, Isabelle thought it was hilarious, leading that boss of yours around on a string without him even knowing."

Caleb felt as though he'd swallowed a chunk of ice and had it get stuck in his throat. "Barillo?"

Deacon looked surprised. "You didn't know? Shit. Yeah, she figured out he liked to stop at a sports bar on the way home to unwind. She struck up a conversation, made friends with him. I mean, he wasn't stupid enough to say he worked for SPECTR, and I'm sure he figured he was being discreet, complaining about his employees in the vaguest way possible. But it wasn't like she was trying to get information out of him, was it? So she'd agree with him when he complained about 'the gays,' and his bosses who wanted him to coddle some guy who shouldn't even be working there, and on and on. And of course, the whole time, she's giving him little suggestions about how to handle things."

"Fucking Barillo." Caleb rubbed his eyes. "He didn't have a clue, did he?"

"No. Never even heard the name Yuri Azarov." Deacon shrugged. "I don't know if Yuri was hoping you'd snap and do away with Barillo or what."

Caleb tipped his head back, trying to think things through. "Yuri sent Ericsson to kill John. And Zahira was next. Was Ericsson supposed to frame someone else? Or did Yuri always expect me to find out somehow?"

"Does it matter?"

"Yes. Ericsson was probably the backup plan when I didn't do in Barillo." God. Yuri's former superiors in Soviet intelligence would have been impressed by the web he'd woven. "So why are you telling me all this? Why betray Yuri and Dru now?"

Deacon's eyes widened, and he gestured toward the city. "You don't know, do you? While you were here, taking a nap, they decided it was time for the fucking apocalypse."

CHAPTER 3

THE FIRE. THE distant sirens.

Dread constricted around Caleb's chest. "Wh-what?"

"It's chaos out there. Yuri is putting NHEs in anyone he passes. There are werewolves running down East Bay Street, for fuck's sake." Deacon shook his head. "I didn't sign up for this."

The ground beneath their feet vibrated, as though a heavy truck had driven past. The pile of steel rattled, and a chunk of concrete toppled from the heap of a demolished wall and rolled across the ground to fetch up against Caleb's boot.

Deacon looked around uncertainly. "What was that?"

"A train?" Caleb suggested. But the tracks running to the freight yard were nearby, and he didn't see anything moving.

No. Not a train. An earthquake.

"Drugoy."

Oh hell. Drugoy must be glutting himself on the demons Yuri had summoned.

Gray's worry thrummed beneath Caleb's, reflecting it back to him. *"They spoke of making this city into a paradise for drakul. Drugoy spared us because he believes he can still convince us to join them."*

I know he's kind of crazy, but he can't really think we'll see demons everywhere and the city in ruins, and decide he's a great guy after all.

"No. I do not believe he would." Gray paused, ruminating. *"Yuri's cleverness*

almost worked. If we had returned their affection, we would have left with them last night. If we had not cared about John."

Shit. *You think John's in trouble?*

"Drugoy and Yuri blame him for our decision. They will try to use him against us, one way or another. Perhaps their plan was to seize him, bring him to us here, and threaten him unless we submit."

It made a horrible sort of sense. *And the chaos—the demons—are meant to draw out John. SPECTR will come for Drugoy.*

"Yes. And Yuri and Drugoy will enjoy this chaos. They will feed well."

Of course they would. It was what Yuri had been doing for months on a lesser scale—summoning demons, then letting them loose so Drugoy would have the challenge of a hunt. No wonder he'd known where to find the werewolves Gray and Dru had hunted together, let alone the sirens.

"What now?" Deacon asked, in a way that suggested Caleb had been gazing off into nothing while having his conversation with Gray.

Caleb turned and stared in the direction of the city. The smoke still rose, even though more alarms than ever split the shrill air. He might be able to find Yuri and Drugoy just by following the noise. Though the demons Yuri summoned and forced into helpless passers-by weren't going to stay put. The path wouldn't be as clear as he'd like. Still, he didn't have any better ideas.

He needed to warn John, before anything else. Tell him to get to SPECTR-HQ and stay put.

Grief seeped into his veins, Gray huddling close against him for comfort. *"John does not want us anymore."*

No. But right now, he needs us.

Caleb held out his hand to Deacon. "Do you have a cell phone?"

Deacon pulled one out of his pocket. "Right here."

The thought of talking to John again made Caleb's gut shrivel. But this was too much and too important to leave to a text. Caleb punched in John's number.

"We're sorry," said an automated voice, "but all circuits are busy right now. Please hang up and try again."

Damn it—the chaos must have spread fast. He typed in a text and sent it, in the blind hope it might eventually be delivered.

Y&D after you. B compromised. Stay in HQ. This is our mess to clean up. -C&G

He tossed the phone back to Deacon. "I haven't forgiven you. But if you want to make things right, get to SPECTR-HQ. Find Special Agent

Noorzai and tell her everything you've told me. Got it?"

Deacon glanced uncertainly in the direction of the chain link fence. "I used up a lot of my TK just now. Maybe if I could get a boost—"

"No," Caleb said flatly, Gray's sharp denial bleeding into his own. "But you can take my motorcycle. Even if the roads are jammed, you might be able to get through on the sidewalks."

The fearful expression didn't fade, but Deacon nodded. "What are you going to do?"

"Yuri's plan was damn near flawless," Caleb said. He dug the keys out of the pocket of his blood-crusted jeans and tossed them to Deacon. "But now he's made a mistake. One that's going to cost him."

"What mistake?"

Caleb's teeth burned as they sharpened. "He didn't kill us when he had the chance."

SPECTR didn't possess the sort of military grade equipment flaunted by most police departments, but they did have an armory with a small amount of body armor and plenty of silver-jacketed ammunition. John strapped on a flak jacket that might hold back the claws and teeth of an enraged therianthrope and loaded every available pocket with more ammo.

Zahira did the same; as she strapped on her jacket, she said, "I'm mad at you, John."

"I know," John said. He focused on checking over his Glock, instead of meeting her eyes. "You have every right to be."

"You used my goodwill." Her voice was tight, words clipped. "You asked me to look up information on the Lake Baikal Vampire, and then asked for my trust. I gave it, because I thought we were friends."

He'd been so angry at Gray and Caleb for abusing his trust. But then he'd turned around and done the same damn thing to Zahira. "I'm sorry. I thought...I believed Yuri and Drugoy were like Caleb and Gray. Weird, but not, you know. Murderous."

Zahira shook her head and left. John hurried to catch up, then fell in beside her.

"You didn't even tell me about the second drakul," she said.

They emerged into the main hall to the elevators. The few field agents remaining in HQ clustered around the doors, faces grim. Some of them had exorcism kits slung over their shoulders, in the hopes that, despite all odds, they might find some possession victims who could be saved. John slowed before reaching the group; once they were on the elevator, there would be no chance for a private conversation.

"Caleb and Gray begged me not to tell anyone," he said in a low voice. "You know what they've been going through here. They'd kept Yuri and Dru even from me, because they were afraid of what SPECTR would do. If I'd gone to Barillo, *they* would have ended up in a cell even if Yuri and Dru managed to escape."

Zahira let out a long sigh. "I know."

"I only found out a couple of days ago myself. I didn't even have a chance to think things through." He paused and looked down at her. "But I'm sorry. I didn't realize you were in danger. I didn't realize *anyone* was in danger. Yuri and Dru played Caleb and Gray, the same way they played Barillo and Ericsson and gods-know-who-else. And I trusted Caleb and Gray's assessment of the situation. I didn't think it would end like this."

She was silent a long moment. The elevator doors opened, and the other agents filed on. There wasn't quite enough room, so they watched the doors close and waited for the next one. "What happened in Ericsson's bedroom, John?" she asked in a low voice. "You went in five minutes before the rest of us."

He took a deep breath, tried not to flash back to that moment of horror and fear. "I saw Gray feeding on Ericsson. Ericsson was already dead, of course—you've seen the size of those fangs. And I...I didn't know the whole story. I didn't know anything, other than I'd ignored the Vigilants' warning about drakul and human blood. And I had to make a choice." He closed his eyes briefly. "SPECTR is more than a job to me, Zahira. My parents...they belonged to one of those religious sects you see all over the rural low country, the ones who think paranormal abilities are a sign of the devil. I became a ward of the state when I was a teen, went to the paranormal school, and then straight to the Academy. SPECTR has been my family, my career, my life."

The lights above the elevator counted down as the car descended. "I knew what my duty was. To take them into custody if I could. Wait until you arrived with backup. Instead, I told them to leave and never come back. That I never wanted to see them again."

"You hoped they'd get out of Charleston?"

"Yes." And because at that moment, he *hadn't* wanted to see them again. Everything hurt too badly. All he'd seen was death and blood, a worst-case scenario where the people he loved most had betrayed everything he cared about.

And now he'd give anything to have them back, to know they were safe and alive, and not devoured by Drugoy.

"Gray is my friend," Zahira said, "but he's also a predator."

"I know that," he snapped, annoyed.

"But sometimes you forget." She glanced up at him. "I've read the reports. When Gray first came into Caleb's body, his reflex was to bite Caleb's sister-in-law, Melanie Jansen."

Goddess, John had almost forgotten about that. "And?"

"We know Ericsson stabbed them in the head, thanks to brain matter on the athame. Who knows what else he might have been threatening in the heat of the moment. In times of extreme stress, the instinct to bite may trigger."

"If that was the case, he would have bitten Barillo," John muttered.

Zahira cocked her head as she glanced up at him. "Maybe he was meant to."

John's lips parted, but he wasn't certain how to respond. Had Yuri and Dru hoped the constant provocation from Barillo would push Gray over the edge?

And then what? If Gray had drained the SPECTR District Chief, all hell would have broken loose. Would Yuri and Dru have turned up offering to help? Tried to convince Gray and Caleb to flee with them? Likely Caleb at least would have thought they had no other choice but to run.

A man could go mad, trying to figure out what Yuri might or might not have planned.

If only he could talk to Caleb and Gray. But he'd been the one to send them away, tell them he never wanted to see them again.

Assuming Drugoy hadn't...

No. He wouldn't consider that, not without proof.

A part of John wanted to believe he'd know on some deep level if they'd died. He still had some of Gray's etheric energy from the last time they'd made love. It would boost his exorcist abilities, but couldn't it also provide some subtle connection between them? Some bond that would ring through him like the alarm of a broken spirit ward if it was severed?

There was no way to know. Either it was true, and Gray and Caleb were still alive, or it was nothing but wishful speculation on his part.

The elevator door pinged open. As they stepped on, Karl jogged up behind them. "Hold it for me!"

"You're coming with us?" John asked in surprise. Karl wasn't a field agent, unless he was needed to sit in on witness questioning. He normally stayed at HQ when it came time for the bullets to fly.

But he had followed Kaniyar when she turned against Forsyth. He'd been there on Fort Sumter that night, gun in hand.

"Barillo wants everyone who can hold a weapon in the streets," Karl said, watching as the floor numbers ticked past. "My family's out there somewhere. Every NHE I stop gives them a better chance of surviving this."

"Inshallah, they'll be all right," Zahira said. John put a hand to Karl's shoulder.

The doors opened and they piled out into the garage. A line of large SUVs stood waiting, along with a couple of the armored transports used when a possessed person refused to cooperate. Barillo stood beside the van in the front, megaphone in hand.

"Is that everyone?" he asked, sweeping an eye over them. "All right. I'll be coordinating from the van. Your mission is simple: take down any NHE you see. Organize yourselves into teams with that goal in mind." He paused. "However, that's just treating the symptoms. We can't make the city safe again until the drakul are removed. Our primary goal, overriding all other considerations, is to end them."

Them.

A murmur ran through the crowd. Barillo scowled. "Yes, that includes Jansen. We have reason to believe he's working with the other drakul. If you spot him, your orders are to shoot on sight."

Caleb came to a dismayed halt when he set foot onto East Bay Street. Cars sat bumper to bumper, completely unmoving, while concerned drivers stuck their heads out the windows or held up their phones, as though that might help them get through the jammed cell network. There were at least two accidents in sight, and he glimpsed distant flashes of red light off some of the buildings, no doubt cast by firetrucks or ambulances.

Damn it. All these people are sitting ducks for demons.

"We could find the demons and eat them," Gray offered helpfully.

Caleb hesitated. They'd recovered enough energy to heal their earlier injures, but they were still running low. For damn sure they needed to feed more if they were to have any hope of stopping Drugoy and Yuri.

Of course, given Yuri could summon NHEs straight from the etheric plane for Drugoy to absorb, it might not matter how many demons they ate. They'd never be on the same level.

We don't have time, he decided reluctantly. *SPECTR can take care of werewolves and ghouls. But we're the only ones who have a chance in hell of taking*

your fire unless you have a clear shot."

They split into two groups, the exorcists swinging wide, making for the silver cords. One of the werewolves left off the assault on the doors, its distorted head swinging toward them. A growl began to boil out of its chest, threatening to erupt into a howl at the sight of unprotected prey.

There came a gunshot, silver-jacketed lead catching it in the side. It let out a yelp—then spun in the direction of its attacker with a roar.

More gunshots, and the other werewolf and ghouls abandoned the hidden prey in favor of the SPECTR agents. John sprinted between overturned cars, making for the shimmering, silvery web of etheric energy binding the NHEs to Yuri's will.

The air dinned with howls and snarls now—followed by a scream. One of the werewolves had reached the other half of the team and flung itself onto an agent, huge jaws latching onto the pyrokinetic's arm.

Fire erupted in its mouth. Within seconds, the werewolf was screaming as well. It jerked back, leaving the agent to take a reeling step away, blood gushing from his mauled forearm.

Damn it.

Then they were out from among the cars and had a clear line to the cords. Offering up a prayer to Sekhmet, John brought his silver athame down on the thread of etheric energy.

It began to unravel under the edge of the blade, one strand after another parting beneath the force of his will. Zahira and the others joined him, and within seconds the werewolf was free.

It staggered back, shaking its head violently. Then it turned in a circle, snarling, realizing the trap and wanting out.

"It's working!" John called encouragingly.

A ghoul was next; it cringed and howled, scrabbling off beneath a truck in an attempt to hide from the sunlight. What had been a united front of teeth and claws and death crumbled rapidly. The NHEs were still incredibly dangerous on their own, but much less so than as a group.

Another ghoul free. A werewolf.

Wait. There had been a werebear. Where had it gone?

A roar sounded directly behind John.

Caleb and Gray move swiftly from rooftop to rooftop for as long as they can, coming to ground only when they spot a lone ghoul or werewolf, hastily killed and consumed. Weariness begins to fall away, the last few superficial cuts healing over at last. But they will need a good deal more if they are to face Drugoy again.

As for how they might defeat Drugoy, when they failed so badly before, Gray does not know, and Caleb has no helpful suggestions. But they have no choice—they cannot wait, while demons tear through the city and Drugoy feeds and feeds. The first earthquake was a warning, a hint of what might happen if Drugoy fully manifests.

"Do you think he would? They might be pissed at us, but at the same time, Yuri at least really likes the mortal lifestyle. I can't imagine him agreeing to become like... that."

A thing of hunger and need, Caleb means. The thing they had become on Fort Sumter, that longed for blood and more blood.

John had brought them back to themselves that day. But should Yuri and Drugoy manifest, they have no John to help them.

"Yeah, well, neither do we."

Gray cannot argue, so he says only, *I do not know if Drugoy will wish to fully manifest. But I do not think it is a risk we can take. We may not be able to stop them now; we would never be able to stop them then.*

They managed to fight Forsyth's drakul only by allowing Gray to fully manifest as well. But they have no convenient bottles of demons to gorge upon this time.

"So that's not happening. I guess we just hope for the best. Maybe we'll get lucky."

Perhaps.

As they move farther into the Historic District, the houses become larger, the lawns wider, until they have no choice but to abandon the roofs and descend to the sidewalk. Fortunately there are few cars, and all of them parked along the sidewalks, unlike the chaos of the main thoroughfares. If any mortals are about, they have chosen to stay locked inside their homes.

"Legare Street," Caleb says. *"Big money area. Maybe they have spirit wards to keep out NHEs? I think there are some private exorcists who hire out for that kind of thing."*

Perhaps. Such wards would not stop Drugoy, but demons are another matter.

The relative quiet ends abruptly with the sound of rending metal from ahead, accompanied by screams and the blare of a car horn.

"Someone's in trouble," Caleb says urgently.

There was no need to point that out. I can hear as well as you, Gray replies, and quickens his pace to a run.

A minivan sits at a stop sign across from a high brick wall pierced by iron gates. Its hood has been buckled by a great weight, smoke and oil pouring out from underneath. Terrified faces stare out through the windshield.

The creature menacing the mortals is larger than an ordinary human, though smaller than the grendel. Its body is gray and lumpen, and a horn protrudes from the center of its forehead, like that of a rhinoceros. Its eyes are tiny, and tusks jut from its lower jaw. Thick-fingered hands scrabble at the seams of the doors and windows, seeking to tear its way in by force.

The scent of damp stone and rotting wood rolls out from it, delicious. *An ogre. I have eaten these before. They are very strong.*

Their heart quickens with the anticipation of feeding. Under other circumstances, this would be a good hunt, simple and straightforward. But as they race toward the intersection, the ogre brings back its fist and smashes through the glass of the back passenger door. The shrieks become abruptly louder, and Caleb's fear seeps into their veins. *"Christ, there are kids in there!"*

The ogre reaches in and wrenches out a small body. The child struggles, howling its terror, kicking and biting as it is dragged from the car. The ogre's cruel eyes gleam, and it opens its jaws to feast on the tender flesh.

Gray roars with all the force in his lungs. The ogre's head snaps up in alarm, distracted from its intended meal. For an instant it hesitates, torn between the wriggling prey and the predator descending on it.

It is a mistake. Gray closes the distance in the blink of an eye, seizes the arm the ogre holds the boy with, and buries his fangs deep in its bicep.

Blood bursts into their mouth, and he sucks it down eagerly. The ogre howls in anguish, drops the child—and hurls Gray away with its immense strength.

Fangs rip free in a spray of blood. Gray smashes into the iron gates guarding the entrance to the old home, which bend beneath the force of the impact. Falling to the sidewalk, he gives his head a shake, blood absorbing and joints healing.

For the most part, the black metal of the gate is formed into slender curlicues, more decorative than functional. But set just beside the lock on each gate, the iron has been forged into the unmistakable shape of a sword.

The child screams. It has fallen to the street and is scooting back as quickly as it can, but the ogre will be on it in moments.

Gray grasps the handle of the nearest sword and tears it free with a scream of abused metal.

"What are you doing?" Caleb demands. *"It's not even a real sword. It's a decoration, you crazy drakul!"*

Gray ignores him. Surging to his feet, Gray puts himself between the ogre and the child. The ogre should flee him as a predator, but either Yuri is controlling it, or it is maddened by the screams of its prey. Hefting the sword, Gray brings it around in an arc just as the ogre charges.

The blade is dull, but combined with his own great strength, it is enough to bite deep into the ogre's neck. The demon's growl turns into a gurgle, and it scrabbles at its throat, crumpling to its knees.

Gray hurls the sword away and falls on the ogre, pressing his mouth eagerly to the wound. Sweet blood pumps out along with its dying heart, energy coursing through him as it is absorbed. The last of the strength leaves the ogre and it slumps dead to the street.

"Get away from my son!" a woman screams.

Startled, Gray looks up, just in time to see a tire iron swinging at his face.

CHAPTER 5

JOHN SPUN, ATHAME slashing blindly in the direction of the werebear's roar. The silver blade caught in furred hide, and it let out a cry of rage and pain, twisting away from the knife. The blade snagged in tendon—then was wrenched from John's hand.

The creature reared up in front of him, blood oozing from one forearm. Huge, a vast wall of muscle and bone, its head a twisted parody of a grizzly. Its jaws gaped open for another roar, revealing jagged teeth, and hot breath reeking of decay blasted into John's face.

He brought up his Glock, firing again and again. The bullets struck the werebear in the chest. Blood spurted from the wounds, but the pain seemed only to enrage the NHE.

The trigger clicked on an empty chamber.

The world slowed around John as the werebear charged. His vision tunneled, and he was intensely aware of the saliva flying from its teeth, the fury in its red eyes. Training kicked in, an instinct he'd honed in the months after realizing sex with Gray boosted his exorcist powers, at least until Barillo had forbidden him to use it.

He flung out one hand, but not to ward off the bear. A spiky rope of etheric energy, similar to what Yuri used to bind the NHEs, burst forth and buried itself in the werebear's forehead.

John had a split second to curse himself—exorcisms, no matter how powerful, had no effect on the permanently possessed. He'd wasted the last instant he might had done something to save himself.

Except the rope…caught.

The werebear rocked back with a scream, as though John had run a pike through its skull. Shock nearly broke John's hold, but he firmed his concentration with a prayer to Sekhmet, narrowing in on the NHE. It struggled like a fish on a line, so he imagined more hooks forming, snagging its substance, entangling it until there was no escape.

Then he wrenched it free.

The werebear toppled as though felled by an ax. For a moment, the infected red tangle of its energy twisted in the air, detectible to John's exorcist senses. But he had no bottle to trap it in, no Gray to eat it. There was nothing to do but release it to pass back into the etheric plane. He relaxed his hold, and the crimson energy flickered, then slipped away, returning to the realm from which it had originally been summoned.

"How did you do that?" Zahira gasped. John blinked and realized the other exorcists who had come to his aid were staring in amazement. "Caleb said Yuri's possessions are permanent."

There came a groan from the pavement before them. Even as John watched, the werebear's form shifted and shrank, becoming more and more human. Within moments, a woman John recognized stared up at him, mouth open in shock.

He and Karl had first seen her behind the counter of Aiken and Daughters Custom Motorcycles. They hadn't gotten her name, because they'd been there for her sister. Isabelle Aiken.

Drugoy's renfield.

"Oh God," the woman babbled. "Oh God, what happened, what…"

John dropped to his knees beside her. "Ms. Aiken," he said, voice firm in the hopes of cutting through her panic, "your sister, Isabelle. Where is she?"

"I don't know!" She was crying in earnest now, great wrenching sobs. "I was on my way to work, and I saw that guy who comes by the shop sometimes, and then…and then…"

John closed his hand around her arm, trying to stave off her panic. "Ms. Aiken, why did Azarov do this to you? Did he say anything?"

"No." She sniffled and wiped her nose. "I'm not even sure he knew who I was."

"She's telling the truth," Karl said. "I don't think she can help us."

John sat back on his heels. The rest of the NHE pack were either dead or run off. An odd stillness had fallen over the street, broken only by the wails of the traumatized woman.

"Noorzai had a good question," Wells said as she joined them. "How were you able to exorcise her?"

"I've been able to exorcise the possessed without using a circle for a while," John said as he rose to his feet. "Barillo forbid me to continue, because it's due to Gray's…energy."

Wells scowled. "Christ, what an asshole. But aren't these supposed to be permanent?"

"Maybe Yuri accelerates the process," John said slowly. "Makes it so the victims can't fight back, and the NHE is in control from the beginning. But there must still be a window. Maybe not forty days, I don't know, but we can still exorcize them."

"The rest of us can't," Zahira said. Her dark eyes shone with a spark of hope as she met his gaze. "But you can. Do you see what this means? Thanks to Gray, you can save them. We have a chance to stop this without a lot of innocent victims dying."

His spirits lifted despite everything. "I'm only one man. And I don't know how many charges I've got in me."

"Saving a few is better than saving none." Wells clapped him on the shoulder. "Let's keep moving."

Caleb pushed to the fore, grabbing the tire iron a second before it shattered their nose. "Whoa!"

The woman tried to wrench the makeshift weapon away. Black hair straggled around her face, and she had a wild look in her eye. "Get away from my children!" she yelled. "Kids, run!"

Of course. Bitterness coated his tongue. Every time he tried to save people—on Fort Sumter, on the drifting boat with Steele, here—they treated him like a monster. Why the fuck did he even bother?

"Geez, Mom, get a grip!" exclaimed the unmistakably annoyed tones of a teenaged girl. "He saved Mahindar, so chill out and stop trying to beat his head in."

A girl of perhaps fifteen climbed out of the van and went to the side of the boy Gray had saved from the ogre. The boy stood up, and though he clung to his sister, he stared at Caleb with wide eyes.

"That was the coolest thing I've ever seen," he said in an awed voice. "Are you some kind of superhero?"

Caleb snorted. "I wish."

Their mother blinked, as though coming out of a haze. "I…oh dear. I'm so sorry." She let go of the tire iron and put her hands to her mouth. "I was in a panic. Mahindar, are you all right?"

The boy, who Caleb guessed to be about ten years old, nodded. "I'm okay. I thought I was a goner for sure, though."

The woman put a hand to her chest. "I'm Mrs. Tavleen Chatwal, and this is my son Mahindar, and my daughter Hardeep."

"Harry," the girl corrected. She ran her eyes over Caleb's form, then tossed her hair over her shoulder. "Cool outfit."

"Thanks," he said.

"Harry, check on Nardev. He's the baby," Mrs. Chatwal added as she turned back to Caleb. "Thank you so much. That thing came out of nowhere. If you hadn't come along when you did…"

For a horrible moment, Caleb thought she was going to break down in tears. But she took a deep breath and visibly steeled her spine. "Just… thank you."

He shrugged. "Sure. Listen, you need to get under cover somewhere."

Harry returned with a toddler on her hip. "Can we go with you?"

"That wouldn't be safe," he said.

"But you beat up the monster," Mahindar protested. He glanced at the ogre, its body already rotting, and looked away with a shudder. "Going with you has to be safer than being on our own."

"They will slow us down," Gray said uncertainly. *"But there are other demons in the area. I can smell them."*

Whiffs of rot and mange and corruption gusted on the breeze. Faint now, but the demons wouldn't stay put. If the rich people were actually hiding behind spirit wards, anyone on the street would end up the target of the feeding frenzy.

Mrs. Chatwal fixed Caleb with a steely eye. "What are you?" she asked bluntly. "I might not have gotten the best look during the fight, but you're not human. But you saved Mahindar, and you aren't attacking us, so you aren't one of those things, either."

Christ. They didn't have time for any of this. "We're drakul," he said. "It would take too long to explain, but we're not like werewolves, or ghouls, or any of the regular NHEs. We hunt them. You don't have to be scared of us."

"I'm not," Harry said quickly.

"We?" Mrs. Chatwal asked.

"I'm Caleb. Gray is the one who fought the ogre. We have a sort of permanent timeshare on my body."

He expected her to back away, maybe go for the tire iron again. After all, he'd just confirmed he was possessed, which was usually enough to send most people screaming in the opposite direction. Not that he could really blame them at the moment.

She seemed to ponder—then nodded, as though she'd come to a decision. "Very well. We're going with you."

"Um…" He wanted to protest. But the smell of demons was getting stronger. If he told her to hide and then left, would something nasty track the family by scent?

If they could find some SPECTR operatives, maybe Caleb could turn the Chatwals over to them. "Fine. But stay out of my way, and for God's sake, run and hide if I tell you. Understand?"

"I understand." Mrs. Chatwal glanced at her kids. "Harry? Mahindar? Do you understand?"

Mahindar nodded. "Yeah, anything you say."

Him, Caleb believed. Mahindar had been traumatized enough for one day. He was less sure about Harry's mumbled "Yes, Mom."

"All right, then," Caleb said. He took a deep breath.

Come on out, Gray. If you're manifested, maybe any demons will at least hesitate before attacking us.

Gray rose up, teeth sharpening and claws slipping free. Their hair swirled and crackled about their shoulders. Mrs. Chatwal's eyes all but bulged from her head at the sight, and Caleb wondered if she was having second thoughts.

"Follow me," Gray told the Chatwals. Then he turned and started down the street, the family scurrying to keep up.

"You're *so* cool," one of the mortal children says breathlessly. "Not like the guys at my high school. They're lame."

Gray moves as quickly through the street has he can, with the mortals clustered behind him. The smallest child was unable to keep up, and when the mother began to struggle holding it, Gray took it from her. It clings to his left shoulder now, body cradled effortlessly in his arm, his other hand free.

"His name is Nardev, and he's a boy, not an it," Caleb says.

Mortal nonsense. Names and genders and all the rest of it. *But very well.*

They have made their way further down Legare Street, in accordance with Caleb's original plan. The demons have left them alone, so far, recognizing Gray as the larger predator.

Yuri might be controlling some of the demons he has summoned, but even he cannot command them all. They passed a pack of ghouls, who fled the moment they saw Gray, and once a werewolf bounded out of an alley, only to turn tail when he growled at it. So far, none have dared challenge him for the mortals clustered tightly around him.

"I am not cool," he informs the child who spoke to him. Harry. Her. "I do not feel heat and cold as mortals do."

The girl laughs. "That's not...I mean, I guess that's why you're walking around Charleston in the middle of summer in all that leather." Her brown face takes on a redder hue. "It looks really good on you, though."

"She's got a crush on you, Gray."

"So you're a vampire, right?" she asks. "I thought they weren't real. Everyone says they're just a story."

"I'll bet the government has been hiding them!" the boy—Mahindar—chimes in excitedly. "It's a conspiracy!"

The toddler grabs a handful of Gray's hair and stuffs it in his mouth.

"You're very good with children, Mr. Gray," Mrs. Chatwal says from behind him. Her breath comes in short pants, as though she isn't used to walking so far so quickly. "Do you have any of your own?"

"I am not capable of mortal reproduction," he replies.

"Really, dude? Not how I would have phrased it."

"Right!" Harry's eyes brighten with excitement. "You bite people and they turn into vampires! Is that what happened to Caleb?"

"This kid needs to lay off the bad movies."

"That is mortal nonsense," Gray says. "I was summoned from the etheric plane five-thousand years ago. I have walked this earth ever since."

"Wow," Mahindar breathes. "You're *old.*"

Harry clasps her hands in front of her. "So, do you have an eternal romance? A great love, reborn life after life, who you meet again and again?"

"Harry," her mother says. "Excuse her, Mr. Gray, she's fifteen. She has...ideas."

The grief they managed to put aside slips back. John's absence is like a cloud over the sun. The colors that have seemed so bright since Gray first awakened in Caleb's body are muted now. "We did have a love," he admits. "But he does not wish to be with us anymore."

Caleb feels very small in the shared space of their thoughts. *"You don't have to answer her."*

But Gray does not mind. It is simply the truth. Sometimes the truth is wonderful, and sometimes painful, but that is the way of things.

"He?" Harry's face falls. "So, you're gay?"

"No. I do not have a gender, and I do not care about such things in others." He pauses. "Though I am learning these things are important for mortals."

"Oh." Her expressions clears. "Agender pansexual it is."

Mrs. Chatwal clicks her tongue. "Harry, leave Mr. Gray alone."

"I don't want to use the wrong pronouns!" Harry protests.

"Same here," Mahindar says quickly. "So do you use they/them?"

It is not something he has given consideration to before. "We are a they, so that would not be incorrect no matter what. But I do not mind 'he.' Mortals change their minds so often as to whether there are three genders, or five, or two. A thousand years yields as many variations."

No one speaks for a few moments. Just as he thinks he has at last escaped the conversation, Mrs. Chatwal says, "We must seem so insignificant to you."

Gray stops. A haze of smoke hangs on the air, drifting from the fires they glimpsed from the steeple. The houses on the street have become less estate-like, more run down, and the windows of one are shattered. The scent of blood drifts from within; someone who could not afford a spirit ward like their neighbors has become prey.

Fire and chaos and death.

Yuri and Drugoy have done this. Out of madness and greed and jealousy, out of malice and cruelty. But also out of ignorance.

"No." He turns to Mrs. Chatwal and looks down at her. "There is another drakul here. He has been in this world mere decades, but in his hubris he has decided mortal lives are lesser because they are short."

If only things had been different. If only he could have made Drugoy understand. There had been such joy in hunting together. Even in sitting silently, much as they had once curled together on the etheric plane, so long ago.

"But they are not lesser," he finishes. "Because no moment in time is greater than any other. Each second is made equal, and the one I experience is no more real than the one you experience, simply because I have seen more of them."

She is silent for a long moment. "I see," she says at last. "How many of you are there? Drakul, I mean?"

The question is too complicated, so he settles for, "There is only one other like me."

"And he did this? I mean, they did this?" She looks appalled. "What are you going to do?"

"I am going to kill them, if I can." The heaviness of it lays on his heart. Drugoy and Yuri have done terrible things. They wished to kill everyone Caleb and Gray loved, to take them away from the network of mortal life that had made Caleb so briefly happy. To take away John and Zahira.

And yet, when they are gone, there will be no one else who understands. No one to hunt with. No one to talk to.

The mortals are quiet for a long moment. "I'm sorry," Mrs. Chatwal offers at last. "That must be hard for you."

The scent of demons strengthens on the wind. Fur and rot and slime, spiked with blood. Howls echo, mingled with growls and the strange whine of ghouls. All underlain with the meat-locker stench of a wendigo.

Demons of different kinds do not hunt together. This must be Yuri's doing.

Which means they probably won't run from us. Damn it. We need to get the Chatwals to safety.

"There are demons nearby." Gray casts about for shelter. Nowhere will be safe for long, but perhaps the low hedge behind the iron fence will do. He hands Nardev to Harry, then strides to the iron gate and rips off the chain holding it closed. "Hide behind the hedge, and I will deal with them."

Uncertainty appears in Mrs. Chatwal's eyes—then vanishes as gunfire breaks out, just around the intersection up ahead. "Go," she starts, but he is already running toward the scent of blood.

CHAPTER 6

GRAY RACES AROUND the corner and into chaos.

Cars line much of the road, either parked along the curb or abandoned by panicked mortals. An SUV with Strategic Paranormal Entity ConTRol emblazoned on the side blocks the road, lights flashing off the spray of glass on the pavement from the shattered rear window.

The agents inside abandoned the vehicle and tried to find refuge behind some of the parked cars. It has not gone well for them, judging by the blood spreading across the pavement.

A ghoul lies dead, body already going to rot, but a werewolf, two more ghouls, and a wendigo stalk the remaining two mortals. A telekinetic seems to be holding off the werewolf temporarily, but the situation will not remain in his favor for long. The wendigo has paused to eat one of the dead agents. As it rips a hunk of meat free, Gray glimpses the dead agent's face. Quackenbush, that was the name on the mortal's cubicle.

"You heard what Starkweather said over the radio!" the other surviving agent says. An exorcist, though not one Gray has ever seen out from behind a desk. "If I can cut those silver cords, we'll have a better chance."

"Damn it," Caleb says. *"John must not have gotten our text telling him to stay put."*

Or he chose not to. John is not one to hide when others are in peril.

For an instant, indecision stutters through them. So long as Drugoy and Yuri are free, John is in terrible danger. None of the mortal agents can stand against a drakul. The only hope is for Gray and Caleb to find Drugoy and Yuri, before they can find John.

"But we can't just leave the Chatwals. And that wendigo is going to tear apart these agents if we don't stop it."

Caleb is right. With a snarl of frustration, Gray launches himself high into one of the palmetto trees lining the road.

The movement distracts the demons, as he hoped it would. The wendigo is nearly below him; it looks up, red eyes bulging from its skeletal face. Lips draw back from teeth like dinner knives.

"It's Jansen!" one of the agents shouts. "Oh shit!"

The telekinetic breaks cover, fleeing...them?

It takes only a moment for the werewolf to catch the man. His screams of pain madden the ghouls, who rush to join the werewolf's attack.

Sick horror flashes through Caleb—but they have no time to dwell. The wendigo lets out a snarl of rage and swipes at them. Though skeletal, it is nearly ten feet tall, and its nails almost snag on their boot.

With a snarl of his own, Gray drops onto the wendigo, claws extended and fangs bared. The wendigo is nothing but skin stretched over bone, but it is nevertheless hellishly strong. It grabs at him with long arms, twisting unnaturally far in their sockets, but the leather of his coat foils its attack.

Frost forms on its skin, making it hard to hold onto. Gray tries to sink his claws in, but the fish-belly white skin tears, and there isn't enough muscle beneath to give a solid hold. He bites blindly, teeth scraping on the bones of its shoulder. The vein is there, he knows it—

The cold radiating out from the wendigo flares suddenly, burning his skin. It slams back into the palmetto, catching Gray between the tree and its own body. The blow loosens his hold, and it wrenches free.

He half expects it to flee, but it turns on him in an instant. A forest of razor teeth flash in front of his eyes—and then he feels them scrape and crunch into the bones of his face.

"It's trying to bite our fucking head in half!" Caleb shouts, as if Gray might somehow have failed to notice.

Pain explodes through their skull, the delicate arch of one eye orbit collapsing beneath the hideous pressure. The wendigo's breath reeks of ketosis and rot, its tongue rasping their skin from bone.

Gray blindly grabs its throat, seeking to tear its jaws free from their flesh. At the same moment, it reaches into the gap where their coat has fallen open and rips aside muscle in search of the organs beneath.

This is not going as well as he had hoped.

He punches his claws as deeply as he can into the wendigo's throat, ignoring the agony it inflects on his body. Cold blood pours over one hand, then the other, and it loosens its grip enough for Caleb's telekinesis to fling it off them.

Gray falls to one knee, gasping. The bones of their shattered eye socket pop back into place, and the deep puncture wounds on their face start to fill in. Blinking, he looks up; the wendigo is clutching at its injured neck, thick blood pouring out of its jugulars. It will heal quickly—but not quickly enough.

Ignoring the blaze of pain in their abdomen, Gray launches himself from kneeling position, tackling the wendigo with all his remaining strength. It crashes back into a car, and he drives his teeth deep into its throat.

The blood is freezing cold, but still delicious. Wounds heal as he feeds, holding the wendigo upright when its legs would have given out.

And it is good. Not as good as when they believed Drugoy was their friend, not as good as when John was with them, but there is still pleasure in the hunt and the fight and the feeding.

The last of the wendigo's energy passes into them. Gray lets it go, and it slumps to the ground, already rotting.

The street is quiet. The second agent, the exorcist, lies dead in the street, her silver athame near her hand. *"She must have tried to free the ghouls from Yuri's control,"* Caleb says. *"Hell, since they've run off, maybe she succeeded."*

The telekinetic is dead as well. *Why did he run?*

Caleb sighs. *"Because we ate a SPECTR agent? Who knows what Barillo has been telling everyone about us. For all I know, he might be making Ericsson out to be an innocent victim."*

Gray has never thought much about fairness. Things simply are. But this does not seem fair, for a man who had no reason to fear them to lose his life out of panic. *It is not right.*

"Mr. Gray?" Mrs. Chatwal calls nervously from the corner. "It got quiet, so we thought it might be safe to come out now?"

Caleb nudges him, so Gray relinquishes control.

"Had a bit of a problem with a wendigo," Caleb says, "But it's safe. Just, um, let me move these bodies before the kids see them."

The woman blanches. "Oh. Yes."

"Yeah." Caleb gestures at the SUV. "But I have some good news. We don't have to walk anymore."

John's phone suddenly dinged with an incoming text message, instantly followed by a chorus of notifications from every other phone in the SUV.

They'd made their way slowly down King Street, following the destruction south toward the Battery. Thankfully they hadn't encountered any more large packs, but there had been a scattering of lone ghouls and werewolves, several of whom John had been able to successfully exorcise. Each took longer than the last, however, and he had the feeling the next time he simply wouldn't have the power left to remove the NHE.

John dug out his phone. The text was from an unfamiliar number, but read: *Y&D after you. B compromised. Stay in HQ. This is our mess to clean up. -C&G*

Relief flooded through him, so strong it stole his breath for a moment. "They're alive," he said aloud. "Caleb sent me a text a few hours ago, probably right after the earthquake happened."

"I told you," Zahira said, but her shaky smile revealed that she'd been worried, too. "What did he say?"

"Somehow, he found out Barillo was compromised." John shook his head. "He thinks Yuri and Drugoy are after me, and wants me to stay in HQ."

"A little late for that," Wells said.

Caleb where are you? John texted. *I'm on King Street. Come meet me.*
I love you.

For a long moment, he didn't think he'd get an answer. Then: *This is Deacon. Caleb borrowed my phone earlier and told me to get to HQ. I'm with SPECTR forces now. Don't know where Caleb is.*

"Deacon? He was the one working with Azarov, right?" Zahira said when John read the message aloud. "Do you think he's lying?"

"Hell if I know." John put the phone back in his pocket in disgust. For a moment, he'd thought he was about to see Caleb and Gray again. Whether he would hug them or yell at them first, he didn't know, but the ache in his heart was all the more painful for having that instant of hope.

"Brandon and Mikki made it to HQ," Karl said, sagging back in the seat.

Zahira clasped her hands. "Allah be praised."

"I'm so glad." John reached around Zahira to give Karl's shoulder a quick squeeze. "I know you were worried."

"That would be an understatement." Karl kept scrolling, then stopped. "Oh shit."

John and Zahira exchanged a look. "Now what?" he asked, though he wasn't sure he wanted to know.

Instead of answering directly, Karl passed him the phone. "Brandon forwarded this. I guess someone with a phone managed to get enough of a signal to upload to social media. The time stamp on it is less than twenty minutes ago."

The image had clearly been taken through an upstairs window. The caption read *Cute goth guy protecting people in #charleston! #earthquake #demonattack.*

"That's Caleb," Zahira said, peering over his shoulder.

John's throat threatened to close up with emotion. "No. The picture quality is too crappy to make out details, but see the way he's holding his head? And his posture, like he's ready to spring into action any second? That isn't Caleb. It's Gray."

Who the people were with him, John couldn't guess. A family, or at least they looked to be: the mother trailing a little behind, along with a young boy. Gray held a toddler in one arm; the kid appeared to be trying to eat Gray's hair. Gray's head was cocked slightly, gaze directed down to the teenage girl walking beside him. Her mouth was open as though she was talking, and Gray was clearly listening to her with the same complete attention he gave everything he did. As though it was the only important thing in the world at the moment.

"I was so wrong," John said softly. "Just before Ericsson shot me, I'd started to put things together. I was scared that maybe Gray and Caleb had thrown in with Yuri and Drugoy. And later, I was scared I'd lost them to bloodlust, and I was just...wrong."

"To be fair, Gray and Caleb aren't exactly innocent in the whole Ericsson thing," Karl said with a wince.

True. But whatever the Vigilant had feared, Gray clearly hadn't gone on a bloody rampage after drinking Ericsson's blood. Instead, he'd tried to stop Drugoy. And now he was out on the streets, guarding a family of complete strangers.

John touched the picture gently with one finger. Caleb was a good guy at heart; he *knew* that. And Gray had always tried his best. If Yuri and Drugoy hadn't shown up, things would never have gotten to the point they did.

John took a deep breath. As of twenty minutes ago, at least, Caleb and Gray were alive and on their feet. "Does anyone recognize the house in the background?"

Zahira shook her head, but Karl took the phone back and peered at it. "Isn't that on Legare Street? The Huger House, something like that?"

"I think you're right. And they're heading south." John's heart quickened. "We'll come out onto South Battery to the east of them. If we head west—"

"Maybe we can meet up," Wells said from the front. "Sounds like a plan. Then what?"

"Then, with any luck, we can work together and take Yuri and Drugoy down," John said.

More than that. He could see Caleb and Gray again. He could tell them he never should have sent them away, that he should have gone with them, or met up later, or something. That he hadn't known the whole story, and he wanted, more than anything, to try again.

But that was too private to say aloud. So he leaned forward, elbows on his knees, and silently willed the SUV to go faster.

"How are you doing up there, Mr. Gray?" Mrs. Chatwal called up from the driver's seat of the SPECTR SUV.

Caleb opened his mouth to correct her, then decided it wasn't worth the trouble. He perched on the roof, one hand curled around the equipment rack for balance. It had seemed a better position to watch for trouble. This way, he could easily spring in any direction, without opening a door and exposing the Chatwals to more danger than necessary.

Than necessary. Right.

Gray hovered just under his skin, ready to emerge the moment they glimpsed a demon. *"We cannot abandon them. And we cannot leave Drugoy to destroy the city."*

I know. Caleb had hoped to find more SPECTR agents to hand the Chatwals over to—assuming any agents didn't start screaming and run the other way at the very sight of him. But South Battery had been startlingly empty so far. No SPECTR, and no demons, either.

Maybe they'd beaten Yuri and Drugoy down here. Hell, were Yuri and Dru even coming this way anymore?

"We're fine," Caleb replied. "Can you turn right onto King Street and take us to Murray Boulevard?" The boulevard ran along the water. Maybe Caleb would be able to find a boat or something to load the Chatwals onto, where they might be somewhat safer. Assuming Yuri hadn't had a chance to pack the harbor with sirens and God only knew what else.

The vehicle made the turn, moving slowly so as not to dislodge him. Caleb tilted his head back and closed his eyes, taking in great, heaving breaths of air, sifting for any scent that might betray danger. He smelled marsh rot and salt, combined with the damp earth beneath the live oaks of White Point Garden to their left. Faint traces of other scents came with the shifting breeze: the reek of demons, ranging from the decay of ghouls to the rotting roses of a succubus.

God, he hoped any of the demons who set a lure would stay far away. He didn't want to have to defend the Chatwals from anything able to turn their own minds against them. Things were hard enough already.

They reached Murray Boulevard. "Left," he called down, before Mrs. Chatwal had the chance to ask.

The sea stretched out on their right, and a median planted with palmettos separated them from White Point Garden. A few cars sat abandoned in their parking spaces, but the road itself was surprisingly clear. Apparently most of the mayhem had been confined north and east of here.

The scent of earth strengthened from the direction of the park. Warm soil, heated by the sun, but mingled with scorched metal and molten rock. Which wasn't a smell that should be coming from the Spanish-moss draped trees.

Drugoy.

"Go!" Caleb leapt from the roof, shouting over his shoulder as he went. "Floor it! Get out of here, as fast as you can!"

Wide eyes stared at him—then the tires screamed as Mrs. Chatwal did as he ordered. For an instant, he let himself hope they would get away unscathed. He and Gray would take up all of Drugoy's attention, who surely wouldn't spare a thought for the insignificant mortals, and everything would somehow be all right.

Drugoy stepped out in the road a few hundred yards ahead, from behind a war monument that had concealed him from view. Even from a distance, Caleb saw his grin.

Then Drugoy dropped to one knee and slammed his hand onto the ground.

The very earth beneath Caleb's feet trembled. Cracks raced out from Drugoy, tearing open rifts in all directions. Birds took flight from the live oaks in the park, wings churning the air, gulls shrieking.

Caleb ran after the SUV, knowing he was too late, praying he wasn't. The asphalt in front of the tires buckled, heaving the vehicle onto two wheels, and for an instant he thought they might make it after all.

The pavement erupted into high ridges, heaving the SUV up from underneath. Tires spun on nothing but air, the engine screamed, and the heavy car began to flip backwards with the shrieking family inside.

CHAPTER 7

GRAY CROSSES THE distance in a second, his only thought to somehow cushion the impact between steel and concrete. There is a terrible sound of breaking earth and groaning metal, and all he can do is to hold his hands above his head and hope as the front of the SUV crashes down.

Caleb's TK surges, cushioning the blow just enough for Gray to guide the vehicle's descent. Even so, it bears him to the ground. Bones snap and muscles scream, the air stinking of radiator fluid and spilling oil. The SUV comes down hard but upright.

Gray blinks. He lies on the broken concrete, the hot engine nearly on top of him, the two front wheels deflated from impact. Bones pop back into place, and he twists his head cautiously to one side.

"Good thing we ate that wendigo."

But the wendigo had harmed them, badly enough most of the energy they obtained from it went to repairing the wounds it gave them. These new injuries are healing, but more slowly than they should. A haze of smoke from the airbags fills the air, blinding him temporarily.

Where is Drugoy?

The door opens, followed by footsteps, Mrs. Chatwal rushing to them. "Are you all right?"

The scent of burning metal and heated stone saturates the air. The ground trembles, footfalls impacting the earth with the rumble and force of heavy machinery.

Drugoy is coming.

"Run," he says. "Get the children, and *run.*"

She doesn't argue. Gray's arms are working again, so he hauls himself out from under the wreck.

Fear washes through them from Caleb. *"Damn it. We need to power up if we're going to fight Drugoy."*

Perhaps they can distract Drugoy, lead him on a chase somewhere. Over water, perhaps?

Doors creak open on bent hinges. Nardev is crying, and his brother hands him out to Mrs. Chatwal. Her face is streaked with powder, cut from flying glass, but she takes the smaller child on her hip and holds out her hand to her older son. On the other side of the SUV, Harry's door swings open, and she begins to climb out.

Drugoy's slim shape appears amidst the thinning smoke.

"No!" Caleb cries.

It happens too fast, even for Gray to stop. Drugoy's arm snakes around Harry's throat, and he hauls her off her feet. She screams and thrashes, but her strength is nothing compared to that of a drakul. He drags her rapidly away from the SUV and into the clear.

"This is why mortals make such bad playthings," he says, cracked-glass gaze fixed on Gray. "They are so terribly fragile, after all."

Harry lets out another cry of terror. Drugoy gives her a rough shake. "Be silent." Blood seeps from where his claws dig into her skin, and she falls quiet. Her eyes squeeze shut, tears leaking out, and a wave of rage rolls through Gray at Drugoy's casual malice.

"Let her go!" Mrs. Chatwal screams, her other two children clinging to her. Gray motions for her to stay back, sheltered by the wrecked SUV. Then he begins to walk slowly toward Drugoy, his hands held out to each side.

"The mortal is of no interest to you," he tells Drugoy.

"True. But she is of interest to *you.*" Drugoy's eyes burn red beneath black glass corneas. "These foolish mortals are your weakness, Gray. I do not know if it is Caleb who convinced you of their worth, but in time you will both come to see we are right."

"What does he want?" Caleb asks worriedly. *"What's his plan here? Or Yuri's?"*

Gray has no answer. The morning wind off the sea stirs their hair, brings with it the cries of the gulls. Otherwise, all is still. "Release her, and we will talk."

Harry tears at Drugoy's grip with her nails, but he ignores her struggles, all his attention fixed on Gray and Caleb. "How did you escape?" he asks. "Did you kill Deacon?"

"No. He released me."

A look of uncertainty flickers over Drugoy's face, so fast Gray isn't certain he read it aright. "Deacon has misunderstood. I will correct him later." Drugoy cocks his head. "Did you like what I made of the city?"

"I did not." Every muscle draws tight, but Gray doesn't see any way to attack Drugoy without risking Harry's life. "This chaos and death is beneath you. When we hunted together, you were strong and certain, but not cruel. What you have done here serves no purpose."

"You are wrong." Drugoy's lips draw back in a grin that has no humor, exposing fangs. "It has a great purpose. I spared your life because I believe you can still learn. This," he gestures at the city with his free hand, "is your lesson. You think to choose these mortals over Yuri and me? Then I will destroy them."

Fear from Caleb, threatening to steal their breath. *"Oh shit. He wanted to isolate us before, so we wouldn't have anything but him. That didn't work, so now he's just going to slaughter anyone he feels threatened by."*

"Yuri and I did not wish to do this, Gray," Drugoy goes on. "You and Caleb left us with no choice. But you have the power to make it stop."

"What do you wish us to do?" Gray asks, even knowing there is no good answer.

"Surrender yourself to me." Drugoy gestures for them to come closer. Gray takes one step, then two, but stops before drawing within reach. "I will release the mortal. You and I will leave this place far behind. We will go somewhere SPECTR will never find us, with just enough mortals to provide hosts for demons. We will hunt and feed, and it will be glorious. And we will remain until I am certain you've learned your lesson." He pauses. "Of course, if you persist in your foolishness, we will have no choice but to repeat this all over again."

The idea of spending years—decades—centuries—with only this monster for company is too horrible to imagine. Of hunting whatever hapless mortals Yuri forces demons into, allowed no pity, no hesitation, for fear Drugoy will do something even worse. For once even Caleb is silent, though Gray can feel his revulsion and terror. It matches his own.

Tears streak Harry's face. She opens her eyes and stares at him, pleading. Begging. Mrs. Chatwal crouches by the wrecked SUV, her other two children in her arms, all of them weeping and afraid. Desperate, but believing perhaps that he can save Harry.

John would do it. Without question.

"Yeah, well, that's why he's the SPECTR cheerleader. He believes in helping people," Caleb says. *"We aren't like that."*

It's true; they are not. Caleb remained with SPECTR because he believed they had no choice, not because he felt the same calling John does. And Gray hunts demons because it is his nature, not because he particularly cares about the mortals they kill.

"I guess neither of us are really the hero type." But there is a dawning understanding beneath Caleb's subdued words.

This cannot be allowed to continue. Drugoy and Yuri are profoundly wrong about everything. And no matter how simple it would be to leap into the bay and swim away, leave Yuri and Drugoy behind, leave the city to its fate, save themselves…they cannot.

"Fuck. I guess hanging out with John rubbed off on us after all."

"Very well," Gray says. "Release the mortal, and we will go with you. We will do whatever you wish."

Drugoy grins in triumph. "Then come closer."

Gray takes the final step to bring himself within arm's reach.

Drugoy lashes out, almost too quickly even for their eyes to follow. His claws catch their throat, ripping flesh and veins and trachea in a blaze of agony. Blood gushes free from their ravaged flesh. Gray heals it as fast as he can, but the damage is great, and their knees strike the pavement as their legs fail to hold them up.

Screams split the air from the Chatwals. Gray blinks sluggishly, sees Harry fleeing toward her family, his blood spattered across her face. But she is free and alive.

Drugoy crouches down so he can look Gray in the eyes. A smile plays on his lips as he licks Gray's blood from his claws. "Do you see? I keep my word."

Veins reconnect, but air still whistles through their torn trachea. They sag to one side, forcing Gray to catch their balance with a hand to keep them from toppling to the ground. He cannot speak yet, but Drugoy must see the question in their eyes.

"Again, this is not something I wished to do. But you have proven yourself untrustworthy. In time, once you earn my faith again, I will allow you to feed as much as you wish. But for now, I think it best if you are weaker. Just in case you get any ridiculous notions of escape, or of fighting me again." Drugoy reaches a hand toward them, and Gray flinches back. "Now come. Let us leave this place together."

"Get the hell away from them," John says, and fires.

John braced himself as he unloaded an entire clip of silver-jacketed lead into Drugoy. His pulse thudded in his ears, and he didn't dare look at Gray after the quickest of glances.

They'd just turned onto Murray Boulevard when the second earthquake hit. As palmettos toppled across the median, John had caught sight of Yuri in the distance, approaching a wrecked SUV.

There hadn't been time to form a plan, just bail out of their own vehicle and move as quickly and unobtrusively as they could, using the trees of the park for cover. John had glimpsed Drugoy take the girl hostage, heard snatches of his words on the wind as he demanded Gray's surrender.

And Gray had given himself over to Drugoy, even though he had to know things wouldn't go well for him.

Now Gray was on his knees, choking on his own blood. The sight tore at John's innards, and if he'd ever, even for a second, forgotten how much he loved Caleb and Gray, how badly he needed them, he knew he never would again.

Drugoy stumbled under the impact of John's bullets. Then his head snapped up, teeth bared. "You dare interfere?"

"We dare," Zahira confirmed, stepping up to John's right. Karl fell in on his left, as did Wells and the rest of the agents who had joined them. A wall of flesh and blood and lead, standing between Drugoy and the huddled family, and John prayed it would be enough.

Drugoy's growl rattled the ground, and John had to lock his knees at the etheric energy rolling off the drakul in waves. He'd felt this same power from Gray, of course, more than once. And yet this was as different in its way as day was from night, heat from cold.

Earth from sky.

"Stupid mortals. Gray allowed you to chain him, to poison his mind, and so you believe you have the strength to defy me." Drugoy glanced down at Gray. "Consider this an extension of your lesson. Remember this moment."

"Oh, hell no," John said. "Fire!"

A fusillade of bullets caught Drugoy, tearing through flesh and bone. Even as fast as a drakul could heal, it staggered him. John reloaded and added to the storm of silver-jacketed lead. The sound was deafening, the stink of cordite saturating the air, but it sent Drugoy to his knees.

Gray stirred in John's peripheral vision.

Drugoy's lips drew back, exposing fangs. The cracked glass of his eyes blazed suddenly. "Enough," he roared. With a tremendous effort, he surged to his feet and into a charge, ignoring the whizz of bullets and the wounds that would have killed anyone mortal.

"Scatter," John shouted.

They dove for what little cover the parked cars offered. But to John's surprise, Drugoy didn't pursue them.

Instead, the drakul paused. As his wounds began to visibly heal, Drugoy's energy became more muted, folding up into Yuri's slender form like an origami box. A moment later, Yuri's cold blue eyes surveyed the scene. He took a limping step forward, then reached out with his hand.

John's exorcist senses showed him the rip in reality even as it opened. Blue light flashed, and he felt power against his skin, spilling out from the etheric plane in the seconds before Yuri tore something through.

"Stop him," he yelled, and got off another shot. If they didn't interrupt Yuri, he'd simply summon more and more NHEs for Drugoy to use to power his healing.

But Drugoy didn't reappear in order to eat whatever hapless NHE Yuri had dragged from the etheric plane. Yuri held it captive in his palm, a haze of angry red energy barely visible in the sunlight even to John. Then, with a snarl, Yuri shoved it at the nearest non-exorcist agent in the group.

Karl.

John tried to yell a warning, but too late. Karl's head snapped back, eyes going wide with horror for an instant before the irises turned yellow. His jaws widened, filled with rows of teeth, and matted hair raced across his skin. Fabric ripped as his body took on new proportions, and a horrible growl escaped him.

"No." Caleb had made it to his feet and stood swaying, hand outstretched and face contorted in horror and grief. "Damn you, Yuri. We're going to tear your fucking head off."

Yuri gripped an etheric cord, connecting him to Karl. But his expression, rather than of triumph, was one of pain. A line of blood ran from first one nostril, then the other.

Karl roared and charged at Zahira. She rolled out of the way and slid beneath one of the cars. John cast around desperately. He was drained, the boost he'd absorbed from Gray the last time they'd made love gone now. At the moment, he didn't have any more talent than a normal exorcist, and even that energy was running low.

He wasn't going to be able to save Karl. Not without Gray's help.

"Stay alive!" he shouted at Zahira, and ran back toward the two drakul.

Yuri gritted his teeth and lifted his hand again, as if he meant to pull more NHEs into the world. Then his expression contorted in pain, and he clasped both hands to the side of his head. "I can't. I'm over-extended," he said. But not to them. To Drugoy.

Yuri vanished, Drugoy emerging with a snarl of rage. Before he could make a move, Gray cannoned into him, and they crashed to the ground together in a flurry of fangs and teeth and hair. They were both hurt and healing slowly, but Gray was clearly the worse off. Within moments, Drugoy had him pinned on the ground.

"That was your last chance," Drugoy said, baring his teeth. "This time, I'll drink until you're dry. Then I'll drain your renfields, and bathe the streets of this city in blood."

CHAPTER 8

DRUGOY PINS GRAY to the ground with the weight of the earth itself. His eyes blaze like the heart of a volcano, and his fangs are bared and ready to bite.

And Gray is weak, painfully so. The scent of werewolf is maddening, but even if he were free, he would never, ever eat Karl, who has been Caleb's friend.

Karl, here with Zahira and John, and other agents who do not seem as afraid of him as the ones they encountered before. If only they had stayed away, they would have been safe. But now Drugoy means to slaughter them all.

Gray struggles against Drugoy's grip, unable to throw him off. There has to be something they can do—anything—

The sound of the gunshot is deafening to sensitive ears. Blood bursts from the hole in Drugoy's throat, and his eyes go wide.

"I told you to stay the fuck away from them," John says.

And for a moment, just a moment, Drugoy's hold loosens as he recovers. Gray falls back for a split second, while Caleb's TK surges and hurls Drugoy from them with all his might. Pain slices through their head, the taste of blood in the back of their throat, Caleb's ability at its limit.

Drugoy crashes into the marble plinth of the Confederate monument. The stone shatters around him, bronze statue toppling to lie in the dust. For a moment, Drugoy doesn't move.

"Is he actually hurt?" Caleb asks incredulously.

So it would seem. Yuri's abilities are greatly strengthened by Drugoy, just as Caleb's are by Gray. But they are not infinite.

"I guess they wouldn't have spent a decade at the bottom of a lake otherwise."

Gray struggles to his feet. But even as he does so, Drugoy manages to stand as well. He glances around him, at the ruined monument, the SPECTR agents, Gray. With a snarl of anger, he bares his fangs, turns—and sprints into the park, vanishing amidst the trees.

Drugoy cannot be allowed to escape. Gray must give chase now, before Yuri recovers enough to summon more demons to fuel Drugoy's healing. This is their only chance to stop the other drakul, and even though they are weak and hurting, at least they must try.

"Gray," John calls.

His name from John's lips feels like a stake through the heart, pinning him in place. Gray turns slowly, sees John jogging up to him, face drawn and eyes bluer than the sky. All he wants to do is catch John up in his arms, hold him close…but he cannot.

"Yeah. That makes two of us."

There comes a scream of metal as Karl rips apart the car Zahira is hiding beneath. John flinches at the sound. "Gray, I need your blood."

This explains it then. John does not want them, but he wants what they can offer him. The realization should not bring more pain, and yet somehow it does. "I must catch Drugoy."

"Listen to me." John grabs Gray's wrist, the familiar scent of his skin and touch of his hand like the kiss of a razor blade against their heart. "I can save Karl, but only with an etheric boost from you."

"Oh hell," Caleb says. *"We were wrong. Yuri's possessions aren't permanent."*

We had no choice but to defend Deacon and the Chatwals.

"I know. But we have to help Karl. Even if…"

Drugoy will feed the first chance he has, even before Yuri is able to recover. And now that they know the possessions can be reversed, Gray no longer has that luxury, unless it is to save the life of another mortal.

Under these circumstances, there is no way to win, save to give chase immediately. Drugoy will surely kill them the next time they meet, otherwise.

For a moment, he is seized with a sense of longing. Everything was so very simple, before possessing Caleb. And it seemed so simple again, with Drugoy and his talk of doing things the drakul way. Hunting and feeding was the answer to any problem.

It had seemed the answer to the problem with Ericsson, but it was not. And it is not the answer now, either.

Gray brings his wrist to his mouth and bites, hard. The pain is almost a shock, massive canines tearing through vein and flesh, but the blood comes.

A queasy look flashes over John's face, but he doesn't hesitate to lean forward and fasten his mouth on the wound.

It's messy and painful, and John manages only a swallow or two before pulling away. "Thanks," he says, dashing his hand across his mouth. "Now, just—just stay here, all right?"

He wishes us to stay?

Caleb is equally bewildered. "John," Gray begins, but John is already running toward Karl.

"We should help him."

Yes. The wound on their wrist is healing only slowly, but they are still better equipped to deal with a furious werewolf than any mortal.

The werewolf has nearly reduced the car sheltering Zahira to a ruin: windows smashed, door torn off, metal dented. The demon is utterly maddened, swiping claws beneath the vehicle in an attempt to reach Zahira, then biting holes in the tires when it cannot.

As they approach, the werewolf catches Gray's scent. Under ordinary circumstances, it would surely flee a larger predator, but Yuri still has it under his control.

It rises to its full height to face them. Its jaws gape, and the reek of mange and rot pours from it. Gray's stomach cramps; he needs so badly to feed, and the werewolf smells so good.

"We will not hurt you, Karl," Gray advises it, just in case Karl can hear him. "We would not, even if John could not save you. Do not be frightened."

The werewolf howls and leaps at him. Its claws slash his face, but it is only one pain among many now, and he pays it no mind. He seizes its wrist, careful not to pull too hard and risk breaking bone, and is rewarded with a savage bite from its teeth.

"Be still. I do not wish to hurt you," Gray says, though of course the demon does not listen. He manages to get both arms around it, pinning its limbs to its sides. It twists madly, biting all the while, and he grits his teeth around the pain. "John, I would appreciate it if you could hurry."

John places his hand on its back. His blue eyes all but glow in Gray's sight, and he whispers something beneath his breath that might be a prayer. Gray can sense the demon unspooling from the body in his arms, until its reddish light forms a tangled, thrashing ball in John's hand.

He cannot resist; he lets go of Karl and snatches the demon from John, devouring it as quickly as he can. Some of the wounds on his face heal shut.

Karl's eyes are glazed with shock and his clothing tattered. He nearly falls, but Zahira is there, as is John. Between the two of them, they ease him onto the grass beside the sidewalk. He is safe, and the Chatwals are safe. John will take care of them.

"We need to leave," Caleb says unhappily. *"Find Drugoy, if we still can."*

Gray takes a step back, then another. He keeps his gaze fixed on John; at least they got to see him, one more time.

As if he hears the thought, John looks up. His eyes widen in alarm, and he stands up, hand out. "Gray, Caleb, wait. Don't go."

Tires scream as four SPECTR SUVs take the nearest corner at a high rate of speed, followed by several armored police vehicles. They screech to a stop, and police and agents in body armor pile out. Sunlight flashes off the muzzles of automatic weapons as they take up position.

"There's the drakul," Barillo shouts from the cab of the lead vehicle. "Open fire, and take it down."

John's throat tore as he let out a scream of denial, but gunfire drowned out any sound he made.

The storm of bullets ripped into Gray's body, shredding meat and bone, pulverizing organs. The impacts hurled him back, spun him in almost a complete circle, black hair flying.

Then he dropped to lie on the broken pavement.

Unmoving.

The shooting stopped, the sound of gunfire replaced by terrified screams. Zahira ran for Barillo's truck, her mouth twisted in fury. The mother from the family threw herself on one of the SPECTR agents, hitting him over and over with her fists until she was dragged off.

It all seemed far away and unreal. All that mattered was the still body lying in a slowly spreading pool of blood.

Goddess. Gray had been hurting before. But surely, surely this wouldn't be enough to kill him, no matter how weakened he'd been previously.

Right?

John didn't remember running across the shattered road. Concrete ripped through his jeans as he dropped to his knees by Gray—no, Caleb.

Brown eyes stared at the sky. Caleb's lips parted slightly, and he heaved in shallow, gasping breaths, even as blood leaked from his mouth and nose.

"Sekhmet, please," John whispered. He caught Caleb's hand in his, holding tight to unresponsive fingers. "It's going to be okay, babe. Just… just hold on."

There came the rumble of engines, no doubt more agents arriving, but John couldn't bring himself to look away from Caleb's face. Caleb blinked slowly, his eyes finding John's gaze. "You…" the word ended in a gasp of pain.

"Don't try to talk," John said frantically. There had to be something he could do, but what? Gray couldn't take sustenance from human blood; John couldn't even offer that much. And the wounds were far too extensive for first aid.

He'd never felt so helpless in his life.

Caleb licked bloody lips and tried again. "You asked us to stay…for this?"

For a moment, John didn't understand what Caleb was asking. Then horror unfurled as he realized the implication.

They thought he'd asked them to stay so they'd still be here when Barillo arrived. That he might have set them up, or at least made sure they remained while the trap closed around them.

"No! Goddess, Caleb, no. I didn't know Barillo was coming. I swear." John tightened his grip on Caleb's hand. "I love you. Both of you."

"Touching," Barillo sneered from a few feet away. John stiffened and looked up slowly, shock starting to give way to pure rage.

Barillo strolled up, flanked by two agents in body armor. One of them held a gun, the other a machete. Their expressions were impassive, but Barillo's eyes blazed as he stared down at Caleb. "Get out of the way, Starkweather. Unless you want your head chopped off, too."

"What?" John leaned forward, blocking them from Caleb as best he was able. "You can't be serious."

"That thing is too damn hard to kill," Barillo said. "But I've never heard of an entity that could live without a head. And if this one can, well, we'll try stabbing it in the brain with an athame and exorcising it the way Ericsson meant to. And if *that* doesn't work, we encase each piece in concrete and bury them miles from one another." His eyes narrowed. "Now get the fuck out of the way, or I'll have you shot."

John's extremities went cold, and the taste of metal filled his mouth. Locking his gaze with the agent holding the gun, he deliberately put himself between them and Caleb. "Then do it."

The agent shifted nervously and cast a glance at Barillo. "Sir…"

"You have your orders," Barillo snapped.

"John, move," Caleb managed to grate out. "L-leave us."

"No." John's heart beat against his ribs, forcing him to take a deep, steadying breath. "I made that mistake once already. I'm never leaving you again, hear me? Not so long as I've got any life left in me."

"I'm done with this," Barillo said in disgust. "Shoot him, then cut its head off. Do it!"

"Stand down," said a voice like the crack of a whip.

Startled, John turned to see a very familiar form walking toward them from the newly arrived vehicles. Though the men flanking her were larger and more heavily armed, there was no question who was in charge. Her black hair was hidden beneath a helmet, but she'd pushed up the bulletproof face shield to reveal her sharp features. Pale scars marred her smooth bronze skin, the remnants of a long ago therianthrope attack, and her dark eyes burned with righteous fire.

"Director Kaniyar?" Barillo said in surprise. "I didn't know…that is…"

Indira Kaniyar stopped and looked down at John and Caleb. "You just can't stay out of trouble, can you, Starkweather?" Without bothering to wait for an answer, she said, "We're heading to HQ. Barillo, get back in your van; I'll deal with you later. Someone get the drakul onto a stretcher. Move!"

"Director—" Barillo started.

She turned on him so sharply he took a step back. "Not another word," she said in a low voice. "You and I are going to have a very long talk back at HQ. Now get in the van as ordered, or you'll be doing it in cuffs. Your choice."

John would have felt pleased at the look of shock on Barillo's face, if the man hadn't just tried to kill him. Now only anger remained. Barillo's mouth thinned, but he nodded stiffly and retreated, taking his agents with him.

"I'd like to ride with Caleb and Gray, ma'am," John said quickly.

Kaniyar looked down at him. "You have a great deal of explaining to do, Starkweather," she said. "But that can wait until we're at HQ. Do what you need to until then."

Kaniyar strode off, firing orders left and right. John sank down by Caleb, holding his hand as they waited for the stretcher.

"Heh," Caleb said, and winced. "Never thought I'd be glad to see her again." His breath caught, and he shut his eyes, then opened them. "Christ, John, this hurts so fucking bad. You've got no idea."

"I know, babe," John said. He bent over Caleb, gently wiping his hair away from his face. "Just hold on."

"I don't think I can." Caleb swallowed hard. "Gray's weak, and it's taking too long. We're going under for a while." A hiss of pain escaped him. "I'm sorry. We're sorry. We never meant—"

"Shh." John pressed his lips carefully to their forehead. "I know. I'm sorry, too." He drew back a bit so he could look Caleb in the eyes. "Go on. I'll be here when you wake up." He bit his lip. "I love you both. So much."

Caleb's lips tried to form a smile. "We love…"

Then he stilled. No breath stirred his ruined chest, and his eyes lost their focus.

Telling himself everything was going to be all right, John closed Caleb and Gray's eyelids to keep the corneas from drying out, and held their hand while he waited for help to arrive.

CHAPTER 9

JOHN SAT SILENTLY by the stretcher Caleb and Gray lay on in the back of the van. Their hand in his was slack—limper even than that of someone in a deep sleep—and the skin against his had cooled noticeably. He kept his gaze directed on their fingers, rather than their unmoving chest, or the pale face, or the bloodied tangle of hair.

Zahira shifted uneasily on the other side of the stretcher. "Are you sure they're…?"

"I'm sure." John brought the cold fingers to his lips. Dried blood coated their fingertips, where Gray's claws emerged when he manifested. "I've seen it before. We just have to wait it out while Gray does his work."

Sekhmet knew, he understood her uncertainty. They *looked* dead. It was hard to believe the men—no, that wasn't right. The *people* he loved were still in there somewhere.

Even more than the claws and teeth, it was a reminder Gray wasn't human. And he never would be, no matter how hard anyone tried to make him.

Even if the person trying was John.

Time and again, he'd asked Gray to behave less like a drakul and more like a human agent of SPECTR. To follow orders. To hunt only when told to—or, after he and Caleb had been handed off to Ericsson and Steele, not at all. And John did it without offering any alternatives, without trying to figure out how to give Gray a way of satisfying inhuman instincts. He hadn't tried to really understand Gray's psychology, just asked him to be patient. When Caleb told him how trapped they both felt, John had heard, but he hadn't really *listened*.

John had tried to stuff a tiger in a business suit and ordered it to sit quietly in a cubicle. Then when it finally bit someone, he'd had the gall to act surprised.

"I should have pushed harder for them," he said, voice low as if they were sleeping rather than as close to dead as it was possible to come. "I asked them to take whatever Barillo handed out and wait patiently until the situation changed. What I should have done was go higher up the ladder. Made noise. Done something."

No wonder things had gone so wrong. It was a miracle they hadn't run off with Yuri and Drugoy the first night they met the other drakul. If not for John, maybe they even would have.

"There's plenty of blame to go around," Zahira said. Dark circles showed beneath her eyes; neither of them had slept in well over twenty-four hours. "Barillo is the one who put you in the position you were in."

"Still, I can't help but feel I wasn't a very good partner. At work or at home." He sighed. "I just…I could have done more."

The van jounced over a speed bump, then started down an incline. The parking deck of HQ, John assumed, since there weren't any windows to see out of. A few minutes later, it came to a halt. The doors swung open, revealing a couple of agents John didn't recognize waiting for them.

"We're to take the drakul to one of the exorcism rooms," one said.

Zahira straightened, weariness falling from her like a cloak. "What? No!"

The agent held up his hand. "Just to keep it out of the way while it comes to. The director says there are too many casualties who can't heal themselves, to take up a bed in the infirmary with one who can."

"It's all right," John said, when Zahira looked wary. "We can trust Director Kaniyar. If she was going to lock them away, she'd come out and say it."

"Special Agent Starkweather, Director Kaniyar wants you to report to the office of the district chief ASAP," the agent went on. "Special Agent Noorzai, report to the briefing room."

John gently folded Caleb and Gray's cold hand on their chest. To his surprise, a glance at Caleb's still face showed a shocking amount of improvement. A furrow gouged in his temple had filled in, and nothing seemed to be actively leaking blood anymore.

"Heal fast, babe," John whispered. Then he sat back while the agents unloaded the stretcher.

HQ was as busy as John had ever seen it; the place looked like a hornets' nest someone had kicked over. Agents raced back and forth, many of them making for the elevator to hit the streets after restocking ammo. Phones rang, updating the situation by the moment. A few civilians were in the mix, including the family who had been on the Battery. The ones who had been photographed with Gray.

John tamped down on the desire to talk to them for now. Kaniyar had given him a direct order, and she expected a prompt response. He made his way as quickly as he could to the district chief's office—her old office, before it had become Barillo's. The door was shut, but Kaniyar called "Come in!" at his quick knock.

She sat behind the desk, looking wildly out of place amidst the chaos of papers and candy wrappers Barillo had piled there. When the desk had been hers, she'd kept it almost completely bare, even the walls decorated in a minimalist style. It had fit her personality: spare and sharp as the blade of a sword.

The dark eyes that glanced over him now were as unyielding as steel. "Shut the door, Starkweather," she said. "I'll get to you in a minute."

There were already two other people in the room. Kaniyar's right-hand man, the empath Pittman, waited against the wall to one side of the desk. Barillo stood across from her, his mouth tight. From what he knew of the man, John guessed he felt humiliated to be forced to stand like an errant schoolchild in front of the principal, and in his own office to boot. Kaniyar almost certainly knew it as well; there was very little she did without purpose.

Kaniyar leaned back in her seat, steepling her fingers in front of her. "As I was saying, Barillo, I entrusted you with a very valuable asset. What did I tell you before I left you in charge of this office?"

Barillo stuffed his hands in his pockets, glowering at the carpet. "You said the drakul might be useful. But that it was also damn dangerous."

John folded his hands behind him and did his best to fade into the wall. He'd assumed Kaniyar had given Barillo some sort of orders in regard to Gray, but he'd never known for certain what they'd been.

"I believe what I said was that the drakul was potentially our best weapon against dangerous NHEs," Kaniyar responded. "I reminded you there is still a great deal we don't know about etheric entities. I showed you the footage from Fort Sumter. And yes, I said Gray was dangerous."

"So why did you let him loose?" Barillo asked.

"Many things are dangerous." Kaniyar's voice was cold enough to chill John, even without being the focus of her displeasure. Yet. "A tank is dangerous. A rocket launcher is dangerous. Your gun is dangerous. A pyrokinetic is dangerous. We weigh the danger to us versus the danger to our enemies, *before* we decide they can't be used."

"It isn't human," Barillo persisted.

"I'm quite aware of that." She tipped her head back slightly, eyes narrowing. "It is my understanding the drakul and his team members were doing quite well at first."

"Yes, but—"

"An excellent solve rate. A high number of fausts exorcised before possession became permanent."

It shouldn't have made John proud to hear it spoken aloud, not now. Not after everything. But he couldn't help the little bubble that welled up in his chest anyway. At least all the hard work they'd done hadn't gone entirely unnoticed.

"While this was happening," Kaniyar went on, "Special Agent Starkweather filed multiple complaints of harassment. What did you do to put a stop to it?"

"I-I told the guys to cool it," Barillo stammered. "Had HR send out a memo."

Pittman gave a small shake of his head.

"Lying won't get you anywhere, Barillo," Kaniyar said. "Perhaps you'd like to tell the truth instead?"

"It was just hazing. Newbie stuff." When Pittman shook his head again, Barillo clenched his teeth in frustration. "Look, people were scared of Jansen, and who the hell could blame them? Maybe it would have been fine if he'd at least pretended to be normal. Instead, he insisted on traipsing around in that getup of his, like an extra from some 90s emo movie. And Starkweather over here was exorcising NHEs without a circle, because apparently that's what happens when you're taking it up the ass from a fucking monster!"

John wanted nothing more than to force Barillo to swallow his venom, preferably along with some of his teeth. It was everything he could do to stay still, not react, and let Kaniyar deal with things.

"Of course no one wanted to be around them," Barillo went on. "Sick fuck like Starkweather? How could you trust a guy like that at your back? Let alone Jansen, the creepy bastard. So if folks wanted to blow off a little steam, I let 'em. You would've done the same."

Silence fell in the office, broken only by Barillo's angry breathing. Kaniyar seemed deep in thought, her gaze fixed on the cluttered desk. Some of the fury eased from Barillo's face, and he shot John a triumphant glance. Certain he'd won.

Barillo had never worked with Kaniyar. He couldn't know what it meant when she went very still.

"Allow me to make certain I understand what you're saying," she said at last. "You held prejudices against Mr. Jansen due to his appearance as well as the NHE inside him. You admit your bias against Special Agent Starkweather is due to his being in a sexual relationship with them. You confess you allowed—perhaps even tacitly encouraged—harassment toward them from other agents."

Wariness entered Barillo's eyes. "I-I didn't say that."

Kaniyar ignored him. "Your prejudices made you vulnerable to manipulation by outside forces—namely one Isabelle Aiken, on behalf of the Azarov drakul."

"I didn't know who she was!" He gestured to Pittman. "Ask him! I'm not lying."

Kaniyar's fist came down on the desk, so suddenly they all jumped. "Are you saying you're stupid as well as incompetent? Does that really seem like a good defense?"

John took an instinctive step back, then stopped. He'd never seen her control slip like this, not even when they were all on the run from Forsyth's goons.

The director rose to her feet, nostrils flared and lips tight. "I gave you what I hoped would someday become SPECTR's most valuable asset. I wanted to leave the drakul in Charleston long enough for the political buzz around the Fort Sumter incident to die away. Handled right, this might have made your career."

She began to pace back and forth. "Instead, you did everything in your power to convince the drakul that SPECTR is his enemy. You played into the hands of the Azarov drakul who most certainly *is* our enemy. And now we have blood in the streets, and damned earthquakes, and you're more interested in covering your ass than fixing what you helped break."

Barillo started to protest, but she held up a hand, and he fell silent. "We have one piece of luck, and one only. Instead of joining in the feast, Jansen and his drakul have taken sides against Azarov. If they'd teamed up, we'd have a very, very big problem right now. As it is, we might have the means to put an end to this and save as many people as we can in the meantime."

Barillo looked poleaxed. "But…it ate Ericsson…"

"And you'd best believe I'll be speaking to Jansen about that shortly." She turned to John. "Are they awake yet?"

"No, ma'am." He bit back on the urge to explain himself, and let her ask the questions.

"Special Agent Starkweather, you withheld information about the second drakul." Kaniyar arched a single, sculpted brow. "Would you care to explain why?"

"I have no excuse," he said immediately.

"I didn't ask for an excuse, I asked for an explanation."

Of course. He'd almost forgotten how carefully she chose her words. He straightened his back and took a deep breath. "Caleb was miserable. Here, at SPECTR, and then later on the grendel case, when the people he thought were his friends turned on him. More of Yuri's manipulation, or at least I'm fairly certain it was."

"I've already spoken to Deacon Ross," she said. "He arrived at HQ just as we did."

How she'd gotten here so quickly, John didn't know, but now didn't seem the time to ask. Likely someone had thought to call her when Gray drained Ericsson. Possibly even Barillo himself.

"Caleb believed District Chief Barillo would try to lock up another drakul, without considering any other alternatives," John said. "He convinced me not to report its existence."

"Given what you've seen today, locking up Azarov wouldn't have been a bad thing."

John spread his hands apart. "We didn't know. He hadn't done anything wrong, certainly nothing to warrant imprisonment. Still, I decided to look into him on my own, just to be on the safe side. I asked Special Agent Noorzai to pull the information on the Lake Baikal Vampire, but I didn't tell her what I needed it for." He sighed. "As soon as I read through it, I started to worry. But it was too late by then. Yuri played us all."

Kaniyar shook her head. "This is a cluster fuck of epic proportions, gentlemen. Barillo, things don't look good for you right now. In fact, it seems you might have ordered Jansen killed as a way of keeping me from finding out just how badly you screwed up."

Barillo opened his mouth, then shut it again with a snap when she glared at him.

"The truth is, I don't have time to deal with either one of you at the moment. If you want any chance of leniency, you will cooperate. Barillo, you'll work the coms and try to coordinate teams. Starkweather, will Gray and Mr. Jansen continue to work with SPECTR for the time being?"

"Yes," he said. "We all want the same thing right now."

"Fine. Go check on them. I believe they put him in one of the exorcism rooms." She turned to the computer monitor. "Inform me when he's on his feet. I have a job for him."

Caleb awoke with a gasp.

His lungs hurt as they struggled to inflate, his corneas felt dry, and his mouth tasted like he'd been sucking on the bottom of an old shoe. His heart beat madly for a few seconds, as though fighting against the inertia of blood gone sluggish, before settling back to its normal pace.

"Shh, shh. It's okay, babe."

He blinked a few times. John's face came into focus above him, as did the rest of their surroundings. They were in a plain room with no furniture, except for a single chair bolted to the floor, and a thin circle of silver sunk into the concrete.

An exorcism room. Oh hell.

"Shit!" He sat up, heart hammering again. "You can't exorcise Gray; you know you can't." Was this Barillo's stupid idea? But no, Kaniyar had shown up, and she knew the score.

Pain and fear tumbled through them, accompanied by a panicked, *"John wishes to exorcise me?"* from Gray. Before Caleb could pull away and get to his feet, John's hand closed on his arm.

"Settle down. It's okay," he repeated. "We're in an exorcism room because we needed somewhere out of the way to put you while Gray did his thing. The infirmary might have been a better place to wake up in, but we've got injured agents and civilians who don't have super healing powers. Plus it gave me a chance to get a nap."

"Oh." That explained the pillows and blankets, though the concrete floor couldn't have been comfortable.

"It's okay, babe," John said yet again. "You're all right." His gaze fixed on Caleb's face, as if drinking in the details. "You're all right."

Then he leaned forward and kissed Caleb hungrily.

CHAPTER 10

FOR AN INSTANT, Caleb wasn't sure how to respond. Then Gray sent a shock of sheer delight through their veins. His uncomplicated joy left them kissing John back with equal fervor. Their heart beat now with a mix of happiness and desire. The need to feel and touch and reconnect.

The smart thing to do would be to put on the brakes. Talking before fucking.

"John has forgiven us," Gray said. Everything right in his world again, or at least this corner of it.

John shoved Caleb back onto the blanket, swung a leg over their narrow hips, and bent down for another kiss. Caleb drew in a deep breath, and Christ, they both stank after a long day of blood and terror.

"We're sorry," he said against John's lips. "We love you."

"I know." John drew back just a little, just enough to stare into their eyes. "I was so scared. Please, I want..."

The stress of the day unraveled. They were safe, at least for the moment, and John was with them, and Gray wanted to touch and feel, because talking was never going to be his strong suit.

To hell with it. Caleb grabbed John's face and hauled him down for another kiss.

And Christ it was good, so good, even on the hard floor, covered in dried blood and God only knew what else. He slid his hands beneath John's shirt, fanning his fingers over the curve of rib and muscle, before shoving the soft cotton up. John sat back and dragged the shirt off over his head, tossing it blindly to the ground. He unbuttoned Caleb's jeans, yanked down the zipper, then tugged jeans and underwear both over Caleb's narrow hips, trapping his thighs together. Caleb's cock popped free, aching with need, precome beading at the tip.

John unzipped, and Caleb reached for him. As their shafts slid together, John bent over him again for another ravenous kiss. The touch sent a wild flare of sheer lust through Caleb, resonating back and forth between him and Gray, building on itself.

"We thought we'd lost you," he mumbled against John's mouth. "Thought we'd never have this again."

"I know." John's breath came fast and ragged. "But we're here now. Together."

"Together," Gray whispered happily, and their nerves came alive with pleasure and joy. Caleb arched his head back, drowning in sensation. Relishing John's weight on his legs, and Gray's presence just under their shared skin. The ache of loss that had hollowed out their heart eased at last, leaving behind only this moment of connection with the two people who mattered more to him than anything else in the world.

John's hips quickened their pace. Caleb didn't try to hold back, just let it all wash over him, until ecstasy took on the edge of primal urgency. His teeth burned as he came hard. It took John a few more thrusts, but then he joined Caleb, moaning into his mouth as hot spunk spilled over Caleb's belly.

For a long moment, there was only the sound of their breathing, raw pleasure ebbing. But God, they were together again, despite everything. It felt like a miracle.

John propped himself on an elbow, so he could look down into their face. "Hey," he said softly.

"Hey yourself," Caleb replied.

"Tell John I also wish to say this."

"Gray says hey, too," Caleb said with a roll of his eyes. John chuckled.

The next moment of silence was far less comfortable. Caleb dragged in a deep breath.

"We're sorry," he said, at the same moment John said, "You scared me."

Gray withdrew a bit, worried. Caleb grimaced. "We didn't mean to scare you. Not today, and certainly not…shit, was it just last night? At, you know. Ericsson's house."

"Not beating around the bush, are you?" John asked ruefully. But at least he wasn't freaking out.

"I don't know how much time we have to talk," Caleb replied. "And please tell me that video camera isn't recording."

"I turned it off manually," John said. "Not that I was expecting anything," he added hastily. "I just didn't want anyone recording you waking up."

"Because it would look creepy and scary," Caleb said glumly. Some things never changed.

John shrugged. "Kaniyar is massively pissed at Barillo. At best, his career is over. I don't think anyone would risk making the director angry right now, so I'm not worried about anyone giving us grief. At least, not at the moment. But I try to plan ahead."

"Boy Scout, always prepared," Caleb said with a wry grin.

John snorted. "Just tell me what happened."

Caleb sighed. John shifted aside, and he began to pull up his underwear and pants. "Ericsson had tried to kill you. And we were sick of doing things the mortal way. Playing nice with Barillo, and not hunting, and all the rest of it. So we went to confront him. Everything happened so fast, and things went sideways, and before we knew it that fucker was threatening to kill Zahira too. Oh, and he stabbed us in the head. It was too much." He looked away from John, focusing on the blank concrete wall. "We wanted to protect Zahira, and you, and ourselves, so we bit him. And neither of us wanted to stop."

John put his hand on Caleb's. Startled, Caleb glanced at him. John's expression was thoughtful, and a bit sad, but not angry. "Okay."

"Okay?" Caleb asked cautiously. "Because you were pretty upset at the time. Not that I blame you—I don't. Neither of us do."

"I thought..." John paused, then sighed. "I was afraid you knew what Yuri and Drugoy were up to. That the idea of an all-you-can-eat buffet might sound too good to pass up."

It shouldn't have hurt, not after what they'd done. But it did. "Christ, John, Ericsson is one thing, but we wouldn't go around eating innocent people! Not anyone who could be saved, anyway. Don't you remember Brimm's attic with all the poor bastards he'd stuffed ghouls into? That was horrible. Gray had never thought about mortal victims before, but as soon as he saw it from my perspective, he was revolted. We'd *never* go along with something like that."

"I believe you." John tightened his grip on Caleb. "Like you said, things happened fast. Yuri played everyone, to the point where no one had much trust left. I let myself doubt, and that was a mistake."

Caleb's shoulders slumped. "Yeah, well. We should have been more honest with you. And we definitely shouldn't have eaten Ericsson. We were so upset we just barfed him all over the yard anyway."

John rubbed at his eyes with his free hand. "Caleb..."

"It's true!"

"You could have put it differently." He let his hand fall. "We both have things to work on, no question about it. But even when I didn't know the whole story, even when I was scared of you, I didn't want to see you locked away by Barillo."

"Why?" Caleb asked, bewildered.

Instead of answering directly, John asked, "Why did you surrender to Drugoy on the Battery?"

"Because he was going to hurt Harry if we didn't." Caleb shook his head quickly when John started to smile. "No, John. You don't understand. I don't give a shit about SPECTR. Right now, I'd throw the whole organization in the sea if I could. And Gray really just wants to be left the hell alone so he can hunt down big scary monsters."

John nodded. "Okay."

"That's not going to change, understand? But maybe...I don't know, after seeing the way Yuri and Drugoy are, it clarified some things. Yuri put the sirens in those women on Ericsson's behalf, and he doesn't even care, because they'd all be dead in sixty years anyway so what does it matter? But suffering is suffering, and no one's is somehow lesser than anybody else's." He bit his lip, trying to think how to phrase things. "Gray thinks mortals waste their lives worrying about nonsense, and they kill each other over stupid shit no one will even remember a hundred years later, and, well...he's not exactly wrong, is he? But that doesn't mean no one else matters. It doesn't mean we can just walk off and save our own skin while people die." He ran a hand back through his long hair, tugging at the tangles in frustration. "Shit, I'm not explaining this well."

John caught Caleb's chin and gently tugged it around so he could look them in the eye. "You don't need to. You both chose to save that girl, even though it meant surrendering without a fight for once, because that's who you are."

Caleb shrugged awkwardly. "We'd rather not do that again, if we could avoid it, honestly."

John leaned over and kissed them. "Agreed. Now come on. We need to let Kaniyar know you're back on your feet."

* * *

Caleb was surprised to find Deacon waiting in the hall for them.

He put out an arm automatically, a barrier between Deacon and John, while Gray growled and rumbled under his skin. "They let you wander around loose?" he demanded.

Deacon held up his hands. One was heavily bandaged, and he looked to have acquired a few more scrapes since they'd parted that morning. "Way to say thanks," he said. "You'd still be chained up if I hadn't helped you."

"Chained up?" John asked with a frown.

"Yeah. Drugoy beat our ass pretty bad last night," Caleb said, as lightly as he could. "Don't worry about it."

John's expression suggested he was definitely going to worry about it. But he only said, "Deacon, you corroborated Ericsson's texts about Barillo to Kaniyar, right?"

Deacon nodded. "Yeah." He folded his arms over his chest. "Like I told Caleb and Gray, this isn't what I signed up for. If I'd realized this was what Yuri and Drugoy had in mind, I would never have gone along with it."

"No, you would have just screwed with my head," Caleb snapped. "Are you lurking for a reason?"

"Kaniyar ordered me to make myself useful. You know, before she arrests my ass for helping out with the demon possession." Deacon gave them a half-shrug.

"And you're hoping if you lend a hand now, maybe they'll go easier on you later." Anger thrummed through Caleb's veins. Yes, Deacon had helped him—but he'd also screwed over the friend who ended up possessed by the grendel. Probably other people, too.

"We don't have time," John said, "We're on our way to see Kaniyar. You can walk with us—maybe we'll find someone you can lend a hand to."

Deacon nodded and fell in behind them like some creepy shadow. The skin between Caleb's shoulder blades twitched. He'd actually liked Deacon, before he knew the truth. But even if he'd been inclined to overlook everything else, something about the way Deacon hovered now put his teeth on edge. Like Deacon was just trying to get an in with another drakul, now that things had gone south with Drugoy.

That will not happen.

It sure as hell won't. "Where's Isabelle?" Caleb asked Deacon. "Does Yuri have her doing his dirty work someplace?"

Deacon shook his head. "I don't know."

"We encountered her sister on King Street," John said. "Yuri had put a demon in her. I was able to exorcise her."

"Her sister?" Deacon asked, bewildered. "Why the hell would Yuri do that? He must not have known who she was."

"Or he just didn't care." Caleb shook his head, anger bubbling inside him.

A lot of which belonged to Gray. *"This is wrong. We would never intentionally hurt Zahira or John."*

"Yuri knew I was going after Ericsson and didn't lift a finger to protect him. Then he put a demon in Isabelle's sister for the hell of it." Caleb glanced back over his shoulder at Deacon. "Maybe he just doesn't give a shit about any of you."

"Mr. Gray?"

They'd passed into the area with the conference rooms while they talked. Startled, Caleb turned just in time to catch Harry as she flung herself into his arms. "You're alive!" she shrieked in his ear.

Sensitive hearing was a bitch sometimes. "Hey, kiddo," he said. "Are you all right?"

"I thought you were dead. I thought the soldiers..." she dissolved into sobs.

Caleb resisted the temptation to point out it was SPECTR agents who had shot him up, at least for the most part. Harry's shout had drawn the other Chatwals from the conference room, where they seemed to be camped out with a group of civilian refugees.

"Harry's okay, thanks to you," Mrs. Chatwal said. She hesitantly put a hand to his arm. "We owe you everything. Everything."

This was getting embarrassing. "It was no big deal. Really."

Harry stepped back, blinking away tears. She had a bandage on her neck, where Drugoy's claws had scratched her, but otherwise she seemed unharmed. Physically, anyway; Caleb hoped she'd find a good counselor to talk to about what had happened. Hell, at the rate things were going, half of Charleston was going to need therapy when this was all over.

"You saved my life," Harry said, voice trembling. "I just...you turned yourself over to that monster to save me."

Caleb shrugged awkwardly. "So hey, this is our boyfriend, John Starkweather. We're kind of back together now."

Harry managed a grin. "I sort of figured, the way he was telling the other one to get the hell away from you."

"Language, Harry," Mrs. Chatwal said. "It's very nice to meet you,

Mr. Starkweather."

"This is Harry, and Nardev, and Mrs. Chatwal, and I assume Mahindar is in there?" Caleb said. Harry stepped aside, and he saw Mahindar in deep conversation with Karl's daughter. Karl's husband spotted Caleb and hurriedly rose to his feet.

"John, Caleb, thanks for helping Karl," he said fervently.

John nodded and shook the man's hand, while Caleb tried to remember his name. "How's he doing?"

"Good. They checked him out in the infirmary, but he's not injured, just shaken." Brandon, that was it, looked troubled for a moment. "He insisted on getting back to work, as a matter of fact."

"Yeah, that sounds like Karl," John said. "We're going to go talk to the director. I'll tell Karl to take it easy if I see him."

"Good luck with that," Brandon said with a rueful smile.

"Want to be of use?" Caleb asked Deacon, who had withdrawn a few steps while they talked. "Help these people. Get them coffee, or blankets, or water, or whatever they need."

Deacon nodded. "I will."

Caleb started away, then stopped. "Oh, and you'd better have brought my bike back in one piece."

Deacon dug into his pocket, pulled out the keys, and tossed them to Caleb. "It's in the garage upstairs."

The door to Barillo's—or maybe it was Kaniyar's now—office stood open. A stream of agents hurried in and out, so they went in without knocking. Kaniyar stood staring at the computer monitor, which showed a map of Charleston dotted with red pins, and issuing a stream of commands into a headset. When she spotted them, she nodded at John to shut the door.

He did, leaving them alone with Kaniyar. She ended her call and turned brusquely to Caleb. "We need your blood."

Oh. He should have expected this, but it hadn't even crossed his mind. "We're pretty tapped out right now."

Starving, more like. He managed so far to avoid thinking about how fucking hungry they were. Gray was running low, and Caleb couldn't even remember the last time he'd had a bite of his own. Not that he needed to eat, apparently, since Yuri had survived for a decade at the bottom of a lake.

Christ. He'd waved goodbye to humanity somewhere along the line and not even realized it.

"Mortals are foolish. You are better off with me."

Hush.

"You seem to be under the impression I'm making a request, Mr. Jansen." Kaniyar folded her hands behind her back. "Exorcists can save those who have had NHEs forced into them by Azarov, but only if they receive a boost from your blood. According to the research Forsyth was able to do on you, it should be safe to ingest."

Caleb nodded, even though he didn't entirely like the way this was going. "Right. Gray destroys any infections the second they enter my system. No need to worry about passing on hepatitis or anything else."

"Good. Report to the infirmary and they'll get started drawing it."

Gray stirred uneasily. *"I do not care for this."*

Considering we drank Ericsson, I don't think we're in any position to refuse her right now. "All right," he said aloud.

"Ma'am." John stepped up beside Caleb. "Gray needs to get his strength back up. I'm not certain when the last pickup for disposal was, but if we have any bottled NHEs in containment, I suggest we let him feed on them."

Gray's interest sharpened, and their teeth burned. Caleb swallowed against the sudden surge of drool flooding their mouth. NHEs were traditionally exorcised into special bottles, briefly stored, and then sent to a facility equipped with a blast furnace for disposal. If the bottles were broken, Gray could absorb the released NHEs in the brief instant before they returned to the etheric plane.

Kaniyar's eyes narrowed in thought. Then she nodded. "Blood first. Azarov is laying low for now, so we have a chance to get ahead of this thing. Once the exorcists are supplied with your blood, you can feed. Understand?"

Caleb nodded. "We understand."

"Good. Do you know where Azarov might be holed up?"

"Not unless he went back to his apartment, which doesn't seem very likely. I'm guessing he's keeping quiet while Yuri recovers." At Kaniyar's questioning look, he said, "Gray boosts my TK, but I can't fly across the city. I can throw things around and jump really far, but there's a limit. At a guess, Dru is probably hunting some of the demons—NHEs—they unleashed earlier, while Yuri rests his brain."

"We'll keep looking for him, then," Kaniyar said, turning back to her map. Assuming he'd been dismissed, Caleb took a step toward the door. "Oh, and one more thing, Mr. Jansen."

Crap. "Yes?"

She met his gaze, her eyes hard and cold as flint. "Ericsson was most certainly guilty of extortion, rape, summoning demons, and attempted murder. Some might say you saved us the cost of a trial." She paused. "I don't like wasting people. But understand; you so much as *think* about biting anyone who isn't possessed ever again, that's it."

Caleb held his hands up. "I swear, we won't. We're on a strict demon-only diet from now on."

"You'd better be. You will work with Starkweather and whoever else I tell you to work with, and they'll handle anyone human who needs to be handled. No more vigilante bullshit. You aren't the goddamn Punisher."

He swallowed and nodded. "Got it. Thank you."

"Get to the infirmary. Starkweather, I want a plan for stopping Azarov on my desk in an hour."

John nodded. "Yes, ma'am. With your permission, I'd like to confer with Special Agent Noorzai and Mr. Jansen."

"Do it."

CHAPTER 11

WHILE CALEB HEADED straight for the infirmary, John headed to the briefing room to find Zahira. She stood near the back, her eyes locked on a map projected on the wall. A quick glance showed John it was identical to the one on Kaniyar's monitor.

"Zahira," he called softly.

Zahira turned, then glanced at Wells, who was at the front podium, giving out assignments. She gave Zahira a brief nod of dismissal.

"Kaniyar wants a plan for stopping Drugoy," he said when Zahira joined him. "You, me, and Caleb and Gray are the closest things we have to experts right now. We need your help."

She nodded. "How are they?"

"Down in the infirmary getting blood drawn." At her frown, he said, "For distribution to exorcists."

"Can they afford to lose it?" she asked as they stepped into the elevator.

"Kaniyar agreed to let Gray feed on any of the NHEs we have in storage." He punched the button for the infirmary level. "I hope we have enough. He's pretty drained, and losing more blood isn't going to help."

They found Gray in a phlebotomy chair, a needle in each arm and a rack of filled vials on a small table. The attendant switched out a full vial for an empty one without disturbing the needle. Gray watched the process with a glum air.

"Gray," Zahira called as they approached.

Gray looked up, and his entire demeanor altered. It was hard even for John to always read the emotion in his obsidian eyes, but there was no missing the big smile slowly spreading over his face. And exposing the savage fangs; the attendant paled and nearly dropped the vial she was holding.

"I can do that," Zahira said, indicating the needle.

The attendant gladly handed her the next empty vial and scurried out. Zahira sat in the chair she'd vacated. "I'm so happy to see you, Gray," she said with a smile of her own. "John was worried about you."

"I am glad to see you as well," Gray said. "I was concerned for your safety."

John gestured to the vials. "Zahira, do you want to drink up now, since we're here? Beat the rush?"

"I can't," Zahira said. "Sorry, Gray, but you aren't exactly halal."

"Oh, right." John felt stupid for forgetting.

"You are here to plan how to defeat Yuri and Drugoy," Gray rumbled. His smile faded into a slight frown. "It will not be easy. Drugoy will not make the mistake of letting us live again."

Cold slicked John's spine. "Deacon said you were chained up. What happened?"

"We fought. Drugoy won." The last two words came out as a growl of displeasure. "He pinned us. Fed from us."

Zahira's brown skin took on an ashen hue. "Oh no. What happened?"

John's heart sank as Gray related the fight. When he was done, Gray said, "When Yuri over-extended his power on the Battery, we had a chance, perhaps, to fight and win. But you needed us. Karl needed us. So we stayed."

And lost what might have been their only opportunity to put an end to things. Damn it. John started to pinch the bridge of his nose, then winced when his fingers encountered bruised skin. They were all banged-up and running on reserves. The fifteen-minute nap he'd managed on the floor of the exorcism room before Caleb woke up hadn't been nearly enough. Zahira likely hadn't even had that.

"We're not in great shape," he said. "But at least this time you don't have to face him alone."

"You didn't have to the last time, either," Zahira said reproachfully.

Gray's expression grew troubled. "We believed everyone hated us."

Zahira glanced up from the vial she was attaching to the needle.

"Neither of us ever hated you. But I am hurt that you and Caleb didn't trust me enough to tell me about the other drakul."

Gray turned his head away. "We made many mistakes. That was one of them. I am sorry, Zahira."

"I forgive you."

John rested a hand on Gray's shoulder, feeling the crackle of energy through his fingers. "We have to figure out how to deal with Drugoy and Yuri, without exposing too many agents to possession. Any force will have to be made up solely of exorcists, and there aren't a huge number of us to go around."

Gray's focus shifted in a way that suggested he was conversing with Caleb. "Drugoy does not like water. It does not harm him, but he is not as strong over water as he is over earth."

Zahira's eyes lit up. "Fascinating! He's the earthquake, and water is his weakness. You're the storm. What's yours?"

Gray cocked his head, hair falling to the side. "I have walked in desert and jungle, upon glacier and field and sand. I did not enjoy the red lands, the places where there is only the eye of the sun. But I was not in a living body. It was not the same, I think."

"Unfortunately, I doubt Yuri is just going to hop onto a boat for us," John said. "But we might be able to lure him someplace. From what you've said, Gray, it sounds as though he'd come after you no matter where you are. Or me, or even Zahira, just to hurt you."

"What about the spirit ward Brimm used against Gray?" Zahira asked as she changed out the vial again. "It was able to contain him, when other wards couldn't."

John considered. Ex-SPECTR agent Howard Brimm had trapped Gray shortly after he possessed Caleb, intending to have a drakul at his beck and call to go along with his army of ghouls. "That was before the forty days were up. I don't know if the timing would make any sort of difference or not, though. I meant to try at some point, just to see if the circle still worked, but never got around to it. The stupid thing was so complicated it would take at least an hour to draw, and there always seemed to be something more urgent."

"It's worth a try," Zahira said. "Though we need to have a backup plan if it doesn't work." She bit her lip. "The best thing would be to lure them somewhere over water without being obvious about it. And without endangering any civilians."

They were all silent for a moment. Then Gray stirred. "Caleb says: Patriots Point."

"The aircraft carrier," John said.

Zahira frowned slightly. "I'm not as familiar with the area as you are."

"The USS Yorktown." John cast back to the tour he and Caleb had taken a few weeks ago. "It's a World War II aircraft carrier, decommissioned and turned into a museum of sorts. There's a destroyer and a submarine as well, but the carrier's flight deck would give us room to maneuver. Not to mention, it's shut down today thanks to Drugoy and Yuri's rampage. Patriots Point is on the other side of the Cooper River, but there's plenty of space around it, so we won't have to worry about civilian casualties. Damage to a historical monument, yes, but I'll take that over loss of life."

Gray's attention turned inward for a moment. "Caleb says there are places to hide exorcists. He believes you could station a sniper on the bridge. A bullet directly through Drugoy's brain would incapacitate him long enough for us to act."

A spark of hope started to grow in John's chest. They might just make it through this intact after all. "How we get him there is the question. We'll make good bait, but he has to know the bait is there to take it."

An alarm began to blare overhead. Kaniyar's voice came over the speakers. "Possible enemy assault. All exorcists to the upper level. Other agents hold position."

Gray receded and Caleb yanked the needles out of his arms, the holes sealing almost instantly. "Looks like we don't have to worry about finding Drugoy and Yuri. They've come to us."

John grabbed the rack of vials. "Zahira, head to the carrier. If things go south here, we're going to need another option, and having Brimm's circle already in place might make all the difference. We'll head to Containment Level and get Gray powered up." Because no matter what else was going on above their heads, if Drugoy was involved, Gray was their best—probably their only—chance of stopping him.

They ran for the elevator. Karl stood in the hall, looking uncertain until he spotted them. "John! What's happening?"

"Drugoy's coming." John shoved the vials into Karl's hands. "Here make sure these get distributed to the exorcists. No more than one each."

Karl paled. Bruises bloomed around his cheekbones and mouth, relics of the transformation the lycanthrope had forced on him. He'd found a spare suit somewhere, but it hung loose on his frame, the sleeves and pant legs rolled up to accommodate for his shorter height. "Got it."

"Then stay back. We don't want you getting furry again."

"Yeah, that wasn't really the type of transition I'm into," Karl said. "Do you need a vial?"

John snatched one up; the contents were still warm from Gray's body. Trying not to think too hard, he uncapped it and swallowed down the contents in one gulp. His expression of disgust must have given him away, because Caleb said, "Now you can understand what Gray's meals have put me through."

John tossed the vial and clapped him on the shoulder. "You have my pity. Let's move."

The elevator whisked Zahira and Karl upward. Containment was the lowest level in HQ. As soon as an elevator returned, John and Caleb climbed on and began to descend.

A jolt shook the elevator, and the lights flickered off, then on, then off again. John stumbled, and Caleb caught him by the elbow. "What the fuck?" Caleb asked.

More alarms shrilled, and the power flickered again. "Possible breach on Containment Level," Kaniyar said over the speaker. "Repeat, possible breach on Containment Level."

John felt the blood drain from his extremities. "Oh hell. What do you bet Ericsson told Yuri everything he knew about HQ's layout?"

Drugoy was the earthquake. How exactly he'd burrowed down to the lowest level, John didn't know—probably by shattering rock and concrete and shifting earth. Now he was loose in HQ.

On the Containment Level, where dozens of bottled NHEs sat just waiting for him to drink them down and regain any energy he'd lost in his digging.

"Not a bet I'm taking," Caleb replied grimly. "It seems like the sort of thing a former intelligence officer would want on hand, even if he didn't have any specific plans to use them at the time."

The elevator juddered to a halt, but the doors failed to open. Caleb growled and wrenched them apart.

Warning lights flashed against the solid concrete walls of a long hall. A guard covered in blood stumbled toward them, his face laid open to the bone by a set of sharp claws.

"Starkweather," he gasped when he saw them.

John ran to him. The man was on his feet at least, though badly injured. "What happened?"

"I was guarding the vault. Just coming on shift." A whimper of pain escaped him. "The wall fell in. It was the other drakul. Azarov. Tried to stop."

Caleb swore.

"Get to safety," John advised the guard. "We're going in."

He drew his Glock and started down the hall, Caleb beside him like a slender shadow. "How are we handling this?"

"Gray and I aren't doing as well as we could be." Caleb's expression was drawn, his mouth set in a line of determination. "Energy-wise, that is. But we're still the only ones with any hope of taking on Drugoy in an actual fight. We'll keep his attention on us, but if you see any chance to hurt him, take it."

If Drugoy managed to get into the vault before them, he'd be able to feast on the bottled NHEs, and the fight would become even more one-sided. And that was assuming he didn't glut himself until he fully manifested.

Goddess, please don't let there have been enough stored bottles for Drugoy to truly become the earthquake. There wouldn't be a building left standing in Charleston.

"If we can lure him away, like we planned, we might not have to fight him head-to-head," John said. "But how do we get him to chase us, without tipping him off about the trap?" Not to mention how they'd get him out of HQ without encountering too many vulnerable people.

"I'm open to suggestions," Caleb said. Then his nostrils flared, and he stilled. A moment later, the scent of petrichor and incense flooded the narrow hall.

"Drugoy," Gray said. "He is nearby. Stay behind me."

John fell in behind Gray. Water filmed the corridor floor now, though where it came from, John didn't know. They were below the water table; when Drugoy broke through the wall, he must have let it seep in after him. How long would it take for HQ to flood?

The hallway let out into a large room. Banks of monitoring equipment lined one wall. Bullets had stitched a line across screens and keyboards, leaving most of them dark and others sparking, the reek of burned electronics in the air. An empty cart stood abandoned near what looked like scanning equipment, no doubt meant to keep inventory of the bottles containing exorcised NHEs. Directly across from the entrance, the wall had partially collapsed, revealing broken concrete, twisted rebar, and shattered stone. Water seeped in, spreading slowly across the floor. Three bodies lay in crumpled heaps, two guards and one in a maintenance uniform.

Yuri stood in front of the vault, a key card in hand. The thick steel door rolled back, the light from within falling across his white hair and arctic eyes.

"Gray," he said, in apparent surprise. "I thought the mortals would have caged you."

John stopped near the entrance into the large room, while Gray paced closer to Yuri. "No. I am free."

Yuri cocked his head, as if listening to a voice only he could hear. "You will never be truly free with these mortals. But no matter. We had thought to come here, gorge on the demons so conveniently trapped in their bottles, then find and kill you. But it seems things are going to become a bit more interesting." His mouth warped in a savage grin. "Race you."

Then he dashed into the vault, and toward the shelves lined with imprisoned NHEs.

"Stay here," Gray orders John, before sprinting into the vault after Yuri.

Freestanding metal shelves crowd the surprisingly small room. Some are empty, but others contain rows of black bottles sealed with silver foil and clay charms. Within the dark heart of each bottle seethes a demon, its essence trapped until it can be destroyed in the heat of a blast furnace.

They should have let us eat them instead.

"Yeah, no shit. Now stop him!"

Yuri casts a glance over his shoulder as Gray closes the distance. Then his fangs erupt, eyes going to black glass and burning lava. His movement is a blur, backhanding Gray hard enough to crack vertebrae and send him to the floor.

There comes the sound of breaking glass, Drugoy smashing the bottles and sucking the unleashed energy into himself before it can escape.

"We have to stop him. Get up; get up!"

Gray's stomach cramps with hunger, and pain flares down their spine as their neck pops back into place. He rolls to his feet, coming into a crouch. If he can wrestle Drugoy away from the shelves, perhaps he can at least stop him from feeding more. With a snarl, he launches himself at Drugoy again.

But Drugoy is smashing more bottles, devouring more demons, growing stronger by the moment. He turns, faster than Gray can track, and punches them directly in the mouth.

Fangs shatter, and their brain hits their skull with enough force to turn their vision white. They crumple into a heap at Drugoy's feet, nose and mouth clogged with their own blood.

"I am finished with you, Gray," Drugoy growls. "I searched for you for so long, but you have proven yourself utterly faithless. You are more trouble than you are worth. We will simply have to start over."

"Start over? What does he mean?"

Drugoy kicks Gray in the side, hard enough to send him flying several feet, ribs snapping under the impact. "After you told us you had inhabited dead bodies, Yuri asked Ericsson what he knew. He spoke of a rumor, another drakul in North America, but inhabiting corpses as you once did. When we are finished here, we will pay a visit to what is left of the Vigilant who once tracked it. Find this other drakul. And, using what you told us of your experience, put it in a living body."

Horror and disgust pour out from Caleb. *"Christ, he can't have us, so he's going to find some other poor son of a bitch to fuck with."*

Coming into a living body had been painful and confusing, but at least Gray had John to help them. Yuri and Drugoy would not help—they would make everything a thousand times worse, until they had another drakul as mad and cruel as themselves.

"No!" Deacon calls from the vault door. "I'm not going to let you."

Gray blinks, vision clearing as their optic nerve heals. Deacon stands in the door, John and Kaniyar behind him with guns drawn.

Drugoy cocks his head, and for the first time, Gray sees uncertainty flicker through his eyes. "Deacon?"

"Do it, Mr. Ross," Kaniyar snaps.

Deacon's TK goes off like a bomb blast, directed into the vault and hurling Drugoy into the wall with bone snapping force.

"I guess Deacon scored some of our blood after all."

So it would seem.

The metal shelves uproot, crashing into one another, glass shards raining down as the bottles explode.

"Gray, now!" John calls, but there is no need for the prompt.

Gray is already feeding.

There are too many demons at once for him to devour them all before they escape back to the etheric plane. Even so, he swallows them down by the handful, by the dozen. Energy surges through him: bones healing, bruises vanishing. Gray rises to his feet amidst the wreckage, black hair swirling around him like a storm cloud. Electricity snaps in the air, arcing from claws and eyes to the broken metal shelves.

He feels good. Better; he feels reborn.

"Yes." / Yes.

They stride across the vault to where Drugoy lies against the wall, still shaking his head in a daze. Gray seizes the front of his shirt, heaves him off the ground, and slams him hard enough into the concrete to leave a dent.

"Everything could have been different," he says, fury riding on the energy sizzling through him. "We might have hunted together across the face of this world, through a thousand mortal lifetimes."

Blood leaks from a cut on Drugoy's head, staining his pale hair red. "You are a fool." There comes a pop as something in his chest snaps back into place. "I tried to free you. They will never let you go willingly. No one knows that better than us." The lake, he must mean. Encased in concrete, crushed and drowning for a decade. "Remember this day, when you are the one trapped alone in the dark."

The ground begins to shake.

For a moment, nothing makes any sense. Drugoy cannot be doing this—he does not have the strength left, surely.

Then there comes the distant sound of an explosion. The shaking increases, and the metal of the vault groans like an animal in pain.

"Someone's set off a bomb!" Kaniyar yells from the vault door, one hand to her headset. "No wait—more than one."

Drugoy grins. "My Isabelle did not fail me," he says, and buries his fist in Gray's gut.

CHAPTER 12

JOHN BIT BACK a cry as Gray's body went flying back into the wreckage. With a snarl of fury, Drugoy turned to the door, where only the thin line of Deacon, Kaniyar, and John stood between him and escape.

"Shoot him," Kaniyar started to say, even as she squeezed the trigger on her Glock.

The emergency lights flickered—then went dark.

Saint Elmo's fire glowed on the jagged points of metal from the broken shelves, and flashes of static arced and popped around Gray, but it wasn't nearly enough to see by. "Hold your fire!" Kaniyar barked, her words almost drowned out by another rumble. A terrifying crack sounded from the room behind them, and for an awful second John thought the entire structure was about to come down on top of them.

The light on Deacon's cell cut through the blackness, shaking madly with the trembling of his hand. "Oh fuck," he whimpered. "Oh fuck fuck fuck."

A pair of glowing red eyes appeared just to one side of him.

Deacon screamed. John barely caught a glimpse of Drugoy's features in the light of the cellphone before Deacon dropped it. John brought up his gun, but he couldn't see anything. He might take the risk of hitting Gray if it slowed down Drugoy, but Kaniyar and Deacon wouldn't recover from a bullet so easily.

There came a sickening crunch, and something slammed into John's body, knocking him back. He skidded across the floor outside the vault, barely keeping hold of his gun in the process. For a confused instant, he had the sense of a vast presence hovering above him; a predator, much larger and stronger than himself, something that wanted only to kill.

Gray, still silhouetted by sparks of static, burst out of the vault with a snarl. At the same moment, a tremor ran through the ground, and the ceiling above them groaned.

A flash of red eyes—then the sound of running steps, retreating. John clutched his gun, tracking Gray's movement because there was nothing else to see in the blackness. Gray dashed a short distance, then stopped.

"Drugoy has fled back into the earth," he growled.

"Starkweather, report," Kaniyar said.

"Alive." John holstered his Glock and fumbled out his cellphone. "But not for long if the roof comes down on us."

The light from his phone found Deacon first. He lay not far away, neck at an unnatural angle, a look of fear and surprise still on his pale features. Drugoy must have snapped his neck, then used his body to clear John and Kaniyar out of the way. As for Kaniyar, she moved stiffly, wincing as she made it to her feet.

John stumbled up. "We have to get out of here." How many bombs had Yuri planted—and how long ago? Was this some backup plan he'd put in place after coming to Charleston, in case SPECTR found him out?

"Yes," Gray growled. "Hurry."

They raced down the corridor, back toward the elevators. "Where are the other exorcists?" he asked as they ran.

"Someone—no doubt Isabelle Aiken—attacked the gate guards by putting NHEs in them." Kaniyar wiped a streak of blood from her lip. "Her possessions weren't as quick-acting as Azarov's, but it was enough to cause a distraction. I assumed Azarov would be with her and sent our exorcists topside. Damn it!"

A scream of twisting metal and grinding concrete sounded behind them, followed by a deafening crash. A wall of grit and dust rushed up the corridor, instantly coating John's skin in a fine haze. He breathed in, choked, and tried to drag his shirt up over his mouth. The whole place was about to come down on them—Goddess, had the civilians at least been evacuated first?

A strong arm swept him up, hefting him off of his feet. He had a confused glimpse of Kaniyar, tossed over Gray's other shoulder, before the drakul began to run.

Another roar behind them, more and more support structures giving way. Smoke and grit filled the air, and through it John glimpsed the ceiling falling in, just as they reached the elevator shaft.

"Hold on," Gray ordered.

John grabbed wildly, blindly, clinging to Gray's slender body by whatever means he could. He felt Kaniyar's arms come around from the other side, their knees knocking together as Gray ripped the elevator doors open and leapt inside.

The whole world shook. Debris fell past them as Gray scrambled up the wall, claws embedded directly in the side of the shaft to give him purchase. They went up one story, two, three—then Gray twisted, kicked open the doors, and swung into the gap. A split second later, the elevator plummeted past them, so close John's hair blew back against his scalp.

"Good work," Kaniyar said, her voice as faint as John had ever heard it.

Back into the shaft, and Gray hauled them up, all of his immense strength and speed bent toward outracing the disaster unfolding around them. Almost to the top now, almost—

Part of the wall broke away under one of Gray's hands. For an instant, they swung free, dangling by one hand, nothing between them and a long drop but five claws. Gray made a sound of effort that rattled in the hollow spaces of John's lungs, before catching onto a second handhold, just below the doors to the garage.

The doors stood open, maybe forced by people escaping the elevator before it fell. With a last burst of strength, Gray dragged them up and out of the shaft.

John let go and rolled free, as did Kaniyar. They weren't safe yet—cracks showed in the garage, and they still had to get to the surface. To his surprise, an armored vehicle idled just a few feet away. The window came down, and Karl stuck his head out.

"Get in!" he shouted.

Kaniyar made for the door. "Is everyone else out?"

"Yes. You were the last. What happened to the other drakul?"

"He's still in play," Kaniyar said grimly. "Let's get the hell out of here."

"Go!" Caleb called. "I'm grabbing the bike."

The motorcycle Yuri had gifted him with was parked just feet away. As Caleb ran toward it, John said, "I'll go with Caleb and Gray. We'll meet you up top."

Karl didn't argue, peeling out in a squeal of tires the second Kaniyar's door slammed. Caleb started the bike, engine revving. "I don't have a helmet," he shouted over the noise. "So just hold on."

John scrambled on, wrapping his arms tight around Caleb's slim waist. A moment later, they rocketed up the curve of the parking garage. Chunks of concrete dropped from the ceiling, but Caleb evaded them with inhumanly fast reflexes. In less than a minute, they emerged into the evening sunlight.

Emergency lights flashed everywhere, and SPECTR SUVs and vans crowded much of the road outside, as if torn between securing the area and falling back to safety. Thank Sekhmet the civilians had gotten away.

Caleb slowed the bike to a sane speed when they reached the street. John let go and looked back.

A huge plume of smoke and dust towered into the sky above HQ. The wail of sirens competed with shrieks of pain on the evening air. EMTs worked on those who had been injured in the evacuation, and Kaniyar issued orders that floated past John like the words of a dream.

"Fuck," Caleb said quietly. John glanced at him, saw his brown eyes fixed on the collapsing ruins of HQ.

"Yeah," John agreed. He blinked back a sudden film of tears. HQ had been his home away from home since he'd graduated from the Academy. Hell, before Caleb and Gray, it had been more of a home than his own condo. And though he knew he should be grateful to be alive, that more people hadn't died, that it was only a building, he couldn't help but feel a wave of grief wash over him instead.

"You okay?" Caleb asked, so quietly the words were nearly lost beneath the chaos around them.

John swallowed hard and nodded. "I'm fine. Glad the civilians made it out."

"You don't have to pretend not to be sad. Not to us." Caleb took John's hand and gave it a squeeze. "I'm sorry, sweetheart. We both are."

"Thanks." He leaned forward and kissed their cheek. At least they were here with him.

The smoke had begun to drift over the ground now, obscuring the area around HQ and the adjoining street. The wind twisted the smoke into odd shapes, until it seemed almost as though something moved within it.

Wait.

The sleek black shape of Yuri's motorcycle emerged from the cloud.

Caleb's body went stiff against John's. "Shit."

Yuri brought the bike to a halt a few hundred feet away. Even at that distance, John could feel the weight of his rage, his hate, like the heat boiling out from a vent of lava.

"Zahira's had time to get to the aircraft carrier," John said through lips coated in dust.

"Right." Caleb's gaze remained fixed on Yuri. "You should stay here."

John put his arms around Caleb's waist. "No. We're finishing this together."

A tiny smile curved the corner of Caleb's mouth. Instead of answering, he gunned the engine.

Yuri gunned his back. Challenge fucking accepted.

"Then get ready for the ride of your life, Starkweather," Caleb said, and opened up the throttle.

Caleb leaned low over the bike handles, John's arms locked around his waist. The wind tore his hair back as he jumped the bike over the curb, dodged emergency vehicles, and aimed toward the concrete river of I-26. The streets were mostly empty, the city locked down tight, but abandoned cars and wrecked tourist buses still turned them into an obstacle course. Christ, he hoped Zahira had managed to get through. If they made it all the way out to Patriots Point and the decommissioned aircraft carrier only to find she hadn't made it, or hadn't had time to complete the circle...

Assuming the circle even worked. Assuming the relatively small amount of water around a permanently berthed carrier would be enough to take the edge off of Drugoy's strength. Assuming a hell of a lot of things, and goddamn this was a crappy plan. The best thing to be said for it was there wouldn't be any innocent bystanders this time.

"Drugoy killed Deacon."

Of all the things for Gray to be uneasy about, that wasn't one Caleb had expected. *You didn't even like Deacon.*

"No. But Deacon was theirs."

I guess Drugoy felt betrayed.

"We would never hurt John and Zahira intentionally, no matter what they did."

Caleb risked a glance back over his shoulder. Yuri wove through the streets with the same ease as Caleb did, his blond hair unfurling in the wind. Yuri and Drugoy were out for blood; they weren't going to stop this time until Caleb was dead and Gray eaten.

Fuck I hope this works.

The on-ramp to I-26 unfurled before them; the interstate looked far clearer than the streets. Caleb opened up the throttle, hoping to get a little distance on Yuri.

A second bike swung onto the ramp, nearly tank-to-tank with them. Though Isabelle wore a full-face helmet, Caleb instantly recognized her silver and purple bike and matching leathers. Her jacket was unzipped, and flapped back to reveal a gun holstered at her hip.

Crap. Better not give her a chance to use it.

She was on the right, not directly engaging, but obviously trying to block him from dodging back off the interstate. Unfortunately, the ramp he needed onto the Cooper River Bridge was less than a half mile away.

No doubt Yuri meant to herd them where he wanted them to go. Up the peninsula and deeper inland. Before, when Yuri had gone down to the Battery and the waterside, he'd been making a point—that he would destroy everything Caleb and Gray loved if they didn't cooperate.

Now he wanted only death. Which meant seizing every possible advantage he could.

Caleb poured on the speed, but Isabelle matched him. He flashed back to the night he and Yuri had raced their bikes up and down this very interstate. He'd felt invincible: fearless, free. Even if he'd wrecked, he would have shaken off the injuries easily enough.

Today, he had John on the back, without so much as a helmet between his fragile body and the roadway. If Caleb screwed up now, it would cost John's life.

The off ramp was only feet ahead. They had to go, now, or what little plan they had would be gone. But Isabelle was in the way.

Fuck.

At the last second, Caleb braked and turned. The front wheel of his bike passed within an inch of the rear wheel of hers. John's arms locked around his ribs in a death grip. The tires broke loose, bounced sideways over the pavement, and for a terrifying second Caleb thought even his inhuman reflexes wouldn't keep them upright.

Then the tires grabbed hold again, leaving behind a smoking line of rubber. He battled the handlebars, dragged them out of a swerve, and back under control.

Isabelle was good, but only mortal. A quick glance showed her bike had shot past the ramp. It wouldn't take her long to get turned around, but every second gave them an advantage right now. As for Yuri, he'd been a block behind them when they hit the freeway. Caleb knew from the ride they'd taken before that his bike might keep pace, but he couldn't overtake them on a straightaway with no traffic. All Caleb had to do was pour on the speed.

John's hold relaxed fractionally. They roared up the curve of the ramp, onto the long span of the bridge as it lifted gracefully over the river.

Almost a straight shot now. Over the bridge, down into Mount Pleasant, and Patriots Point Park was right there on the water. They just had to stay ahead of Yuri for a little longer.

They came over the crest of the bridge, beneath the enormous towers. In front of them, a scattering of abandoned cars from some earlier wreck sat across the road. There was just enough space to maneuver a mid-sized car between them.

Or there would have been, if there hadn't been a werewolf hunkered in the gap, gnawing idly on one of the dead drivers.

Caleb braked hard, swearing furiously at the werewolf. "John, can you drive the bike?"

"Yes."

"Then take over—we'll get the werewolf out of the way, you get through, and we'll catch up with you on the other side."

He was off the bike before John could argue they take the time to exorcise the werewolf. Hopefully the damn thing would just run, as soon as it caught wind of Gray. He let Gray take over, and the lycanthrope looked up from its meal in alarm.

Yuri's motorcycle roared over the crest of the bridge.

Gray spun to face it. "John! Go!" But the damned werewolf was still sitting there, and Yuri—

Was heading straight for Gray.

Caleb reached for his TK, but the bike was traveling too fast even for his enhanced reflexes. He glimpsed Yuri leaping off, a split second before it plowed into him. Pain exploded from groin to chin, and it launched Gray and Caleb from their feet. Caleb caught a crazed image of the towers spinning above—then growing farther and farther away, as they plummeted over the side of the bridge and toward the river two hundred feet below.

John sat frozen, the bike rumbling beneath him, staring at the point where Gray had stood only moments before. The hit had been savage, and striking the river from this height would do an incredible amount more damage. And even though he knew Gray and Caleb would get through it, his heart pounded and his mouth went dry, because Yuri…

Was still on the bridge. With John.

Yuri rolled to his feet, road rash vanishing as he healed. He turned toward John, and from behind him there came the sound of another motorcycle as Isabelle arrived on the scene.

As before, he could feel Yuri staring at him. Plenty of NHEs had wanted to kill John, but somehow this felt different. He'd never truly felt like *prey* before.

Then Drugoy unfolded, the scent of broken rock and hot earth blotting out even the stink of the marsh.

He had to go, while he still could.

The werewolf let out a yelp and fled Drugoy's presence, leaving the way through clear. John gunned the motorcycle and took off, as fast as he dared.

It wasn't going to be fast enough. He'd never ridden seriously, and even if he had, Isabelle was a pro. Whether she or Drugoy ended up at the handlebars, John had no chance of outrunning them. Still, it would take precious time for Isabelle to stop the bike, pick up Drugoy, and get moving again. Caleb's motorcycle had the advantage in speed so far; maybe it would be enough.

Sekhmet, Devouring Lady, just let me keep ahead of them long enough to reach the carrier. Please.

Once past the blockage, it was a fast drop off the bridge and onto the highway leading to Patriots Point. He risked a single glance back at the river while he could still see the water, but it would have been hard to spot Caleb and Gray even in the best of circumstances.

And of course, they might not even be on the surface. They might be floating along the bottom toward the Atlantic, bones broken and organs pulped. It could be hours, longer, before they healed.

Which left only John and Zahira to face Drugoy and Isabelle.

Goddess, he hoped Brimm's circle worked.

The area was eerily deserted as John guided the bike down the wide road and into the parking lot. Ordinarily the place was packed with tourists looking to take the ferry to Fort Sumter, or a helicopter ride above the harbor, or visit one of the military vessels in permanent dock here. Now, there were only gulls picking at stray french fries, accompanied by a lone egret making its way through the marsh grass along the river. Across a few hundred feet of shallow water, the enormous bulk of the USS Yorktown dwarfed everything else in sight.

Zahira's sedan was parked as close to the ticket booth as possible. John steered the bike around the back of the gift shop, past a barrier open just wide enough for the bike to pass through, and onto the pier leading out to the carrier. As he did so, a purple and silver motorcycle entered the lot.

Isabelle and Drugoy had arrived.

CHAPTER 13

JOHN GUNNED THE bike down the pier. The flags lining the bridge snapped in the ocean breeze, seeming to urge him on. Instinct, or some whisper of his sixth sense, caused him to glance back when he was midway across. Drugoy and Isabelle had reached the pier, Isabelle tucked on the bike behind the drakul. For just an instant, John thought Drugoy hesitated, red-hot gaze sweeping across the lapping water, before following John onto the pier.

Isabelle leaned around Drugoy, something in her hand. John just had time to see the glint of sunlight on the barrel of her gun before she fired.

The bullet struck the railing, and John swore. He was so close now, the bulk of the carrier swallowing the sky in front of him, blocking out the light of the setting sun and casting an enormous shadow over everything around it. The pier ended in a second one set at right-angles, which ran alongside the vast ship. Steel staircases connected to the carrier itself, arranged to allow tourists easy access at multiple points.

The leftmost stair would take him straight to the flight deck, where Zahira hopefully waited with the spirit ward complete. John abandoned the bike and ran toward it—

Bullets struck the concrete only a yard in front of him.

He stumbled back. The motorcycle was nearly on him. Drugoy's pale hair streamed in the wind, his teeth bared. So close, John could see the furious glow of his eyes, could *feel* the energy boiling out of his slender frame. The scent of hot earth and melting stone saturated the air, and the reptile part of John's brain screamed at him to run blindly from the predator poised to eat him.

He had only a split second to make a decision. Isabelle would shoot him if he took the exterior stairs to the flight deck, but there were interior routes that would get him there. The problem being it would take much longer.

No choice existed. John sprinted for the nearest stairs, swerving when another bullet struck the metal. Even as he reached the top, he felt them shudder beneath Drugoy's step.

The stairs let out into the cavernous hanger bay. Historic aircraft on display lined the port side, with exhibits on carrier history and the Battle of Midway crowded to starboard. Greenish light from the overhead lamps lent the deserted space an eerie air, and John's footfalls echoed strangely as he pounded up the center of the wide room.

John cast about wildly, trying to remember where the stairs leading in the direction of the flight deck were. He and Caleb had taken the tour, but he'd never imagined his life would depend on recalling the ship's layout. Up, he needed to look for arrows pointing up—

"Why do you bother running, John Starkweather?" Drugoy called from behind him. "Your time on this earth is already so short. What difference does a few more seconds make?"

John threw himself between two of the displayed fighters. Adrenaline coated his mouth in copper as he drew his Glock.

There came a tremendous screech of metal on metal. Before John could so much as flinch, the propeller torn from another plane smashed into the one he hid against, showering him in glass from the shattered canopy. He ducked into a ball instinctively, and glimpsed Drugoy's black-clad legs as he came around the other side of the plane.

Instinct took over; John fired before he'd even made the conscious decision to do so. The bullet tore through Drugoy's knee, and the drakul let out a howl of rage as the injured limb buckled beneath him.

It wouldn't slow Drugoy down for long, but a few seconds was all John needed. He broke cover, running for the steep stair and the sign pointing up: *Tour 3, Flight Deck/Bridge.*

More exhibits, and thank the Goddess the way through was marked with clear yellow arrows. If he got lost in the maze of tiny rooms, he'd be a dead man.

Drugoy's roar of anger echoed behind him. The doorways between rooms were almost oval in shape, meant to form watertight seals in an emergency. John's foot caught on the lip of one, and he went sprawling, leaving skin behind on the ugly green tiles of the floor. He was up and running again in an instant, but the stumble had cost him precious moments.

Because Drugoy was coming.

As John entered the Pilot's Ready Room, a splotch of red caught his eye amidst the industrial green of floor and walls. He tore the fire extinguisher free just as Drugoy arrived, and directed a full blast right into the drakul's face. Drugoy jerked back instinctively with a snarl, flinging up one arm to protect his eyes. John hurled the canister at him, then bolted without seeing if it made contact.

Down a narrow hall, through a series of control rooms whose informational displays remained on, recorded voices issuing orders to emptiness. And there, at last, a narrow stair accompanied by a sign with an upward-pointing arrow and the words *Flight Deck*.

The stair was barely wide enough for a single person. As John started up, Drugoy burst into the tiny compartment, glaring at him through the empty space between risers.

John lunged up the last few steps, but he wasn't fast enough. A hand grabbed his left foot, claws puncturing through his shoe and into flesh. John fell, chin clipping one of the steps—and then screamed as Drugoy buried his fangs directly into his calf.

Agony exploded up John's leg, centered around the two enormous fangs driven deep into the muscle. He felt the suction, Drugoy seeking to drink, maybe by instinct and maybe just out of the desire to hurt John. For a moment, John couldn't do anything but cling to the stairs with his free hand, his thoughts blotted out by a white wall of pain.

He'd run, and he'd fought, but it hadn't been enough. His strength had found its limit. He was going to die here on this stair, in fear and anguish. Drugoy would leave his drained corpse behind and find Zahira. If she wasn't able to lure him across the spirit ward, or if it failed to contain him, she'd die too. And then Drugoy would hunt down Caleb and Gray, and finish what he'd started.

Their light would go out, drained away and absorbed into Drugoy's essence.

In his mind's eye, small and clear as a photograph, John saw Caleb laughing as they climbed these very steps only a few weeks ago. Saw Gray's happy smile when he beheld Zahira and John in the infirmary earlier today.

John twisted his upper body around, brought up the Glock he'd somehow managed to hold onto through everything, and fired at Drugoy's head.

The angle was bad, pain and the faint thought not to shoot his own leg keeping the bullet from going straight through Drugoy's brain. Instead it ripped across the back of his skull, blasting away bone and blood and a spatter of gray matter.

The fangs released, and Drugoy toppled back off the ladder-like stairs, striking the floor below.

The Glock fell from John's fingers. His strength was ebbing, his calf on fire. Blood poured from the deep puncture wounds, filling his shoe and dripping onto the stairs. A groan escaped him as he dragged himself up the last steps, and the flight deck opened before him.

The setting sun turned the sky into a blaze of orange, gold, and deep blue. The light tinted the pale gray decking, splotched here and there by rust along the seams. More historic aircraft dotted the vast platform of the flight deck, along with displays including missiles and a jet engine removed from its housing.

And there, thanks be to Sekhmet, was Zahira.

She looked to have just been putting the finishing touches on the complicated circle Howard Brimm had once used to trap Gray. Exhaustion showed in every line of her body; making the circle must have been an enormous undertaking. But when she saw him, she rose to her feet and started in his direction. "John!"

"Stay there!" He held up his hand and began to limp toward her. Pain exploded up his leg, and he nearly fell.

Ignoring his order, she ran to him, the edges of her hijab fluttering in the unending wind. She got one arm under his shoulder, keeping him from going to the ground. "You need a hospital."

He gritted his teeth. "Get to the other side of the circle. Drugoy's right behind me."

She whispered a prayer. "And Gray?"

"Somewhere in the river."

Somehow, they made it the last few yards, until the circle was between them and the entrance. John closed his eyes as a wave of dizziness washed over him. His throat ached with dryness, and he distantly wondered if he was going into shock.

Zahira tensed against him. "John. Look."

Drugoy emerged onto the flight deck, an expression of utter rage written across his features. His own blood stained his hair red, and John's coated his lips and chin. Glowing eyes fixed on them, then narrowed. "And so we come to the end of this foolishness," he said.

He began to stalk toward them across the deck, making a direct line for their position. John held his breath and prayed Drugoy's attention would be too focused on them to notice the light chalk marking the pale gray of the deck.

"He's not shaking the ground with his steps," Zahira whispered. "I mean, the deck. I think Gray was right—he's weaker over the water, away from the earth."

"You are mortal," Drugoy said, drawing ever nearer the line of the circle. John forced himself to look up and stare at Drugoy's cracked-glass eyes, terrified of drawing the drakul's attention to the circle. "Your lives are *nothing* compared to that of a drakul. You are weak, and afraid."

"Maybe," John said. "But Gray still chose us. So what does that make you?"

Drugoy rushed forward with a roar of fury.

A wall of shimmering light burst into being around Drugoy as he charged across the circle. He struck it—then wrenched back and away with a startled cry of pain. "What is this? What have you done?"

"It's working!" Zahira's grip tightened on John.

Drugoy's roar of fury was loud enough to vibrate the rotors of the helicopter on display. It echoed from the bridge tower, off the gun emplacements, and across the harbor. He dashed again for the edge of the circle, and again was driven back by pain.

"Shoot him," John said. "Right through the head—every time he gets up, shoot him again, until help can get here."

Zahira nodded and let go. John leaned heavily against a display sign, unable to keep his balance otherwise. As Zahira unholstered her Glock, he caught a flash of sunlight off metal near the entry to the flight deck.

"Down!" he shouted.

He tried to lunge away, but his wounded leg betrayed him, and he fell heavily to the rough decking. The bullet tore through the display sign above him. Zahira put the bulk of the copter between her and the shooter.

"Drop your weapon!" she yelled.

Isabelle walked out onto the flight deck, her gun trained in their direction. "Drugoy, are you all right? What did they do to you?"

John dragged himself on his elbows to the meager shelter offered by the nearest jet. His throat was seared and cracked as the desert floor, and he had to swallow twice before he could speak. "More worried about Drugoy than your own sister?"

From his vantage, he could see Isabelle's legs as she moved across the deck toward Drugoy. "Kim? If you've hurt her, you fucker, I'll rip out your eyeballs."

"We aren't the ones who hurt her," Zahira called. "That was all Drugoy. He put a werebear into her."

"Liar," Isabelle said. "Dru, tell them."

Drugoy had bent to the deck, and for a moment John thought he was cringing back from the pain of the circle, just as Gray had when he was trapped. Then there came a loud creak, followed by a groan of metal as Drugoy forced his claws into a seam and began to peel the deck plate free.

No. "Zahira," John croaked, but it was already too late. The sheet of solid steel popped free, taking part of the circle edge with it. The light of the ward flared—then vanished.

Drugoy was free. All their effort had been for nothing.

"Get back, Isabelle," he snarled. "These two belong to me."

"What were they talking about?" she called, but he ignored her, striding toward where John lay helpless.

Zahira's Glock barked, followed by the click of an empty chamber. She was out of ammo. As Drugoy's form drew closer and closer, John struggled to think of something, anything, he could do to save them. To at least give Zahira a chance of escape, if not himself.

But there was nothing. He'd only delayed the inevitable after all.

An anti-aircraft gun came sailing up and over the side of the deck and landed directly on top of Drugoy.

Gray's vision tunnels red as he climbs over the rail and onto the flight deck.

Caleb's TK had cushioned their fall into the river, saving them from the worst of the impact. By the time they had surfaced, the current sweeping them toward the ocean, it had been easier to simply swim for the carrier than return to land. The whole time, hoping against hope that John had evaded Yuri and Drugoy on the bridge. That Isabelle had not shot him. That he would join Zahira aboard the great ship and trap Drugoy until Gray arrived.

The ship had been easy to climb, hauling himself over its barnacle-encrusted waterline, claws sinking into the welds between plates until he reached the gun emplacement just below the deck. And found his worst fears on the verge of taking place.

John lying bleeding onto the deck, his left leg so covered in blood it was impossible to even tell where it was coming from, his skin perilously white. Zahira, tossing away her useless gun, pulling out her silver knife for a final stand. Isabelle, a look of uncertainty on her face, her weapon pointed at the ground but liable to fire at any moment.

And Drugoy, bearing down on John and Zahira with murder in his eyes.

Drugoy means to kill them, to take them away from Gray and Caleb, and the rage the thought ignites is incandescent.

Gray leaps down and seizes the enormous gun, tearing it free of its mooring in a single heave. Caleb joins in with his TK, and together they hurl the gun over the side, tumbling end over end, until it smashes down atop Drugoy.

Gray springs over the side in an easy leap, landing between John and Zahira. *"John needs help,"* Caleb says urgently. *"He's bleeding out—we've got to get him to a hospital as soon as we can."*

The gun crashes to the side as Drugoy shoves it off of him.

Then we must kill Drugoy as quickly as possible. Aloud, Gray says, "Zahira, help John. I will deal with Drugoy."

He doesn't wait for her to reply. Standing up, he reaches for one of the helicopter rotors hanging low over their heads. It comes free with a squeal of tortured steel, and he strides to Drugoy with it in his hands.

Drugoy is badly hurt. Yuri's exorcist ability has recovered somewhat over the hours, but when his eyes flash blue and he reaches up to summon a demon from the ether for them to eat, Gray swings the rotor and slams it as hard as he can into the back of their head.

"Try summoning an NHE with your skull staved in, asshole," Caleb snarls.

The blow sends Drugoy flying across the deck and into one of the jets. The chains holding the aircraft in place rattle with the force of the impact.

Gray tosses the bent rotor aside as he crosses to Drugoy. They must end this, as soon as possible. John is hurt, maybe dying; he needs the help of other mortals.

Drugoy stumbles upright. The wounds on his face have yet to heal, a great flap of flesh hanging free where the edge of the rotor cut through muscle and ligament. "Curse you," he says, spitting the words like venom. "We survived the lake. We won't die at the hands of a pathetic excuse for a drakul like you."

He seizes the jet engine sitting by the plane, ripping it free of the chains holding it to the deck. Gray charges, meaning to stop him, but Drugoy heaves the engine directly at Gray's face.

Caleb surges to the fore—but his TK is spent. Pain slices through their head as he tries to use the power, only to be obliterated by an even larger agony as the engine smashes into their face.

The blow carries Gray backward, into another jet. Its steel skin crumples beneath the impact, and for a moment there is nothing in the universe but agony. The jet engine falls to one side, and Gray collapses to the deck. Caleb's thoughts riot through their skull, fragmented by neurons misfiring as they struggle to heal.

Blood spreads around them in a pool, a great gout of it pouring from their mouth. Their lower jaw is shattered to fragments. Fangs fall out, one then the other, their body fighting to replace and regrow their best weapon before it is too late.

Drugoy takes a step, swaying like a drunken mortal as he, too, battles to heal. Yuri's blue eyes flash, and they draw a demon from the etheric plane and devour it, then another.

They will not stop. They will continue to summon until they are healed. And they then will kill Gray and Caleb, and John will die, along with Zahira. They will find the other drakul, wherever it might be, drag it from its ignorance and peace, and into a living body.

Drive it as mad as they. Swim together in rivers of blood.

"Drugoy!" Isabelle's scream is raw, echoing off the jets.

Yuri's hand falls, and Drugoy turns his head to watch her approach. She holds a cellphone in one hand, her gun in the other, and both are shaking. "It's true, isn't it?" she asks, thrusting the phone at him as though it were a weapon. "Why did you do it? Why did you hurt Kim?"

Drugoy's brows draw together. "Who is Kim?"

"He doesn't even care that much about his own renfields," Caleb says, almost in wonder.

Drugoy believes mortals do not matter. That they are there to serve him, or to be ignored. And though there is much to be said for ignoring mortal nonsense, there are consequences for it, too.

The phone falls to the deck. "My sister, you son of a bitch," Isabelle says, and fires.

The bullet takes Drugoy through the lower part of the head, severing the spinal column where it enters the skull. And even as he staggers, limbs beginning to collapse, Gray heaves himself up off the deck.

With the last of his strength, he catches Drugoy's body in his arms, and keeps running.

The world spins around them, shouts and cries echoing, accompanied by the beating of helicopter blades in the wind. Drugoy tries to twist in his arms, and for an instant their eyes meet.

A long time ago, they hunted in the etheric plane. And sated, curled together in peace.

"Goodbye, Drugoy," Gray says.

His foot hits the upper rail, propelling them into the air and off the deck. At the same instant, Gray drives his regrown fangs deep into Drugoy's throat.

Then they hit the river, and the water closes over them both.

Grit flew into John's eyes as a helicopter landed on the flight deck. SPECTR agents swarmed onto the deck, and Kaniyar shouted orders. Isabelle dropped her gun and held up her hands, her expression a mask of utter defeat.

"Hold still, John," Zahira said, from where she was applying pressure to his leg. "Just wait for the medics."

"No." He shook his head. "Gray. Where…?"

They were close enough to the edge that he could lift his head and see out into the heaving water. The last of the light was almost gone, but it was enough to show him a great stain of red spreading slowly from the point of impact, marking where the two drakul had vanished.

A titanic bolt of lightning exploded from the surface of the river, into the clouds above. The flash blinded John, the crack nearly deafening. A moment later, a great gust of wind roared across the harbor. The sunset vanished, eaten up by a storm wrack that grew from nothing to nearly covering the entire harbor within seconds.

Rain sheeted down, followed by more blasts of lightning. A wave of weakness passed over John, and he lowered his head to the deck even as the medics arrived.

"Don't be afraid," he told Zahira. "It's just Gray." Then the blackness of the sky slid like ink into his skull, and the world fell away.

CHAPTER 14

THE STORM RAGED throughout the night, giving way to a gentle rain that lasted for the next two days. John spent most of that time either in surgery or deeply asleep. Eventually, he awoke to find Zahira beside him, watching the rain beat against the window.

"Gray? Caleb?" he managed to ask, though he had the strange feeling he'd done so before.

"Still no sign," she said, which made no sense, because the signs were surely all around them. In the rain tapping on the glass and the wind whistling through a gap where the window didn't fit well. "None of Drugoy, either." She glanced at him with a tired smile. "Good news, though. Thanks to the vials of blood, all of the victims we know of have been tracked down and exorcised. There might be a few stragglers, of course, but I think we can safely say it's over."

It wasn't over, of course, not really. SPECTR HQ was a smoking ruin; images of the dust cloud rising above it played day and night on the television hanging in one corner of the room. At first the painkillers made it hard for John to follow what the newscasters were saying, but eventually he realized Drugoy and Yuri had inadvertently done SPECTR something of a favor, at least PR wise. Vague rumors of compromised agents had no power against the stark footage of an attack on a government building, especially when accompanied by images of flags lowered to half-mast in honor of the Charleston dead.

Kaniyar took full advantage. Camera crews were conveniently on hand as exorcists risked their lives to save some of the last possessed victims, and video of heroic EMTs played side-by-side with tears of gratitude from survivors. The first few times, John expected the Chatwals to appear, but they never did. Was Kaniyar worried their story of Gray would complicate things, or did the media itself naturally shy from anything that might add nuance to what seemed to be a straightforward tale of heroism and bravery? At this point, no one might even want to hear a story of being saved by an NHE, only to have SPECTR open fire on him.

Karl came to pick John up the day he was discharged. "Where's Caleb and Gray?" John asked, as soon as he walked into the room.

"Hello to you, too," Karl said. "Why yes, I did bring you some real clothes to wear, so everyone doesn't have to see your ass hanging out."

John frowned at the suitcase in Karl's hand. "You didn't have to pack that much."

"I kind of did." Karl sighed. "Kaniyar's orders. Get dressed, and I'll take you to her."

Unease played over John's nerves as he sat up and swung his legs carefully over the side of the bed. The left was heavily bandaged. According to the doctors, Drugoy hadn't damaged any of the major nerves, but the scarring within the muscle itself might present an issue down the line. Having come so close to dying, a bit of a limp seemed a small price to pay.

"Why won't you tell me about Caleb and Gray?" he asked as he took the shirt Karl handed him.

Karl sighed and glanced at the door. "They dredged the bottom of the river around the carrier," he said carefully. "A few human bones were recovered, in an advanced state of decay. Almost as if whoever they belonged to had died a long time ago."

A chill ran up John's spine. When the body possessed by an NHE died, the corpse behaved as if the person had died the day of possession, however long ago that might have been. "Who did they belong to?"

Instead of answering, Karl went to the window and looked out. He inspected the outside of the sill carefully, then tapped his finger against it. "Our esteemed director supervised the lab testing herself. According to the circulated results, they've been matched to Caleb Jansen."

John stared at Karl for a long moment. "That can't be," he said numbly. "I saw the storm, Karl. I saw—"

"I have to bring the car around," Karl said abruptly. "If you've got what you need from the suitcase, I'll meet you out front. Before you leave, you might want to check out the view one last time."

The moment he was gone, John limped over to the window. But it wasn't the view he was interested in. Instead, he looked down at the sill, where Karl's attention had been so unnaturally focused.

Scored into the concrete ledge were a set of fresh claw marks.

"Where are we?" John asked as Karl pulled the sedan into what looked like a half-completed sub-division just off Highway 17. "I thought we'd go to whatever temporary headquarters Kaniyar has set up."

The sun had set as they drove across the Ashley River, leaving the peninsula behind them. Bats swooped through clusters of moths beneath street lamps, and a few security lights showed on some of the empty houses, but for the most part the only illumination came from their headlights.

"She wanted a bit more privacy," Karl said wryly. "Here we are."

He pulled up to one of the driveways. Most were empty, but this one held a compact SUV with a motorcycle trailer hitched behind. As the headlights swept over the bike, they revealed the familiar custom paint job of lightning across the tank.

John's heart beat faster. Karl threw the sedan into park. "I think they're waiting inside. Just let me get your crutch."

The garage door eased open as John hobbled up to it, Karl trailing behind him. The slowly ascending door revealed three pairs of legs, but the moment he spotted the heavy boots with their silver buckles, he forgot any of the others existed.

"Hey," Caleb said. And then he couldn't say anything else, because John's mouth was on his.

Halfway through the kiss, John felt the surge of energy, Gray showing up long enough to give his own greeting. Static sparked over the fingers John had buried in their hair, the crutch dropped and forgotten on the floor. Gray firmed his hold, lifting John just off his feet, and for a time there was nothing but breath and lips, and the steady beating of their hearts.

Eventually, the sound of Kaniyar clearing her throat broke through John's haze. Gray very carefully lowered him, then folded back away, leaving Caleb to cradle John.

"Pretty good kiss for a dead guy, huh?" Caleb asked with a crooked grin.

"Yeah." John laughed. "You were at the hospital. Why the hell didn't you wake me up?"

Kaniyar sighed heavily. Caleb hastily bent to retrieve John's crutch. "You needed the rest. And, um, we weren't strictly supposed to be there."

"I'm glad you're all right, John," Zahira said from where she stood to Kaniyar's other side.

"Same," he said fervently. "So why are we meeting here?"

"Dead guy," Caleb said, raising his hand. "I can't really wander around the city without giving up the game."

The yellow light of the garage gleamed from Kaniyar's black hair, finding the first threads of silver. She looked more tired than John had ever seen her, and a sliver of guilt worked its way under his skin. Most of what had gone wrong could be laid at Yuri's door, but he bore his share of responsibility.

"I'll do what I can to help, ma'am," he said. "But you have to understand, it's my duty to advocate for Caleb and Gray. I dropped the ball on that before. I made bad decisions, and I want to make up for that if at all possible. But not at their expense."

"Duty?" Caleb asked with an arch of a brow. "Damn, Starkweather, you know how to lay on the romance, don't you?"

"Thank you for making your opinion clear," Kaniyar said dryly, "but I've already spoken with Mr. Jansen. Sorry—Mr. Gris."

"Michael Caleb Gris, pleased to meet you." Caleb tipped an imaginary hat at John. "I already have a new driver's license, social security card, and birth certificate. I didn't ask how she managed that on such short notice."

"Which just goes to show you can learn," Kaniyar said. "I have a new assignment for you, Starkweather. As Mr. Gris has already agreed, I hope you will as well. While you were in surgery, we had a very long, very serious talk about what happened and how we might take the opportunity to make a course correction, as opposed to losing a valuable asset."

"That would be Gray," Caleb put in.

Kaniyar shot him a quelling look. "My take is that the drakul will perform better outside of a traditional structure. As far as most of the world is concerned, Gray and Drugoy killed each other, and Jansen's death has been confirmed through DNA testing of the recovered remains. Given the trauma of your wounds, both physical and emotional, you've decided to take an extended leave of absence. Most of your belongings have been placed into storage, and your condo put up for sale."

John's lips parted in protest, but he caught the words back before he could speak them. He understood—they couldn't stay in Charleston after what happened—but it was still a blow.

Caleb shifted from one foot to the other. "I'm sorry," he said. "We're sorry. We should have asked you. If you don't want—"

John seized his hand. "It was just a place," he said, meeting Caleb's eyes. "You and Gray are my home."

The smile that spread over Caleb's face was like the sunrise.

"Take some time off," Kaniyar said. "Go on a road trip. I recommend south. Savannah is nice this time of year."

"Lying," Karl murmured.

Kaniyar cracked a smile. "Savannah is hot as balls this time of year. Go where you like. If you come across any possessed who can be saved, I trust you can handle it, Starkweather. If you can't, that's what you have Mr. Gris for."

John tightened his grip on Caleb's hand. "That can't be all."

"Of course not. You'll have a handler—who, I haven't decided yet—who will contact you when needed. Any NHEs who pose too big of a threat to our human agents are now your problem. A good thing Caleb can get by without sleep, because you could be called on to travel to any point in the lower forty-eight at any time. I hope you enjoy long drives."

Silence fell. Caleb met John's gaze uncertainly. "Are you okay with this? I know it's a lot, especially after everything we put you through."

"You're worth it." John took a deep breath, feeling a stress he hadn't even realized he carried slip away. Turning to Kaniyar, he said, "Thank you, ma'am."

"SPECTR will benefit," she replied. Then her expression softened. "And Gray did save me from being crushed under a ton of rubble. Circumstances allow me to be generous." She nodded to Karl. "I'll wait in the car why you make your goodbyes. Starkweather, Gris, I'll be in touch soon."

She strode to Karl's sedan without a backward look. "I'm guessing we shouldn't linger," Karl said wryly. "It was a pleasure, John, Caleb. I hope to see you again."

"Karl. Give my best to your family." It was against etiquette to touch an empath, so John was surprised when Karl stuck out his hand. He went to shake, and found himself pulled into a quick hug.

"Take care of yourself," Karl said. Then he let go of John and embraced Caleb. "Look out for him, okay?"

"We will."

Karl left them with Zahira. "I heard from Harry," she said.

Caleb's face lit up. "How is she?"

"Good, all things considered. The whole family is in therapy, but they're strong." She smiled at him. "A lot of people owe you their lives."

"I just hope they're okay." Caleb shrugged awkwardly. "Can I be honest for a moment? John excepted, you were the best thing about working at SPECTR. If you ever have any drakul questions, just shoot me an email."

"Do you have an email?"

"Fuck, I knew there was something Kaniyar forgot."

Zahira laughed. "The devil's in the details, as they say."

"Thanks for everything, Zahira," John said. "You're the best partner we ever had."

"You're like brothers to me." She blinked rapidly. "Inshallah, we'll meet again."

"I'm certain of it," John replied.

"And if Kaniyar doesn't give you a promotion, let us know," Caleb added.

Then he was gone, and Gray unfurled. Lightning danced in his depthless eyes, and he inclined his head to Zahira with an odd air of formality.

"Drugoy did not understand," he said. "Our mortals are ours to protect, not to possess. If you are ours, then we are yours no less. If ever you have need of us, call, and we will come."

Her dark eyes welled. "Thank you, Gray. May Allah bless you and reward you with goodness, and guide you to the right path."

A few minutes later, the sedan pulled away, taking Kaniyar, Karl, and Zahira with it. John turned to the SUV, hand once again wrapped in Caleb's. "Did you do the packing?"

"Karl and his husband did most of it," Caleb said. "Honestly, I'm cringing at the thought of opening the first suitcase and finding lube and sex toys."

John laughed. "Hopefully the embarrassment will have faded by the time we see them again."

"Yeah." Caleb squeezed his hand. "Okay, now that Kaniyar is gone…are you really okay with this?"

"Are you?" John countered.

Caleb nodded. "Gray can't fucking wait to hit the road. The only time he's ever stayed in one place before, it was because he was staked."

No wonder he'd been so unhappy. "I'm good," John said after a moment's consideration. "It's all a bit sudden, mind you, but fuck it. As long as I'm with you two, I'll be okay." He paused. "Though you're going to have to drive, at least until I'm off the painkillers."

"Need me to carry you to the car?"

"Nah. I'll make it."

They climbed into the SUV, John settling into the passenger seat. "Nice of Kaniyar to provide this," he said, running a hand over the spotless new dashboard.

"Not bad," Caleb agreed. He cranked the engine, then glanced at John. "Which way?"

John tilted the seat back and closed his eyes. "So long as I'm with you, it doesn't matter. But I'm guessing Kaniyar said south for a reason."

"South it is, then," Caleb said.

John was asleep by the time they hit the interstate.

Caleb glanced in the mirror, but traffic was light. A single pair of red tail lights showed on the horizon ahead of them, but otherwise they might have been the only ones on the road.

Gray hummed just beneath their skin, a contented cat.

You okay? Caleb asked.

"John is with us again." Joy, and a sense of completion, darkened by a single shadow. *"I will miss Zahira."*

Me, too.

"And I will miss Drugoy."

Caleb let out a long breath. Once they'd been reassured John would be okay, the only thing he'd been able to think about for the last few days was Drugoy and Yuri. About how different everything could have been.

We'll probably never meet another living drakul.

"You are likely right," Gray agreed. *"But as we have eaten the two we have encountered, perhaps that is for the best."*

Caleb snorted. *You have a point. So you're good?*

"We are free, Caleb. That is all I have ever wanted."

Yeah. Caleb shifted lanes to avoid a bit of debris in the road. *We are. I'm glad Harry and her family are going to be okay.*

"Helping them…it was a good thing."

Yeah. It was.

Warmth spilled out from Gray, like a hug. *"There will be more good things. We will hunt. We will make love with John. We will live as we were meant to."*

Caleb glanced at John's sleeping face. *Yeah,* he said with perfect honesty. *It sounds like heaven.*

Gray curled up into a happy ball at the back of their consciousness, going dormant. A smile stretching his mouth, Caleb settled in, guiding the car deeper into the southern night.

The adventures of John, Caleb, and Gray will continue in SPECTR Series 3.

SHARE YOUR EXPERIENCE

If you enjoyed this book, please consider leaving a review on the site where you purchased it, or on Goodreads.
Thank you for your support of independent authors!

ABOUT THE AUTHOR

Jordan L. Hawk is a non-binary queer author from North Carolina. Childhood tales of mountain ghosts and mysterious creatures gave them a life-long love of things that go bump in the night. When they aren't writing, they brew their own beer and try to keep the cats from destroying the house. Their best-selling Whyborne & Griffin series (beginning with Widdershins) can be found in print, ebook, and audiobook.

If you're interested in receiving Jordan's newsletter and being the first to know when new books are released, please sign up at their website: http://www.jordanlhawk.com. Or join their Facebook reader group, Widdershins Knows Its Own.

Made in the USA
Columbia, SC
21 September 2018